Undaunted: One girl, many morons, and the search for Mr. Right

Rachelle Chedore

Undaunted: One girl, many morons, and the search for Mr. Right.

Copyright © 2016 Rachelle Chedore

First Edition.

Print ISBN: 978-0-9953372-0-6
E-Book ISBN: 978-0-9953372-1-3
E-Book ISBN: 978-0-9953372-2-0
Audio Book: ISBN 978-0-9953372-3-7

Prologue

Growing up, I always imagined what it would be like to start a family of my own. I knew someday I wanted to be a wife and mother. And of course, it wouldn't hurt to have a cute little puppy running around as well. That would be ideal. I mean, what girl doesn't dream of these things? And let's not forget the big fancy wedding that is supposed to precede all this. I had the standard clipping of the amazing wedding dress – the one I would have to find an exact replica of when my day came – and a few bridal magazines stashed under my bed with pages folded for the ideas I liked.

There were also boards hanging on my bedroom walls plastered with sticky notes, lists and drawings. It may have looked a little bizarre, like a wedding bomb exploded in there – but it helped to keep me focused.

Now don't get me wrong…I wasn't fixated with being married or anything. Honestly I wasn't. Sketching tons of pictures of myself with the love of my life at a chapel with all the fancy trimmings did not make me obsessed. Besides, it was abundantly clear to everyone he liked me. *Not* that awful girl Amelia.

I mean, what did she have over me? Sure she had long blond hair and could sing (in her mind anyway) like Mariah Carey – but she wasn't very nice and didn't have my fashion sense. And most importantly, I'm not even sure she liked him. Not like I did. There was really no comparison.

Anyway, I was talking about my lifelong dream. The one that seemed utterly hopeless. I was eighteen and never had a boyfriend. I hadn't even gone on one little date.

I know – it's ridiculous. Especially with my green eyes, copper hair, and cute figure. It was time to change my status. Yes, I Reanne Riley was tired of being terminally single.

But how is it, while I'm sure plenty of my male friends liked me, not one of them had enough gas in their tank to ask me out while the light was green light? It certainly wasn't due to a lack of opportunity. Maybe I kept attracting the ones that were clueless. Or crazy…

Chapter One

Not Happening

When I was sixteen, there was this guy named Ken. We always sat close to each other in class and we'd occasionally chat after school. I'd say we were slowly becoming friends, though not close by any means. After a while he developed feelings for me. I'm not being conceited – it was fairly obvious. He always initiated the conversation. It didn't matter where I was or whom I was with, he'd show up and hang out even if he didn't have much to say.

"Hey Ken – how are you?"

"I'm well. I'm well," he would reply awkwardly. And that was it.

I'd try again. "What's new?"

"Nothing much." Oh brother.

Hmm…now that I think about it, that's a bit stalker-like isn't it? I need the Jaws tune right about now while I do a voiceover. He's slow. He's a third wheel. He's…silent stalker Ken!

Ok, I'm kidding. He was a decent guy, really. The point I'm making is that he liked me. But what did he do about it? Nothing at all.

I admit I didn't think about him that way at first, but with his constant loitering and having the occasional interesting thing to say, he kind of grew on me. So I became flirtatious to help the poor guy stop tripping over his tongue and let him know he wasn't sitting in the love boat alone. I gave him an oar to go forward.

This guy wasn't getting it. He didn't need a paddle; I think he needed a heavenly voice to give him a signal or at least some billboards with flashing lights. Anything other than my flirting, which didn't do the trick. What did the guy want me to do? Ask *him* out? I don't think so. Not that there's anything wrong with a girl asking a guy out...I just didn't think it was necessary. I gave him enough encouragement. He was probably shy, poor thing. Anyway. As time went on, so did my interest in a possible relationship with him. The light turned red and I left.

Then there was Alex Sherman. Now Alex I didn't even like. Not the slightest little bit. In fact, I'm only mentioning him because...well...you'll see. Alex was a bit stocky, wore glasses and had a sandpaper personality. He rubbed everyone the wrong way. Not that he was a bad person, he was just very intelligent and he knew it. One couldn't have a conversation with him without being overpowered by his opinion. That and the fact I wasn't even remotely attracted to him meant he didn't stand a chance. He had bright red hair and the freckles to match making him the perfect carrot top. He was also accustomed to being the center of attention – the influence of his parents allowed him to be the popular guy who sang, spoke and led activities at the summer art camp we attended. I suppose he thought he could impress me. It may have worked if he wasn't so blasted annoying!

'Where is the tape for his mouth? Does he *ever* stop talking?'

These were the thoughts running through my mind whenever he came over while I *tried* to enjoy my bland lunch. As I sat at the table with my friends I'd be suddenly blinded by the shock of red on his head, glittering in the sunlight as he parked himself across from me. And what's worse, he asked questions while I was eating. Questions!!

You see, I wore braces at the time and anyone who has ever suffered through years of wearing those *knows* food always gets stuck in them. It was particularly worse for me because I had the clear kind, and unfortunately, the food caught there was very noticeable. *Ugh*. So I didn't want to talk while I ate.

Unlike Ken, I didn't give this guy any signals at all and he just forged right ahead. Wouldn't leave me alone. We're talking about a case of too much self-esteem. Any more and his head would have exploded in balloon bursting fashion. I wish I had a pin; I'd have gladly popped it for him.

You know how some say if you ignore a problem it might go away? Well this one didn't. He tried becoming friends with my brother Jaden, which is hilarious because Jaden couldn't stand him either. In fact, his attempt at friendship with my brother created issues between the two of them, which is a whole other story.

Jaden of course told me everything Alex said and we laughed about it. We weren't being cruel – Alex is just the type of person you'd want to prank or see trip. If there's someone incredibly obnoxious in your life, then you know what I mean.

Since his attempt through my brother was unsuccessful, Alex got his best friend involved. I know; this guy *actually* had a friend? Ok, that *is* a bit mean. I'll take it back. But yes, he had a best friend. His name was Neil.

Ah, Neil. At six feet tall with a medium build and sandy hair, Neil was easy on the eyes. If you could tolerate his nose, that is. It was wide and flat and didn't really fit his face. Other than that he may have been a package deal. His intelligent gray-blue eyes were piercing and deep with flecks of green – the way an ocean might look, shimmering on a beautiful summer day.

Wait…are you wondering why I was hung up on his nose? You think I'm too picky? You're probably right. But it wasn't just his nose; his best friend was Alex for Pete's sake! That alone has to tell you something.

Anyway, I didn't know Neil well. I probably only spoke to him once or twice at camp. So it was quite a surprise to see a random email from him a few months later.

I just walked home from school on a cool October day. My cheeks were rosy from the blustering wind, my hair in disarray. I threw my book bag onto the chair by the door and decided to check my email before tackling my homework. Ok – I'll admit I had no intention to do homework – I planned to organize my wedding stuff. But that's neither here nor there.

I opened the email and wondered how Neil got my email address. A few quick inquiries revealed that my email had been passed around at camp. Jeez, you can't trust anyone, can you? It was only meant to go to the close friends I made. But I suppose it was my own fault – I should have paid better attention to where it went. Instead I'd been busy admiring ingenious outfits other girls had worn, and was trying not to gawk at the ugly ones.

At any rate, I found out later Neil got in contact to check me out on Alex's behalf. Some best friend Neil turned out to be. He was more like a backstabbing vulture that swooped in first.

Subject: From Neil Malcom
Hey Reanne,

This email probably comes as a surprise, since you may not remember me. We met at camp and spoke briefly (briefly, due to the fact I was in a relationship and spent most of my time with her).

My girlfriend however has tossed me aside like yesterday's news and I'm taking this time to re-establish old friendships and make some new ones. I'm not looking to start another relationship,

just hoping to get to know you better. Feel free to ignore or
respond, as you see fit.
Neil.

Hmm, funny he didn't bother to mention Alex. Like I said
– vulture. But I was ok with him. I replied to the email and things
accelerated from there…and it was perfect he only wanted
friendship. As much as I anticipated the day I would *finally* have a
boyfriend, I had no interest in dating *him*. Did I mention he looked
kind of old? Not prune-like old but he could have passed for thirty-
four.

When I first saw him I thought he was a camp supervisor
rather than a teen attending. I preferred to find someone who
looked a little more my age. And aside from his resemblance to a
father figure rather than a friend of mine, I liked his writing style.
As well as his commitment to his former relationship. Quite noble,
I thought. Where's the white horse? The guy sounds like a knight.
Right?

Of course I didn't make this assumption from just one
email. I have more sense than that. I began thinking of him this
way after dozens of emails. Dozens of emails that left Alex in the
dust. Alex who? Exactly.

Well I guess we should give Alex some credit, shouldn't
we? He persisted in sending the odd email here and there. I recall
one specifically where he disagreed with something I wrote and
turned it into this huge debate, where he got so angry – like a red

eyed bull – because I wouldn't concede to his point of view. Yeah, like *that* would win me over. He called me 'the straw that broke the camel's back.' He even suggested we take the debate over to the phone, to which I replied that I wasn't much of a 'phone person.' But he insisted. After all, he was used to having his way – except when it came to getting girls to go out with him. There he failed miserably.

So we had this phone conversation and let me tell you – it didn't go well. I'll spare you the details, but I was quite happy to have it over with. I followed it up with an email, again emphasizing that I preferred email to the telephone.

He wasn't satisfied with this answer, especially since a girlfriend from camp phoned one night and we had a great chat for five hours. I happened to let this information leak out to him in an online conversation he started. Yes, I know. I'm so bad. But truly, the guy had it coming.

Alex faded from the picture after that but unfortunately stayed around. He was like a little rock lodged somewhere in my shoe. You know – that tiny little pebble that irritates you as you're walking? You're aware of its presence, but you just can't find its exact location to get rid of it. No matter which way I shook the shoe – Alex popped up from time to time. Maybe he was more like a weed that kept growing back after I hacked it down. Or a pest I couldn't exterminate. You get the idea…irksome.

Chapter Two

To Prank, Or Not To Prank

Neil and I enjoyed our budding friendship over the months that followed. It turned out we had a lot in common. We were both avid readers, had a thing for history and loved Picasso (ok, so maybe I wasn't *as* interested in history as he was – unless you count fashion throughout the ages…and maybe I didn't know *that* much about Picasso – but I liked to draw clothing designs and wedding scenes. Same difference).

He also had a penchant for pulling pranks on people, which I was a little wary of, but other than that we clicked very well. He even asked for my home address, which I have to tell you – I was quite excited about.

Isn't it natural to give more information to each other as you become closer? It made sense. We lived a two-hour car ride apart so why not send the occasional letter to each other the old-fashioned way? Snail mail could be just as fun!

Secretly, I thought he might want to send me a gift. It was February, and he knew my birthday was around the corner.

Now…I know how this sounds and I wasn't being greedy. Honestly, it was just a thought. *He* requested the information. It's not like I said, "here are my details, send something nice if you know what's good for you."

My birthday falls just before Valentine's Day as well – but I wasn't expecting anything for that.

Ooh, maybe it would be a two-in-one gift!

As luck would have it, something arrived in the mail right on my birthday. I awoke to the smell of bacon wafting through the house, and headed downstairs toward the kitchen where mom was drinking coffee from her *# 1 Mom* mug I gave her. Dad wore the ugly holy track pants (mom and I tried to toss them out a million times. We even tried to burn them once but dad appeared just in time and all we managed to do was add another hole). I don't know *why* he liked them so much.

He sifted through the mail, dropping each item onto the countertop with a thud. "Bill, bill…another bill…this one is for Reanne…bill…"

I slid past him in my socks, grabbing the envelope. "Thanks dad."

"Happy birthday love!" Mom was usually the first to say it and dad followed suit.

I beamed at them and chatted for a few minutes, but didn't stick around for very long – I wanted to see what I got. The envelope was very thin, so I imagined a gift card inside.

I was right – it was a card. *Just* a stupid card. Oh well, at least Neil remembered my birthday. It's the thought that counts, right?

Then I noticed the swirly script on the upper left corner of the envelope. Neil didn't send it at all. It was from Alex.

Strange, I mused as I studied the card. There were red roses on the front and printed text inside, which read:

Roses are red
Violets are blue
The only thing I want
Is you

Please say you'll be mine
Love Alex

I was flummoxed. Had Alex gone mad? And talk about corny – he didn't even personalize it with a message of his own. My nostrils flared. How *dare* Neil give that pest my home address! It was betrayal at its peak. Neil built my confidence to help Alex all along. The dirt bag.

All right. I have to deal with Neil. That much was certain.

But what was I supposed to do about the card? Oh…you think I should have ignored it? Yes, well. I guess that's what an intelligent girl would have done. Not me though, I was too shocked to think straight and it felt like someone poured a bucket of ice water over my head. I was so engrossed in my friendship with Neil I kind of forgot about Alex. Not that it was difficult – Alex is someone you'd want to forget.

Since I knew further encounters with Alex were inevitable, ignoring his…er…love note seemed like a bad idea. I didn't want him to become an enemy. So I sent an email thanking him for the card. To be polite, you see.

He emailed back to find out what card I was talking about, as he hadn't sent one, and did I mean the card I sent *him*?

Wait. What? Why did he think I sent him a card? I promptly told him I hadn't given him one. *As if.*

Alex phoned the next day to investigate the situation. As you can imagine, I was thrilled to hear his grating voice. Have you guessed what happened? Neil sent the exact same card to Alex and me to make it look like we were asking each other out.

I was going to kill him.

I sat on my bed, twisting the telephone cord around my finger, wishing I could twist it around Neil's neck.

"Reanne, I was taken aback by the card. I thought it was incredibly forward," Alex's voice drifted down the line.

What a dingbat. Alex thought I would actually chase after him? After all my effort to dodge and ignore him in the past? Please.

So, what could I say without being rude? That I would have never given him a card in a million years? That, if he were the last man on the planet I'd die and have the card buried with me before giving it to him?

It was completely true but I couldn't say it. I decided to stick with a neutral answer. "And I was surprised to see a card from you. I'm glad I emailed you so we could straighten this out." *Now let's get off the phone and never speak again.*

A birthday card really did come from Neil afterward followed by a gloating email – he was so proud to have pulled one over the both of us.

Then Neil and Alex joined forces to pull a prank on me. This actually happened a few days after the first incident. Would you please remind me why I thought I enjoyed being Neil's friend? And why I didn't tell Alex where he could go right off the bat?

You see – there was this other guy at camp, Dan. He liked me too, no surprise there. Dan seemed strange though – I mean, this guy literally followed me all around without uttering a word, and ducked behind trees or buildings whenever I turned to look at him. He too, tried to go through Jaden by letting him know he wanted to go out with me. I'm thankful my brother tipped me off. Dan was avoided like the plague…until the day he accosted me while I chatted with a friend at the edge of the field.

It was a blistering day and we lounged beneath one of the Weeping Willows, watching the leaves dance and float like wind chimes whenever a slight breeze kicked up. The cabins weren't air-conditioned, so we found the best spot to cool down.

"Look out, Dan's coming," came my friend's urgent whisper. I peered through the hanging leaves to see him walking toward me intently.

I got up and started off in the opposite direction as I normally would, but then he ran. So I ran. Yeah – if you're thinking it's freaky – it was. He caught up and breathlessly shouted (seriously who *shouts* when they're standing right in front of the person?), "Will you go out with me?" Little beads of sweat formed on his brow.

"No," I said, at a loss for words.

"Oh. Oh, ok." He walked away with his head hanging and I felt bad. But that was it and he quit chasing me. If only Alex could be so easily deterred.

Anyhow, Neil knew about this. One evening while I chatted with Neil online, Dan popped up with a request that I add him to my friend list. I don't know why I did it. Sometimes I'm just too nice for my own good. I didn't realize Dan's request was live, so the moment I accepted it, he began typing at me. I relayed bits of the conversation to Neil simultaneously.

Reanne says,
Hey Neil, Dan just added me and started chatting.

Neil says,
What's he saying?

Reanne says,

Something about how much he really enjoyed getting to know me...how funny. Oh wait, he mentioned he's really glad we've started dating. That's freaky. What should I say?

Neil says,

I don't know, maybe you should try to get rid of him.

Reanne says,

Ok, I just told him we're not dating and I'm only interested in friendship. Now he's saying he doesn't think he can live without me.

I couldn't wrap my head around it. He looked sad when I rejected him at camp, but I didn't realize he was suicidal. I guess you never can tell with these lunatic types.

Reanne says,

NEIL! What should I do?

He said he's going to kill himself!!!!

Neil says,

Think he'd really do it?

What a horrible thing to say!

This carried on late into the evening. I was concerned for Dan but also creeped out! Neil tried to help me (if you could call it that) through the situation until midnight when Neil finally admitted that cyber Dan was actually Alex. Ok, that did it. Wouldn't you want to get even at this point? How much can a girl take before retaliation comes pouring out in volcanic fervor? They say 'Hell hath no fury like a woman scorned.' Maybe they needed to see what that would be like.

Except before I knew it, the weekend arrived and my friends were over to celebrate my seventeenth birthday. I looked forward to it for quite some time and I was in my element as friends came shrieking through the door, leaving melting snow in their wake. Plans of revenge were quickly forgotten. Why would I waste time thinking about those Neanderthals when the girls and I were going to get into some good gossip, good food and a few games? The night couldn't have been better.

Especially since my mom Karen hosted the party. She had everything meticulously planned. And the games! They were a blast.

"I'll set the timer after I pass out the pencils and papers. The goal is to jot down anything you can think of concerning Reanne. Likes, dislikes, hobbies, and so forth," mom instructed. "Whoever has the biggest list will win the game. Ready, go!"

I watched in fascination as everyone scribbled furiously. Some girls petered out quickly while others like Rhonda wrote until the buzzer sounded.

"I win!" Rhonda exclaimed as she read out her impressive list, which included things I told her ages ago, things *I* even forgot about.

Of course Rhonda would win, she's a fantastic friend. And talented too – she can compose music like nobody's business. In fact, Rhonda's the one who first encouraged me to attend the summer camp, though she didn't have to do much to convince me. We were inseparable and always had a lot to say to each other. Even if we weren't talking we'd have those comfortable silences. I liked to think of us as the dynamic duo. We've known each other *forever*. We also had a motto. It was "there are plenty of fish in the sea." We said this to one another whenever we suffered a major letdown from meeting another deranged guy or if a good one got away.

Rhonda always had my back. Particularly when it came to fending off Erin who could be quite vicious when she was in a foul mood.

Speaking of Erin, she was at my party. I didn't want to invite her but she was part of our group and it would have been snobby not to. I met her at the beginning of high school and we were very close until I found out she was a lot like a coin. Two faced.

Erin was infatuated with getting married, even more than me. It's true. She always brought tons of bridal magazines and newspaper clippings to my house and littered them all over my bed. And at her birthday and any other function at her house, all of the activities were wedding themed. A little over the top if you ask me. At least I kept my interest on the subject controlled and moderate…for the most part. Anyway, Erin was the drama student in our group and she served her role well. She always blew everything out of proportion.

"I *can't* believe it. *Seriously*. I'm leaving, this is *ridiculous*!" Erin erupted as we played the next game.

"Chill out Erin, it's no big deal. This is supposed to be *fun*," Rhonda reminded her.

Erin moved to a corner where she pouted profusely and threw a tantrum like an over-tired toddler. I didn't know what her problem was – I really liked the game! Each of us had to wear a sign on our back with the name of a notable character printed on it, with clues listed beneath to help us guess who we were. I was Queen Esther from Biblical times – thank you very much. And Erin was Jezebel. She really shouldn't have taken it so personally. It was just a joke!

"Will you girls be all right for a few minutes?" Mom shrugged on her coat. "I'm popping out to the store."

We were in the living room listening to music and finishing our pizza. In fact, we were all a bit tired and would probably relax until she returned.

"We'll be fine," I answered. At least, we would have been fine if my sumptuous birthday cake hadn't been sitting on the table in plain view. It's the ultimate temptation and I eyed it surreptitiously while my friends chattered.

Gosh it looks good. Strawberry shortcake is heaven on earth.

Just look at those juicy glazed strawberries and swirls of whipped cream! I was beginning to salivate. *I wonder if I could just sneak one. No one will miss one little strawberry, surely.* My hand inched toward the cake. *Or maybe that dollop of icing.*

"Reanne!" Rhonda's voice was sharp and I jumped in fright. "Will you come here a moment? I want to show you something."

I subsided in relief. She hadn't seen me. "What's up?" I asked as I wandered over.

"This!" Julia exclaimed. She grabbed my arms and swung them behind my back, which was quite startling. I didn't know Julia very well – she came with Rhonda.

"What the –?" I was so confused. That's when Erin grabbed a piece of cake and tried to dump it on my head. The nerve. Well I was too quick. I jerked away with lightning speed and grabbed a piece of my cake too (oh the horror). I swooped around with the grace of a jungle cat and slam-dunked my piece of cake onto Erin's head – while the piece she intended for me hit Julia in the face.

Stunned at the turn of events, they both stood there silently while great globs of icing trailed down their hair, neck and clothes.

"You guys look rather fetching," I joked. It was that or cry – half my cake was mashed on the floor.

"Girl you fight too much," Julia muttered when she found her voice.

Yes, I do. And she'd do well to remember it in the future. After desecrating my cake in such a manner, I left them to clean the mess before mom came back while I showered upstairs. Bits of cake had splattered into my hair upon impact with Erin.

I came down feeling refreshed as Erin and Julia dumped the last drops of icing into the trashcan. They looked pretty miserable and I suppose I could have left the cake-covered girls that way for a few hours. Didn't they deserve it? But I graciously let them wash off too.

What was with everyone anyway? It was like some sort of conspiracy. Or maybe a pranking epidemic, although how Neil affected my girlfriends, I had no idea. But it *had* to be his fault. He started it and somehow I needed to get even.

I sat at the computer and emailed him about my birthday bash after everyone left. He replied and also mentioned the 'Dan' incident. He thought it would be fun for he and I to team up and prank Alex next.

Now there's a thought. At least I can get somebody back.

Re: Operation Alex.

What do you have in mind?

Reanne.

I stared at my screen and tapped my fingers along the desk as I considered what Neil suggested. I mean – it *was* a good idea. Neil wanted me to pretend to be very upset with the both of them over what they did while he took it further with Alex. The idea was to make Alex feel bad enough to write an apology email or possibly send a gift!

That's what he wrote: *If he's feeling really guilty, maybe he'll send you a little something.*

Now, I know what you're thinking – I was after a gift again. But really, I just wanted to have my own fun. It's the only reason I would agree. I zapped up a quick reply, setting things in motion.

Then I felt prickles of uncertainty. Had I done the right thing? What if Alex told everyone about it? I didn't particularly care what Alex thought of me, but did I want to have my character possibly slandered to others? Nope.

So I changed my mind. I emailed Neil to call it off.

Subject: Don't shoot me

Neil, you're going to shoot me – but I've been thinking about this and I can't go through with our prank. So I'm terminating it. I

repeat – don't continue. Let's try to get him another way some other time. Maybe we can find a way to make him jump or something?
Reanne.

I emailed Alex next; laughing about the prank they pulled on me to show how good natured and forgiving I am. Problem solved. Right?

Not at all. I still received a pompous, derogatory email from Alex. Typical attitude from him, but surprising as I thought I had cleared the air. I was quite bewildered until Neil's email came just after it.

RE: Don't shoot me
REANNE!!!

How could you do this to me??? I jumped online and everyone started talking to me right away, including Alex, so I didn't read your email until after I started talking with him. Besides that, Ms. Weak knees, I emailed him last night about how you were initially laughing, then started to get upset and how you had now blocked me and wouldn't talk to me etc.

And then you, the spineless wonder, had to get cold feet and send him an e-mail totally counteracting everything I had accomplished! That e-mail was a masterpiece and you ruined it! This whole prank was going to be a thing of beauty and you ruined it! I can't believe this.

So I'd already started into my conversation with Alex playing it up that you were furious with me, had me blocked and so on. Imagine my shock when he says, "man, she didn't seem that upset with me! She actually sent me an e-mail laughing about it and telling me how great it was!"

So I was like WHAT? Oh great! First I thought maybe it was one you sent before we planned this prank. But then I jumped into my inbox and read this and my jaw dropped! I couldn't believe it! We had the perfect prank going and you dropped the ball. Unbelievable.

So I'd already gone too far with the prank without knowing you'd jumped ship on me to go back, so I kept steaming ahead playing it up with Alex. I figured I could at least have my own little bit of fun even if you cancelled out most of my fun, Ms. Turncoat. Alex was so concerned about the two of us being on speaking terms and so convinced of his own skill at convincing you to forgive me that he told me he'd e-mail you and clear things up between you and I. Try to find out what's going on. So of course I let him.

What's more, I'm not going to send this out right away. I'm going to save it for a little bit and let Alex' e-mail get to you and run its course. I at least intend to enjoy the thought of confounding you both a little bit over this before letting you terminate the prank. Meanwhile I'm going to go to bed grimacing in pain at the thought of all the fun you spoiled on me...it was perfect!
BANG!!
Neil.

PS. I'll get over this. Sometime. At least, you can hope so.

PPS. There's no non-psychological prank you can play over the net. Think about it. What are you going to do? Splash a "virtual pie" in his face? Really now. Guess we'll just have to wait for the fun to start at Convention. 'Till then I guess I'm on my own eh?

Thankfully this email arrived before I had the opportunity to respond to Alex. So I told Alex what really happened and forwarded Neil's email for good measure. Hey – what do you know? Alex, in turn, took my email and showed it to Neil and was quite prickly about it. Probably because he thought this would definitely seal his inability to go out with me. Not that he *ever* had a chance, but I suppose he thought he did. So as you can see, I pranked Neil in the end – without even meaning to. I must be good. You have to be, to do it unintentionally.

Anyway, we put the silliness behind us and Neil and I continued to email each other over the months. What started out as emails zinging back and forth with table tennis zeal, soon carried over to phone conversations. Talk about fun! This was a guy I could really talk to. We talked about God and our convictions, our friends, and hobbies – though I refrained from sharing my interest in weddings. Men seem to get spooked by a mere reference to it.

We also discussed our fears. Well, the poor man didn't really have a choice when it came to the fear conversation. While we were on the phone one evening, this giant black insect appeared out of nowhere and flew around my room. I let out a blood-curdling screech, which I'm surprised didn't deafen Neil.

"Attack!" I yelled to my dog Snowflake who rested at the foot of my bed. She just gave me a blank stare before laying her head down and stretching out. The black beast continued to career around the room, terrifying me. "Get it Snowflake!" I tried again, to no avail.

Neil waited politely while I screamed and chased the insect around the room myself, so I could kill it and flush it down the toilet. I know, I know; flushing it was excessive. But I had to make sure it was dead. Have you ever tried to kill a wasp? You can hammer it with a gigantic shoe repeatedly and it can still get back up. I know – I've done it. I had to make sure this one didn't do the same.

Neil's fear was a little deeper than mine. He was quite hurt from his previous relationship and didn't know if he could trust another one to work out. I felt bad for him. I didn't know what it was like having never even *had* a boyfriend to break up with. I always thought when the person and the timing were right; I'd know it and that would be it. Sometimes the conversation got a little heavy – but we were very good a cheering each other.

"I have to tell you about Pebbles," I told him during one of those heavy moments. She was our hamster and my family had her many years ago when we lived in an apartment. She was quite cute and fluffy. I was the one that named her – I got it from 'The

Flintstone's.' My brother always tried to take the credit, but *I* am the brain of the family.

"My dad is a big softie," I continued, "and he thought Pebbles was cramped in her cage. I guess the light bulb clicked in his head one day and he decided to move her and her shavings into a laundry basket."

"Why a laundry basket?" Neil was intrigued.

"I don't know but that's my dad for you. I guess he thought it was a decent size and he wasn't worried about escape because the little holes in the sides of the basket weren't large enough for her to crawl through."

Neil snickered.

"Needless to say, she *did* get out of the basket on the very first night my dad moved her. And," I paused for effect. "She made it into my parents' bedroom. Mom woke up yelling in the middle of the night because Pebbles sat on her chest, staring at her with beady little eyes." This really happened. I'm not sure who was more terrified, Pebbles or my mom.

"So your dad put her back in the cage," Neil stated.

You would *think* so.

"No. He put her in the laundry basket the second night and used board games to cover the top. He didn't think she was clever enough to get out with a moveable lid."

Neil chortled with laughter. "Your dad is quite the character." Which is very true. So many of the family jokes are about dad. If there's a mishap or something goes wrong, we call it 'pulling a Tom.' He doesn't mind: he's a self-proclaimed klutz. Ok, not 'self-proclaimed' per se. But he's become accustomed to the teasing, which is only right since he can be quite the tease himself.

"I guess the little fur-ball had more brainpower than dad, because she did get out and we never saw her again."

Chapter Three

Progression

I couldn't believe how close Neil and I became throughout the year. With the many conversations and easy banter, he was right up there with Rhonda. They each had their own pedestal in my life. It was perfect having a male and female friend I could talk to about anything and bounce ideas off of. It gave me different perspectives to contemplate.

Like with the new guy in class, Justin. I told Neil about him right away. Neil thought Justin was definitely interested and he agreed Erin was jealous. Seriously, if looks could kill, I'd be dead. Her eyes burned holes through the back of my head during math – I could feel it. What was her problem anyway? She always wore nice clothes and her parents bought her everything. Did she have to have attention of every male as well? Although, I guess I couldn't blame the poor girl for being envious. She wanted the attention of every man, but she *never* got it. It just really annoyed me that she always expressed interest in the same men as me. She went after every guy I ever mentioned when I thought we were actual friends.

Anyway, Justin and I started spending a bit of time together after class and he even chased me through the school halls trying to tickle me. Except it was destined to fail. When he found out about my friendship with Neil, he got jealous. At least, I think that's what happened.

I wasn't about to give up my best friend to get a date, although I probably needed to consider drawing back at some point. Would *I* want my future boyfriend to be closer to another woman than he was to me? No. But it wasn't a concern right then because Justin didn't ask me out. Oh, he constantly stared at me and showered me with compliments, but didn't make a move.

This just proves there must be something seriously wrong with men. Neil double-crossed Alex, Justin didn't like Neil, and Alex was jealous of everybody, yet *no one* asked me out. I just didn't understand guy world.

So Justin faded from the scene and Neil and I had fun together on the rare opportunities we had to socialize in person. There were always art conventions and conferences taking place and everyone looked forward to going because you could see old friends and go to the mall to grab a bite to eat between the meetings.

At one such gathering, Neil and I found each other right away while Erin shot vibes of resentment at me with her laser-like eyes. I watched her uncertainly, because I was sure she would tear her clothes and transform into a chest beating, longhaired Hulk at any moment.

"MG!" Rhonda ran over in excitement and squashed me in a bear hug.

Ok, I've just realized another reason Erin couldn't stand me. And it wasn't my fault. 'MG' stands for 'Madame Gorgeousness.' It's a nickname Rhonda dubbed me with a while ago when she first noticed I was receiving a lot of male attention.

"You look like an angel," Neil complimented when Rhonda released me.

Erin began glowing with radioactive rage.

But I *did* look like an angel; I wore my new white, lacy outfit from *Tristan of America* and my white strappy stilettos, which were killing me. But I refused to complain – it's the price you have to pay sometimes for a bit of style and height. And I *needed* a bit of height standing next to Neil.

"So – where to for lunch? How about Kelsey's?" Rhonda *always* suggested the same place.

"We went there last time – I feel like having buffet," I countered. Buffet was clearly the better option. You can eat whatever you want and as much as you want…but no one seemed to care.

"Kelsey's it is then," Rhonda beamed.

We agreed to meet there at 1:30 p.m. and Neil went off to invite a few others.

I guess Alex caught wind of those plans because he showed up too. Figures.

Outside the restaurant, I was cold. The forceful wind (unusual for the end of May) whipped at my clothes and stung my cheeks. I rubbed at the goose bumps rising along my arms, which only succeeded in warming one patch of skin at a time, for about half a second. I know I should have had a jacket – I just couldn't bear the thought of ruining my outfit.

Alex had been gazing at me for a little while and finally offered his. I hesitated, not wanting to give him the wrong idea if I accepted it, but not for long. I didn't want to look like an ice sculpture in a few more minutes, either. With the jacket draped around my shoulders, my arms tingled as they warmed. Then my senses were assaulted.

Oh gross. *Did something die?* A foul, wretched odor darted straight to my nose and activated my gag reflex.

"Are you ok?" Rhonda's face was etched in concern as she peered at me.

"Um..." Yuck. *Yuck.* It was body odor. No, worse than that. *Ew.* It smelled as if a skunk trawled through a dumpster, then jumped into a pile of excrement and died.

Didn't Alex have access to a shower? Or at the very least – a puddle he could roll around in to take the edge off? I saw one near and should have shoved him in. Instead, I removed the jacket and handed it back with a quick, "thanks, I'm warm now." It wasn't true but I was more content to freeze than stink with him.

I suppose I should have just told the truth. It's a crime to smell like that and I might have done society a favor in telling him so, but I couldn't bring myself to do it.

"We're here!" Neil and a few others finally arrived and we went in. I sat as far away from Alex as possible. Obviously.

"I got my license!" A girl named Carry with big teeth and short hair boasted at the other end of the table. "Look how great my picture turned out," she said, passing it around.

"Mine is horrible," I mumbled.

"*You*, took a bad picture? Yeah right, let's see."

Well that was sweet of Neil to say. But there was absolutely no way I would show him the photo. Ever.

I had been *so* excited to go for my written test that I stayed up late the night before, studying. I gave myself a passing glance in the mirror the following morning then sailed through the door. I would have taken more care if I realized I was getting a photo I'd be stuck with for five years. They really should have emphasized this information in Drivers Ed…because it's more important than parallel parking, and I *still* can't do it properly (and haven't needed to), so what's the point?

I ended up with a mug shot. It was a close up (I mean, *way* too close) with my hair pulled back from my face instead of my preference – down. There were also exhaustion-induced rings beneath my eyes. I seriously didn't notice those rings when I left the house. I looked like a raccoon. With swollen and puffy lips. Don't ask me how *that* happened.

Neil wouldn't leave me alone. "Come on, it can't be that bad."

Over my dead body. I was flattered he thought so, but I wouldn't show him the picture or he couldn't live to talk about it. So really…I did him a favor.

Time to change the subject.

"Hey Neil, did I tell you about the time Jaden went for his license?"

"No."

"My mom and I went with him to get it. All the way there he hopped in his seat with excitement but we didn't realize there was a strike going on at the time."

"Why were they striking?" He seemed interested in my story!

"I don't know, but Jaden had a big smile on his face as we drew closer to the building. He couldn't wait to get out of the car. The smile faded a little but remained as we drove up to the people holding picket signs, lingered as we drove past them, and then completely dropped as we passed the building and left."

"When did he get it?"

"About a month later."

"That's good." Neil eyed my purse. "So, can I see the picture?"

"No!" *Honestly.*

We dispersed after lunch. Neil and Alex wanted to go to Starbucks so Rhonda and I decided to venture off on our own to check out the shops. The wind died down making it a decent day to go for a walk. I whipped out my Versace sunglasses and put away my Coach scarf. I bought them on sale at an outlet, but don't tell anyone. And I must say, Rhonda looked pretty hot as well in her new dress and Prada heels. She could afford the Prada at full price since she entered a musical composition into a contest and won (that and the fact her family is rich). And why not look our best? Neither of us ever had a boyfriend – we were each determined to get one. Now that I think about it, isn't it odd that *no one* in our circle of friends ever dated? I guess our standards were higher when it came to finding the right guy. We didn't have five-minute relationships in middle school for the sake of it like everyone else.

Actually, Rhonda *couldn't* have a five-minute relationship because her dad was strict, and I just wasn't interested back then. Ok, that's not quite true. The truth is, I was always the shortest kid in class (and got teased mercilessly because of it) and didn't start catching up until I was fourteen, and by then all the nice boys were taken…except for Jeremy White whom I almost went out with, but nothing came of it. I don't know why that didn't work out.

"Oh wow. Reanne – look!" Rhonda's eyes sparkled.

She spotted a bridal shop. And…wow. Just, wow. There was a gorgeous gown in the window. It's like a fairy godmother popped up onto my shoulder and commanded me to enter. And let's face it, who am I to argue with my fairy godmother? When you're given such noble, worthy instructions…you just…do it.

Ten minutes later, Rhonda sat on the couch and I was feeling more beautiful than I've ever felt. It was perfect. The bodice was snug and covered in sequins and jewels. Talk about bling. The full-length skirt cascaded like a waterfall of lace and silk. And the tiara. Oh don't get me started on the tiara. I felt like Princess Diana. I was finally a blushing bride and I couldn't stop looking into the mirror.

I gasped.

Oh no. No, no, no. I stared at the shock of red hair and freckles in horror. Alex was gawking at me through the shop window; I could see his pudgy face in the corner of my mirror. I had to get out of sight. Fast.

I leaped off the stool in one mad dash and huddled into a ball of crinoline on the dressing room floor. Maybe he only passed by and didn't really get a good look at me. It could have been anyone, right? There were plenty of pumpkin look-alikes around town. A minute passed. I poked my head out and a pair of red, six-inch heels came into view.

"Excuse me, if you're not taking the dress, please *carefully* step out of it and leave our store," the sales clerk requested with a tight smile.

I glanced up – the real brides all gaped at me, and Rhonda scooted away on the sofa as if we weren't together.

An interested babble began going around the room and I heard whispered comments like "deranged," and "serious issues." Excuse me; *I* had issues? The woman who murmured it sounded like Bridezilla. I looked at her expecting a severe face or even a hideous snarl – but the woman was actually quite stunning.

The dress she had on was not. *That* was revolting. The empire waist made her appear ten pounds heavier than she probably was and the little slab of fabric across the top was too tight. Her bulging, lumpy breasts looked as if they were about to split the dress.

She seriously had to pick something else. She *had* to…unless she planned on being the entertainment at her own wedding.

"Hello there," I gathered my dress and stood. "Yes you. Hi," I gave a friendly wave. "I was just noticing your gown and – "

I didn't finish because she turned and walked away. I stared after her in mystified silence. Some people can be so rude. Well fine. I only wanted to help. Her groom was destined to take off in the opposite direction during her debut down the aisle…and it wasn't my problem.

"Reanne, we need to go or we'll be late for the convention." Rhonda's hand landed on her hip as I stepped back into the dressing room. "And why did you dive off like some lunatic?"

"*Lunatic?*" I echoed, affronted. "I saw Alex! Just outside." I caught her expression. "Don't give me that look, he was *there*."

So Rhonda didn't think Alex walked past but I still needed reassurance. "Do you think he'll tell Neil?"

"No."

"What if he thinks I want to marry *him?*"

Rhonda huffed in exasperation. "Stop being paranoid."

Easy for her to say…she wasn't being stalked by a carrot top. I finished getting into my Tristan outfit – quite sad and dull looking compared to the gown I had on – and we made our way to the convention.

When we arrived, Neil and Alex were behaving normally – well, whatever you would consider normal for Alex.

"What took so long?" Neil asked.

He had *to ask.*

I darted a look of appreciation at Rhonda when she said, "we lost track of time." And it was totally true – I would have convinced Rhonda to get into a gown as well if we weren't interrupted.

Neil grinned at me and looked a little smug. I didn't think it was paranoia; he really looked like the cat that swallowed the canary.

Throughout the meetings I kept firing distrustful looks in his direction, which he ignored (or genuinely didn't notice). Maybe I was safe after all.

I'll have to be more cautious in the future.

And by that I mean sticking to visiting bridal shops in my hometown. Alone. It's difficult though. Have you ever been out and you've seen a perfect outfit you *had* to look at, even though you knew you couldn't afford it? Or you've had a sudden craving for fries and you've driven to McDonald's like a maniac until you had some? Well that's what it's like for wedding gowns and me. Ok, fries too. I think it's just this innate drive that all people have. There's something dear to each of us and that's what gives us the zap of strength to get through each day. I knew you'd understand. We all have our guilty pleasures.

A week after the convention I received a letter in the mail from Neil. And yes, I can assure you it really did come from him. Not Alex, or Neil pretending to be Alex. Anyway. It was a pleasant note reviewing the weekend and the fun we had. And asking why he hadn't been invited to my wedding. Har-di-har. What a dork.

Chapter Four

Summer

Things heated up when camp rolled around once again. I anticipated the activities and fellowship, and Neil looked forward to tricking people. Do boys ever grow up? I don't think so. Plus, he *actually* thought I would help him. I'll admit it was entertaining while we discussed possible schemes to play out, but he should have known by then I wouldn't participate in reality. He referred to us as 'conspiratorial co-prankers' and began making cryptic calling cards we could leave in our wake. Seriously. Neil made business size cards with an image of a cheeky little devil in the center and a lightning bolt emblazoned on the side with a caption reading – 'How does THAT strike you?' Didn't he remember what happened when we tried to prank Alex? It wouldn't go over well. I also didn't want to jeopardize my camp experience by being kicked out if we were caught.

One thing he wanted us to do was to put confetti on the cafeteria fan so it would fly everywhere when someone turned it on. I'm not sure how he planned to accomplish this since the fan was on the ceiling, twenty feet up. Neil was tall but he wasn't *that* tall, and I doubt a ladder would have conveniently materialized against the wall. He also wanted me to betray the girls by rigging the toilets so water would spurt back at them when they flushed at night. I'm pretty certain a riot would have ensued. And if they realized I had anything to do with it I would have squealed like a songbird so the lynch mob could go after Neil. Hmm. Now *there's* an idea.

I contemplated a few of his schemes – he made it sound like it would be a hoot and gave me half the calling cards he designed.

Oh. And he brought giant super-soakers to camp. You know, those huge water guns that hold about a gallon of water? During downtime at camp, he strutted around with it brandished and shot any innocent person in his path. He even hit Rhonda, poor girl. Rhonda was really obsessed with her hair and didn't want to get it wet. So what did he do? He aimed it right at her head. I knew his actions were intentional and she was going to kill him…after she went back to her cabin and spent hours wringing it out, trying to flatten it again. I was protected though – we had a pact so I was free to walk around and not worry about being targeted.

Camp was a blast that year – there was even a beach day. The guys all went together at the beginning of the week, and the girls went the day after. We went on this old yellow bus. It was loud and creaky – I questioned our safety. It was this enormous, belching monstrosity you could hear coming from a mile away. No wonder the guys easily ambushed us.

We pulled onto the campground and descended the steps, completely oblivious to the army-clad men sneaking out of the forest. Suddenly they were running at us and screaming like a bunch of ninja banshees while we halted in shock. Their faces were painted in green and black streaks, some of them wore bandannas…and they *all* had water guns. Neil was at the forefront as their ringleader and I swear he was strutting about like Rambo. Girls scattered like bugs as bullets of water pelted the bus. One startled girl almost nosedived down the stairs right in front of me.

I eyed Neal indignantly. *Why don't I know about this? We're supposed to be in on it together.* But I was just as gobsmacked as everyone else.

In the corner of my eye, I saw Alex round a building with a water gun almost bigger than him. The little twerp aimed it right at me so I jumped the last step of the bus and ran. His stubby little legs moved surprisingly fast as he gained momentum. I glanced over my shoulder as I headed for the cabins…and you should see this guy run. It was like being chased by an Umpa Lumpa on Red Bull. I only needed him to sing some silly song and he would have stepped right out of a scene from the movie.

I panted as I ducked out of sight near the bathrooms.

I think I lost him.

A few moments passed before I checked the coast. It was clear. No super-soaker-crazed maniacs in sight. I released my breath and tiptoed toward my cabin, the one at the end of the strip. I squinted, as there appeared to be a big black can next to it.

Just about there. Almost to safety, I thought in relief.

Hang on a minute. What is *that?* A huge truck tire, filled with cement was parked right outside my door. I grabbed the edge and pulled. It didn't budge. I propped my back against the door and kicked at it with my feet. The stupid thing wouldn't move. How on earth did it get there?

My hand flew to my chest as Neil stepped out of the shadows and nearly gave me a heart attack.

"Oh, it's just you," I breathed.

A wicked grin split his face as he produced the king of all water guns and doused me with it. The hose connected to a large backpack that kept pumping the water out. I spluttered and put my hands up in an attempt to block the flow while Neil sprayed and laughed gleefully until I was little more than a drowned rat. I stared after him mutinously, the water dripping from my nose, as he sauntered off looking for his next victim.

He was *going* to regret that.

The next day was a busy one. Organized activities were taking place with a variety of fun stations set up. Everyone was occupied.

I was alone, hovering at the entrance of Neil's cabin that he shared with some other guy. A thorough sweep of the area had been conducted to ensure its desertion. There was no way I would mess this up.

My body tingled with exhilaration and a bit of fear as I crept to the door and grabbed the handle. *I'm really doing this.* My heart thundered in my chest. *I'm breaking in!*

I stepped back from the door and surveyed the open window above the bush one last time. I really didn't want to pick the lock on the door. *Can I fit…? No. The window will definitely be a tight squeeze.* Getting stuck would be way too compromising.

I didn't exactly know how to pick a lock, but I heard a credit card is quite handy for this sort of thing. I took my debit card out of my pocket (it's all I had) and touched the handle with my right hand.

The door clicked as if being opened from the other side and my heart slammed through my chest.

"Ouch," I grunted as I careened into the shrub and scraped my knee. The debit card was discarded in the dust.

In plain view.

Crap.

I could only hope it would go unnoticed. My legs curled into my chest while I waited silently for the angry shouts of discovery. Minutes passed and nothing happened. I could see from my vantage point through the foliage that no one was there. I completely overreacted. The cabin was empty and the door was unlocked. It must have opened when I hit the handle.

I stood and dusted the debris from my hair and clothes, feeling a flood of relief. The debit card went back into my pocket.

Well…I'll never understand how anyone can break and enter on a regular basis. It nearly killed me, just there.

I stepped inside the musty cabin and glanced around. Clothes were scattered about; books were strewn across the dresser. The odd board game littered the floor and beds, but there wasn't anything I really wanted to take.

How disappointing.

And then I spotted it. The lone super-soaker ensconced in a heavenly light. Well actually, it was just sitting in a sunbeam shining through the window, but I knew with absolute clarity what I needed to do. The perfect pay back. I snatched it up and retreated to the safety of my cabin.

Ha ha! I pulled it off! It was my turn to gloat – but not right away of course. I wanted him to sweat a little wondering what happened to it.

Later that day, Neil emerged from his cabin in a panic.

Yes! I reveled from my hiding spot. *This will teach him.*

He began his futile search in the surrounding area of the crime scene and eventually extended it to other parts of the campground. He didn't say anything to anyone and people looked at him oddly, while I snickered. *Yes, yes!*

As the hour wore on, my pleasure began to fade as Neil became increasingly anxious. He was really worried. Blast my conscience!

Ok. I didn't want to walk up and admit I took it. And I *certainly* wasn't ready to return it.

How can I indicate that it's just being borrowed?

I thought hard. And then, like a flash flood, it hit me. The cards! I completely forgot about the calling cards. I hadn't used any yet.

My face fell as I realized I needed to sneak back in. *Darn.*

If looks could kill – I'd be dead. Neil was furious I had taken his precious water gun. What audacity! If anyone should have been steamed, it was I. After all – didn't he drown me earlier? Didn't he block me from my cabin with a two-ton tire?

"I could have you kicked out of camp for this," Neil hissed heatedly in my ear as he thrust the card at me.

Jeez. Some people can give it but they can't take it…what a baby. Suddenly, my conscience cleared. He deserved it.

"When am I getting it back?" he sulked.

"Maybe never!" I retorted. I knew he wouldn't *really* have me kicked out of camp because I would never speak to him again. Besides, he knew I'd give it back. Eventually. But not until I was finished with it.

So. You probably think I took immense pleasure in drenching him, and I'm sure that would have been fun. But that's not how it happened. I didn't do it. Oh, I suppose I could have blasted him with it myself but it just seemed so much sweeter to give it to

Rhonda and let her do the deed later that evening. After all – she was the one walking around with an Afro the size of New Jersey.

She spent the evening armed with the water gun and snuck up on Neil while he talked with another guy. She was so close, aiming it at his back; her finger poised on the trigger. It looked like she was going to get him. It really did.

"Hey, let go! Let. It. GO!" Rhonda grunted and strained.

Neil spun around and wrestled the gun away from her…and shot her in the head again, increasing the volume of her hair by another two inches. Poor girl. She screeched, stomped her foot and ran back to the cabin in hysteria. I don't know how she ever got her hair back down to normal. I of course, was out of sight. I refused to be victimized by the waterworks any longer.

Throughout the rest of the week, Neil and I were inseparable. I chose to forgive his treachery. I *did* get even so I felt pretty good. We spent the remaining time at camp hanging out and laughing, to the point that people began to look at us suspiciously. As if we were a couple.

At least…that's what I gathered from the Spanish drummer leaning against the cafeteria wall. He kept smiling at me as I waited for my food. "Neil's a pretty great guy, eh?" His eyes gleamed. "You must really *like* him."

Well of course I liked him or we wouldn't have been friends. And what was I? Chopped liver? I liked to think I was pretty great too.

The line moved forward and I grabbed a tray. I guess plain ham sandwiches were on the menu. Again. Oh well. I took one and found a table.

"Hey Reanne." Neil came over and sat next to me as I dug in. I glanced at him – and he looked a little perturbed. "You didn't grab my lunch?" He stared pointedly at my plate.

"Um…no." Was I supposed to? No wonder people thought we were an item. *Why* would I reserve his lunch? Maybe if there was one sandwich left and I knew he'd be joining me, then that would have been different. Rhonda and I didn't get meals for each other.

Perhaps he asked me to and I forgot. Yes, that had to be it.

Neil stood impatiently in line while the guy against the wall struck up a conversation with him too. "So, you like Reanne, eh?"

Although at that exact moment, I'm not too sure he did. The line had grown – quite a bit I noticed – and Neil didn't seem pleased about it.

I guess I should have saved his lunch. I shrugged in guilt. *Too late now.*

"I can't believe camp is over," Rhonda sighed. "I'll miss it." The last day arrived and we were packing our clothes.

"It went too fast," I agreed.

"Is this the last bag?" Jaden entered the room and lifted Rhonda's huge Louis Vuitton case.

"No, I'm just finishing mine," I told him. Once that was taken to the car we made the rounds and said goodbye to our friends.

"So this was fun," I gave Neil a hug. "It's kind of sad it's over."

"I know," he nodded. "Do you have any plans for the rest of the summer?"

"My parents rented a cottage for the last week. It should be fun. You?"

"There's a trip planned to an amusement park. A few of us are going." His eyes lit. "Hey, would you and Jaden be interested in joining us?"

Excitement bubbled up until I remembered how far he lived. "I'm not sure how we'd get there," I said simply.

Neil was confident. "I'm sure we can figure it out."

"Then we'd love to go. Thanks," I added.

"No problem." He winked at me. "Anything to get you there."

It turned out Alex lived thirty minutes away from me and was taking a group to the park in a rented van. Neil arranged for Jaden and I to drive to Alex's house and go with them. Oh joy, I really looked forward to *that*. Had I been aware of the arrangements before Neil bought the tickets, I might have said no.

This day is gorgeous!

The sky was bright as Jaden and I stepped out of the car. I smoothed my cute coral skirt and adjusted the white lacey top. I don't mean to brag, but I designed the outfit myself and had it put together by a professional seamstress. And it looked *awesome!*

Jaden tapped on the front door three times before Alex flung it open. "Come in!" He gestured toward the family room. "We're still waiting on a few others."

We sat on the green and beige sofas and made small chat until everyone else arrived. Before we knew it, it was time to go.

Alex blatantly checked me out as I climbed into the van. "Neil will be impressed," he said as I slid into the back seat. Then he waggled his bushy red brows suggestively.

Who said I wanted to impress anyone?

Instead of dignifying that with an answer, I popped my earphones in and tuned him out. Ah, *much* better.

Alex hopped into the front seat and the van began rolling along. Occasionally I caught sight of Alex's lips moving as we made the journey to the park, but I couldn't hear him. Just like a pantomime. I only turned the music down if it looked like someone else tried to get my attention, but things were pretty quiet for the most part. I even fell asleep.

I yawned and looked around in bleary-eyed puzzlement. *Where am I?* Oh right. The amusement park. I perked up and clambered out of the van the moment it stopped. I had to move fast…the van had become stinky. Which came as no surprise since Alex was in it.

My eyes darted around in wonderment at the massive roller coasters shooting up into the sky. *This will be a blast!*

Jaden zoomed past me when he spotted a few girls from camp.

"Howdy," Neil drawled as he appeared next to me. He wore a black, patterned shirt with jeans, and his face was laced with adventure (or was it deviousness?). My stomach momentarily swooped with misgiving but it didn't look like he had a prank up his sleeve. Which was good for him. I didn't want to push him off a roller coaster, but I would have if provoked.

"We're splitting into groups," Neil instructed.

Jaden, being the popular guy that he is dashed off with two girls and of course Neil and I stuck together. I think Alex trailed after Jaden's group. Yes, that must be right since Jaden told me later that Alex was angry because the girls ignored him. I was baffled by Alex's reaction – you would think he'd be used to it by now.

Neil and I sat side by side and buckled up in preparation for the first ride. We lifted off, then zoomed and rotated like a psychotic spinning top. It wasn't really my thing, but Neil loved it.

I love the rides that drop. I mean, really drop – the ones where your stomach clenches and your heart stops. And what better way to get that death defying experience than to bungee jump? I know. I must be crazy. But I just love heights. Or rather – plunging off of them, which is why I convinced Neil to try that next.

"Are you sure about this?" Neil mumbled as we ascended in a stretcher-like contraption.

"This will be great. I know it!" We could see the entire park as we climbed higher and higher. "Just don't look at the lake," I said while grinning stupidly. I of course stared straight at it to heighten the thrill.

The rides below grew smaller and smaller until they all looked like tiny ants. Neil tightened the arm looped through mine. "I can't believe I let you talk me into this," he choked out through gritted teeth.

"Juuuust relaaax," I soothed. Then I pulled the ripcord.

A scream tore through my throat as we plummeted toward our deaths. My arm went numb as Neil squeezed it, hard. I heard him bellow next to me, but all I could focus on was the lake quickly coming upon us. I squeezed my eyes closed, knowing the contact would be like smacking into concrete.

I screamed again…or maybe I never stopped…as we swung forward and arched high into the air just moments before disaster.

"Wahoooooooooo!" I yelled, completely exhilarated.

Neil released my arm (which would need to be amputated now, due to a severe loss of circulation) and extended his own out front.

Hmm. I gazed at Neil appreciatively. *He looks like Clark Kent.*

"You were right," Neil asserted with shining eyes. "This *is* great!"

I beamed back as we sailed toward the lake again. "I'm *always* right," I said a bit cheekily.

"Is that so?" Neil tilted his head toward me.

Oh my goodness. My eyes widened. *He's going to kiss me!*

My breath caught in a mix of anticipation and fear. My best friend was about to go for it, bouncing from a bungee.

My first kiss!

Except it wasn't. He turned away and let out a roar of laughter as we zipped past the water again and slowed down.

I shook off the disappointment that followed. It would have been all wrong, anyway. I mean – you shouldn't kiss your best friend just because you have a near death experience together. Exactly. Besides...I bet it didn't even cross his mind. I was being silly.

Or was I? We left the bungee area and Neil wanted to visit an ice cream stand like a sugar-crazed energizer bunny getting a high before the next ride. "Are you having any?" he asked.

"Naa. Maybe later."

"Want some of mine?"

"I don't have a spoon," I said simply.

"It's ok, I don't mind sharing with *you*."

"Whaaaat's uuup?!" Jaden called as he and the girls headed our way. I swiveled around to look at them as they drew near.

"Hey – can I have some?" Alex asked, spotting the ice cream. I guess he assumed the answer was 'yes' because his hand went sailing toward the spoon.

Neil dodged him. "Not a chance."

And who could blame him? It's one thing to share with me but no one would want the spoon back after Alex.

Chapter Five

The Cottage

I breathed a contented sigh as I stood outside the cottage and took in my surroundings. There was silence all around me but I knew the swampy ditches teemed with life. Frogs, salamanders and all sorts of critters lurked just beneath the cloudy surface. The landscape reminded me of visiting my grandparent's cabin when I was younger. We'd go on long weekends; I was always armed with my buckets and nets and a grin would poke through my mud-streaked face as I presented them with whatever toad or turtle I captured. Not that I would do that now, of course. I'm much more mature and refined. It just felt nice to reminisce. I was Indiana Jones – the female version – and this world was mine to explore.

I sighed again and fixed my eyes on the lake with longing. It sparkled as though covered by millions of diamonds and a fish splashed in the distance. *Diving in from dad's new speedboat would be so refreshing right now.*

He bought it earlier in the summer and it was very attractive. All shiny and bright – it was his new baby. Seriously.

He took better care of that thing and paid more attention to it than Jaden and I.

Ok…maybe I'm exaggerating a little. But he spent hours cleaning it, making adjustments to it, and basically not letting anyone near it while he worked, which was a little annoying since we all wanted to see it.

The benefit from all his labor, however, was using it at the cottage every day. It was already mid-week and we had been on the boat half a dozen times, flying over the waves while the wind whipped our hair. Occasionally we rested in the middle of the lake while Jaden back flipped off the edge of the boat.

"Show off," I'd mumble. I didn't attempt it.

Even Giselle cringed every time he made that potentially fatal leap. Giselle is a family friend, has been for many years, and my parents invited her to stay in the adjacent cottage with her three sons. Her husband Martin couldn't attend due to work obligations, which I actually think worked out really well. Snowflake wasn't fond of him at all and growled every time she saw him. I think it's because Martin never let her sleep on their bed when they looked after her for us. Giselle didn't mind though, and allowed her to have Martin's spot if he worked the late shift.

One night Giselle and Snowflake were snuggled in bed when Martin came home and found his pillow outside the bedroom door on the floor. He assumed Giselle was angry with him and slept on the couch. It turned out Snowflake dragged the pillow there. Everyone always laughs at this story and Martin will too…but I always catch him giving Snowflake the evil eye during the retelling.

"Can we go fishing? Please! Pretty please!" Giselle's youngest bounded up to my dad and tugged his shirt.

"In a bit Jared," dad answered absently as he fiddled with the lawn mower. "This blasted contraption isn't working!"

That was the only downside to having the boat. I'm not opposed to fishing as long as I don't have to spear the worm myself, and as long as the fish actually stay far away from me as they're being hauled into the hull.

This of course was never the case with the boys. They giggled uncontrollably as worms were thrust in my face and slimy, writhing fish slapped against my legs. I couldn't help but flinch and jump away.

Other than *that*, all enjoyed the boat and the cottage. Except for maybe my dad when he struggled with the mower. I watched him in a mix of amusement and concern as he poked at it. It seemed to be working just fine and I gasped as his finger loomed dangerously close to the blade. "Dad! Look ou – "

He moved his finger out of the way. *That was close.*

The only teeny thing that niggled me during this vacation…just this one little thought, is that it would have been nice to have a boyfriend present. I didn't *need* a boyfriend obviously, but the idea of having someone to snuggle up with next to the fire really appealed to me.

Instead I sat by the fire alone that evening, watching the marshmallow at the end of my stick shriveling as it burned. Ok, not *alone* alone. My family was there, and Giselle's family and my dog. But having Snowflake nestled against me was *not* what I had in mind.

She gave my hand a friendly lick as if sensing my thoughts. "You're a good girl," I murmured and gave her a pat on the head, before getting up and heading to my room.

I awoke the next morning to the sound of distant chatting, instead of the usual chorus of crickets and birds. *What's going on?* I thought groggily, squinting at the clock.

Ugh, 6:30 a.m. Why would anyone *be up at this time?*

I flung myself against the pillow, fully intending to pull the covers over my head and drown them out.

A muffled laugh drifted down the corridor and I paused. The blanket remained suspended over my head as I craned to hear. *What's going on out there?*

I was torn. I had to make a paramount decision. Go back to sleep, which my body desired to do, or be nosey like those poor saps in films who don't mind their own business and then get caught and tortured by terrorists. *Obviously* I would go back to bed. I'm not a moron. Clearly my body needed the rest.

You know, I couldn't fall asleep with the racket anyway. I swung my legs over the side of the bed and stumbled out – where I nearly tripped over Jaden's black Nike shoe.

"Arghghghgh," came my garbled moan as I caught my balance.

I didn't know why his shoe was in *my* room but I'll tell you one thing – I planned to shove it down his throat the moment I saw him.

Ok, deep, calming breath. I'm not a morning person. But I'd be fine once I had coffee. I mean – I wouldn't *really* choke my brother with his own shoe, no matter how appealing the thought.

I kicked it aside and stumbled into the hall where I passed the little mirror by the front door.

"Gaaah!" I caught sight of my reflection. Hair stuck out in every direction and a bird might have been nesting in it too. I took a few quick swipes at it with my hand and smoothed it down a fraction before continuing out the door. *It's just my family*, I reassured myself. *They've seen this a zillion times.* Besides, I didn't need to dress up just to see a toad. I assumed that's what all the fuss was about.

The boys went on about it all week, saying how big and fast it was – maybe they caught it. I actually wanted to see this.

I hastily ducked through the door and collided with some klutz on the porch. Ok, I still needed that coffee.

"Hey, watch where you're going," I snapped. I could feel a scowl on my face.

My expression must have changed to one of astonishment as I found myself gazing into a pair of grey-blue eyes, obscured partially by a shock of light brown hair.

"No. I don't believe it!" I reached out and pinched.

"I believe the point of that exercise," said Neil, bemused, "is to pinch *yourself*." His lips twisted into a wry smile. "Surprised?"

Surprised? Was he kidding? I was stunned. I squealed excitedly and then shrieked in terror when I remembered the condition of my hair.

I look like crap!

I left Neil in a cloud of confusion as I stormed back to my room, this time actually tripping over the stupid shoe and banging my elbow. I felt a surge of outrage.

"JADEN," I bellowed. "JA-DEN!"

He appeared around the corner and crouched as the shoe whipped past his fat head.

All right, I know I overreacted…but my elbow throbbed, and someone should have mentioned Neil was coming. I mean, who *does* that? Who in their right mind invites a guy over without giving a girl any notice?

"Cool, you found my shoe, I've been looking for that." Jaden was *so* oblivious. "And you might want to fix yourself up, I invited Neil for the day. He's going home tomorrow morning," he added before ducking out like the rat he is.

I had to remain calm. So what that I nearly broke my neck? So what that Neil saw my hair looking completely dysfunctional? Jaden tried to do something nice for me – I reminded myself. And how did I repay him? By nearly knocking him out with his own shoe. It *really* shouldn't have been in my room. I should have aimed better.

Stay calm. This is no big deal. I can salvage this.

I attacked my hair with a boar bristle brush like never before. It ran through my hair a few times before it snagged and tangled.

Oh come on!

I tugged in one direction and then the other. It seemed to be coming loose, one more little yank and it would be free. Then I heard the snap. Great. Just. Great. My hair ripped.

I pulled the small clump from the brush and exhaled. This is what happens when you rush. My mind raced through hair care articles I previously read before recalling a tip about combing from the bottom up. I tried again.

Oh forget it! Minutes later, I was no further along and more frustrated than when I started. It was no use. There wasn't enough time and I was still drowsy, which didn't help.

I pulled a vintage silk scarf from my drawer and wrapped it around my head. Done. Out I go.

"Sorry about that!" I laughed as I stepped onto the porch. "Neil?" I looked around in bewilderment. He was gone. The guy had more moves than Houdini.

Then I spotted the candy wrappers alongside the cottage and my ears tuned in to the ruckus coming from the same direction. I followed the trail of litter, and once I focused, I'm surprised I didn't hear the noise sooner. I mean honestly, you could hear it a mile away. I rounded the corner to the back of the cottage, and there they were. Giselle's sons climbed all over Neil like a little band of monkeys while he stood there, letting them.

My heart warmed. It's so nice to see a man having fun with kids! Neil was a youth leader in his local church, so it was good to see him in action.

"Swing me! Swing me!" chanted the youngest boy who was perched on Neil's shoulders. His legs flailed about in front of Neil's chest and his hands were wrapped around his head, nearly gouging his eye. The middle boy clung to Neil's leg like a leach. I thought I'd see blood suckers if I looked closely enough. The last boy stood to the side and kept yelling "my turn! My turn!" like an annoying broken record.

I'm not opposed to kids having fun or anything. It's great. It's just that…Neil had only been there a few minutes and the boys were totally monopolizing him.

No, it just wouldn't do. Neil was only staying one night and I couldn't have them demanding to be zoomed around like airplanes until he collapsed.

I'll give them a bit more time, I decided generously. *Let them get it out of their systems.*

I stared at my watch, my foot unconsciously tapping, and interrupted after precisely sixty seconds. "Hi!" I cut in loudly.

Neil pried the children away, except for the one still clinging to his leg, dragging behind him as he made his way over. "Good to see you," he hugged me.

I caught a big whiff of something spicy and woodsy and wondered what scent he wore. Not that it would do him any good here. If he didn't replace it for insect repellent – and fast – the bugs were going to get him.

"What *is* that?" Neil's nose wrinkled in disdain as he sniffed the air around me.

"What's *what?*" I asked, slightly offended.

I know I didn't look the greatest, and I certainly hadn't doused myself in perfume like he had, but was it really necessary to comment? Honestly, what did Neil expect – that I would look like a beauty queen in *that* setting on a surprise visit?

"Cottage life suits you," he quipped with a gleam in his eye. "And I like your fragrance, what is it?" he asked with a straight face.

"Insect repellent," I replied pleasantly as the flies began to descend upon him in a thick, bloodthirsty cloud. He was suddenly serious about liking my scent and I tossed him a nearby can. "Knock yourself out," I said with a smile. "Before the bugs do."

"You might want to hang on," I advised wisely. The mid-day sky became overcast and the water was choppy. The boat dipped precariously over the waves and the cool water splashed our faces.

"Do you need me to hang onto *you*?" Neil projected over the roar of the wind. *Har-har. Like I don't know how to stay in my own boat.* Dad smashed the boat into another wave and my bum flew off the seat before colliding with it again. It was dangerous, yet Neil and I grinned at each other like idiots.

"Tom, we should head back. This isn't safe." Poor Giselle sat miserably at the back where she sported two yellow life jackets.

"It's ok," said dad easily. "I've done this before."

The boat rose again before pounding down into the water. We nearly capsized.

"Tom." There was a definite edge to her voice. "I've had enough."

Dad didn't seem to hear her. "Who wants to ride on the sea biscuit?" He cut the motor.

"I'll go first!" Dad tossed it into the water and I hopped on with determination. I was *really* good at staying on the sea biscuit. My fingers wrapped around the smooth handles and locked in an iron grip. Once I get a hold of something, I usually don't let go. Just ask anyone from my elementary school days.

There's this huge hill on the playground of my old school that iced over every winter. Kids always went mental, diving down it and hollering with glee until grade six boys claimed it for themselves. They wouldn't let anyone else have fun. Of course a few brave souls tried it anyway, only to be immediately tossed off.

And then I came along. Little me in grade four. The hill sloped away from someone's back fence and I inched along it undetected until I was able to lace my fingers through the spaces in a superglue grip.

As soon as I was discovered, I had an entire brigade of boys pulling at my legs, trying to peel me off. I held on as tightly as I could, delivering the occasional kick. I think I even nailed one guy in the head before he slid away – which I was quite proud of.

Well what did they think would happen? I'd easily let go and whistle a merry little tune all the way to the bottom? No way. I adhered myself to that fence all through the lunch hour until the bell rang, and they dubbed me 'Poligrip' for the rest of the school year (the adhesive that helps elderly people stick their dentures to their gums).

I would deploy Poligrip again.

"Ready?" Neil called out.

"Go for it!" I shouted back.

He nodded at dad and away we went. Giselle still clutched the side of the boat and she appeared to be telling them off.

My eyes stung as the wind hit my face and water poured over my head. The sea biscuit bounced along like a skipping rock but I held on through every jarring, jerky movement.

I'm doing so well! I laughed aloud and swallowed a mouthful of lake water. *Ew!*

At least twenty minutes passed. My hands were hurting and I suspected there might be a few blisters afterward, but I didn't care. I would stay on it all day if I had to. I was *going* to do better than Neil.

Just then, the biscuit hit a monstrous wave that sent me rocketing through the air and I slammed into the murky depths. I emerged with my hair plastered to the side of my face.

"How did I do?" I asked as Neil hauled me into the boat.

Dad held up two fingers.

Yes! I resisted the urge to pump my fist into the air. "Twenty minutes. I knew it!"

Neil stifled a laugh.

"*What*?" I glared at him. "You think *you* can do better?"

"Sorry to break it to you hun," said dad kindly, "you were only *two minutes*." He wiggled his fingers.

How*? How* could that be? It felt like much longer and I would have the aches and pains tomorrow to prove it. Oh well. I took solace in the fact that Neil would likely last two seconds. He wasn't used to it like I was.

Neil reigned in the sea biscuit and took his place. And as he settled himself in – the waves died down and the sun poked through the clouds. I glanced around in confusion.

No. No way.

The boat roared to life and away we went. With Neil soaring behind it on a smooth glassy surface.

This is officially unfair. I rode behemoth waves while he sailed along. For crying out loud, he looked comfortable enough to take a nap out there.

Five minutes passed, then ten, then fifteen.

"STOP THE BOAT," I yelled. Neil tugged the rope to pull himself in, and as he stretched one long, lean leg into the boat, I gave him a push. Just a friendly little shove – I didn't *mean* for him to flip over the side. Well, ok. I did. I mean come on – who has clouds part and winds die down for them like that? So *randomly?* Completely annoying.

I was almost satisfied with his overturn into the water until he popped up and dragged me in with him.

"Don't beat yourself up," Neil consoled as I slapped water at him. "You tried."

Uh huh. I pushed his head under water and followed as dad anchored the boat.

I opened my eyes in the manky depths and searched for a set of illuminated toes. I thought it might be fun to give Neil a little scare.

Hang on a minute. *What if toe-eating fish actually live here?* A sudden vision swam before my eyes. Divers finding my skeleton at the bottom of the lake and everyone at my funeral tragically commenting to one another that it was "such a sad way to go."

Trying not to panic, I headed to the surface with Neil emerging just seconds later. No wonder I couldn't find his feet. He was probably attempting to do the same to me.

Actually, I'm *glad* I didn't try that. It wasn't the way I wanted to spend the entire day with him.

The rest of the day blurred past in a jumble of jokes and conversation. At suppertime, I helped mom prepare the meal while Neil wandered off with Jaden for some 'guy talk.' And afterwards, there was a big fun bonfire where Giselle's boys continued clamoring for Neil's attention. I could barely stay awake – I was completely fried. Needless to say, I went to bed that night and fell asleep almost before my head hit the pillow. I was gone. Totally and completely gone.

And so was Neil. He got up early the next morning to make the long drive home and by the time I came out, I missed him. It would have been nice to say a proper goodbye in the morning, but it worked out in the end. I couldn't have seen Neil anyway. I woke up with a bunch of nasty little welts on my face – a mosquito attacked me while I slept. When I finally found it, I squashed it. Twice. Stupid bug.

Subject: (None)

It was great seeing you at the cottage, I had a wonderful time. Please send my thanks along to Jaden for the invite (although I'm really surprised you didn't invite me yourself! Tsk tsk Reanne!). We'll have to fix that. You can make it up to me by planning a trip to my neck of the woods sometime. ☺ At any rate, I just wanted to let you know how much I enjoyed our time together this summer. Talk soon, and good luck getting organized for school!

Neil.

Chapter Six

Transition

I finally got my braces off. *Finally.* I felt dazzling and wonderful and…well…free! What a great way to begin the school year.

To celebrate, Rhonda and I went shopping followed by a trip to the salon for some extreme pampering. My teeth were finally released from the prison that held them hostage for three years, yeah!

"How about this one?" Rhonda asked.

"Umm…I'm not sure if that look is really *in* at the moment." Our feet were submerged in water (awaiting pedicures) and Rhonda pointed at a picture of a glamorous woman sporting a sleek, short bob.

"Of course it is!" Rhonda's voice throbbed with intensity. "Many women have this look and it's fab!" She touched her own hair self-consciously. "I'm tired of these nightmarish curls and I'd like to try this. I've been wanting to do something new for a while now."

"Really? You never mentioned it." I admired her mane of hair as she examined the photo. "I don't think you should. You have amazing hair and you can enhance it so much with just a bit of gel or mouse."

The problem was getting her to regularly use the products. Without them, she resembled an electrocuted hamster. So I guess she had a point. Still…it was worth a shot to convince her otherwise. "You just have to get into a routine with styling your hair and it would be fine."

"No. I'm doing this," she said with a note of finality. "It will really suit me."

My brow creased dubiously. "If you say so."

I tried desperately not to laugh. Or wince. Or…anything. It was really difficult. Rhonda sat there staring at me like a skinned rabbit. It didn't look anything like the picture. Oh, there were a few similarities, like the slight fringe sweeping across her brow and the angled hair along the right side of her jaw, but that's where it ended. The other side looked like it had been hacked with a weed whacker and the back was just as patchy. And far too short to fix.

"So how does it look?"

I didn't know what to say. I really didn't.

"It looks lovely – I like the shade you chose."

Rhonda peered at me anxiously. "I don't mean my nails, you dope! What do you think of the *hair*?"

I stalled.

"It looks horrible doesn't it?" Rhonda wailed. "It didn't turn out at all!"

She was crestfallen. I needed to redeem the situation. "Ok…maybe if we get you a nice stylish hat – "

"I've ruined my hair!"

"It looks…er…not too bad." Who was I kidding? It absolutely was. "All right, the positive thing to remember here is that it will grow back. In fact, it will probably grow out in no time at all!" I smiled encouragingly.

"*Not* in time for the wedding." Rhonda hit the magazine in frustration. "Stupid trendy style," she muttered. "Stupid moron stylist. I'm going to sue!"

She really should have sued.

Poor Rhonda. She was bound to scare all the guests upon their first encounter with her at Erin's wedding, which was scheduled for the last weekend in September. I know – I couldn't believe Erin was engaged either. The story is that Miss Obsessed fell for the first guy to pay her any attention over the summer, and he proposed after two weeks. She hired a whirlwind wedding planner and set up the date just as quickly. My jaw hit the floor when she gathered a group of us together at her house to share the news. I mean, that was pretty fast. She wasn't even old enough to be legally married. She needed her parents' consent, which of course they gave because, let's face it, they've never said no to anything she's ever wanted.

"Erin, are you sure you don't want a longer engagement and spend a bit more time getting to know one another?" I asked from my spot on the luxurious, feather filled couch. She shook her head resolutely.

"What about our last year of school?" Rhonda exclaimed. "What about all the *fun* you're going to miss?" She flapped her Dior clad arms. "What are you going to do for a *career* without your education?" Her voice rose passionately. It's amazing how Rhonda can sound *exactly* like her dad at times. "Without a solid education you won't get anywhere. Where's your *ambition* girl!"

"I have ambition." Erin's chin jutted out. "I don't need to finish the last year, I'll skip it and become a famous actress. I have *connections,* you know."

I muffled a snort. She was completely serious. And delirious.

"*Anyway*," Erin glared at me, "there are *other* things to discuss."

I have to admit I was a teeny bit envious. Not about her nonexistent career in acting – but the wedding. The large, extravagant wedding she was about to have. We spent hours listening to her describe every little detail and it all sounded really amazing. Except for the part where she asked Rhonda to be her maid of honor. I caught the terrified expression on Rhonda's face before she composed her features…and that was the second time I had to quell a giggle.

Who would willingly submit themselves to slavery? I could see Erin on the day – *fetch me this, get me that – where's my bouquet?* I know traditionally the maid of honor plays a large role in the scheme of things, but Erin would drive hers straight into a mental institution. She'd have a request every five seconds. Rhonda declined. Naturally.

So Erin pinned her gaze on Julia, who immediately lit with joy. "I'd love to!" She gushed. I just hoped Erin remembered to keep her far away from the wedding cake.

Now, I wasn't interested in being Erin's maid of honor, but I was a little surprised she didn't even consider me. I would have been a far greater asset to her than Julia, who was completely clueless when it came to weddings. Although, I guess it wasn't that shocking she didn't ask me – Erin was unmistakably irritated by the sight of my teeth. She glared at them during later dress fittings as if staring long enough would make the metal reappear. Why do some brides feel threatened by members of their bridal party? I don't understand. Especially when her parents spared no expense. Erin selected the most sensational wedding gown ever, yet you should have seen the dresses she chose for us – they were a bright, puke green.

And if picking ugly gowns and scowling at my teeth weren't bad enough, Erin glowed at the sight of Rhonda's hair and said it was perfect. What a liar. The only thing that could have made Erin any happier is if someone walked up to Rhonda with a razor and added a bald spot as well.

For some reason – the only thing Erin wasn't obsessive-compulsive about were the shoes. She actually let us select our own. We couldn't believe it.

Since the shoes were the only items that would look good – Rhonda and I went shopping and really made an effort. I bought Fendi on sale (shhh) and Rhonda purchased Christian Louboutin – she got the most beautiful classic pumps. Erin was going to bubble over like a popped boil. *Ha!*

The day dawned and getting ready was chaotic. Her majesty Erin bossed everyone about and girls vied for space before the bathroom mirror to do hair and makeup. Rhonda and I beamed at each other like mischievous kids until it felt like our faces would fall off. As we zipped up our Frankenstein dresses, my eyes darted toward the creamy closet doors where our shoes were hidden.

Stop looking! An inner voice chimed. *You'll give it away.*

Nearby, Erin pursed her lips and studied her reflection in a full-length mirror.

She looked amazing. Her hazel eyes gleamed and her hair cascaded in a shiny auburn waterfall of ringlets. Her veil was dotted with iridescent pearls and a similarly designed necklace graced her neck. Her dress of course fit like a glove, but it wasn't the gown or any of the accessories that made her so stunning. She was radiating with an inner happiness.

"Allo?" A light tap sounded at the door before a mustached man with a French accent stepped into the room and began snapping 'getting ready' shots.

"Here's your bouquet, Erin," came Julia's doting voice.

Girls scrambled together to adjust Erin's veil and train while the flash went off.

"Zees way, mademoiselle." Before we knew it, the photographer ushered Julia out onto the landing and directed her toward the winding staircase. "Suivez-moi," he beckoned the rest of us.

This is it! I clapped my hands.

Rhonda was already strutting about the room in her shoes like a catwalk model, and I was overjoyed to be joining her in just a moment! I opened the closet doors and gasped.

Where are my shoes?

They were gone. I knew instantly that someone stole them.

Shoeless and miffed, I dashed out onto the landing and peered over the wooden rail at the bridesmaids positioning themselves on the stairs. They giggled and held up their flowers in a neat row as the photographer counted "un, deux, trois." The flash went off again and my eyes zeroed in on Julia.

Julia.

Standing there with a grin plastered all over her stubby face, her villainous brows highly arched.

"Are you coming or what?" called Erin, spotting me.

"Yeah…" I forced a smile. *If she damaged my shoes, she's going down…*

"Reanne! Get over here!" My attention snapped back to Rhonda, waving at me from the bedroom.

"Rhonda! You'll never believe this! *Julia,*" I spat the word "took – "

I stopped dead as Rhonda pulled the shoes from behind her back.

"Here you go." She handed them to me in excitement. "I thought Erin was about to find them earlier so I hid them under the bed. Sorry, what were you saying?"

"Um…nothing." I slipped them on and admired myself in the full-length mirror.

Rhonda draped an arm around my shoulder and grinned wickedly. "Ready dahling?"

"Ready!"

We sauntered out onto the landing with our dresses hiked up…just a bit.

"Took you long enough," said Erin shortly. She glanced away before whipping her head around again to get a better look at us. We watched in delight as her gaze flew right past my Fendis and landed on the Louboutins. Her eyes bulged in the most unbecoming way. Bahahaha!

I stood there cheerfully awaiting her reaction to my shoes, but…there wasn't one. She didn't even notice them. What *nerve*. Although I guess I couldn't blame her. My shoes were nice – but

Rhonda's were to die for. And by the look on Erin's face, someone was definitely about to die. I quickly distanced myself from the Louboutins; Rhonda was on her own.

The church filled with guests wearing fancy suits and hats while the bridal party mingled in an out of the way section of the foyer. "Places people, its time!" Erin nudged me out of a conversation I was having and I hit the brakes in annoyance.

"Erin, not all of the guests are here yet. Besides," I raised my brows, "isn't your wedding planner supposed to tell us when to go?"

She winced. "Oh. Right."

To be honest, I wasn't in a hurry to get inside the main sanctuary. Of course I looked forward to the vows and everything, but I wanted to keep talking to the incredibly hunky groomsman I was paired with before the day became swallowed by the ceremony, more photos, and speeches.

As Erin went to pester the wedding planner, I turned back to my groomsman and bestowed him with a dazzling smile. "So how do you know the groom?"

"We were on the same junior baseball team back in…"

I stared into his dark eyes, the color of rich chocolate and admired his voice. *It's so sexy.* His hair was too. It fell in soft curls along his brow and I was *dying* to know if it was permed or natural.

"…And we've been best buds ever since…"

Maybe I've been a little hard on Erin, I found myself thinking as I watched her jab a finger at the wedding planner and raise her voice a few paces away. *She's been really stressed out with the wedding, yet she still made the effort to pair me with this great guy. She didn't have to do that. And not just any guy...one that could easily be a GQ model.*

"...Then this other time we..."

I pulled my gaze back to the gorgeous specimen before me as he reminisced. *I mean, just look at him. He's George Clooney, but younger. The stubble he's sporting would make other men look gruff, but on him it's so rugged.*

"...It was hilarious and my girlfriend couldn't stop laughing when I took the..."

I wonder if he's actually related to George Clooney. I glanced discreetly at the Rolex poking out from beneath his suit sleeve. *Yes! At Erin's wedding, it's entirely possible! I'll just ask him if...hang on a minute...*

Something he said wormed its way into my consciousness. I shook my head. I must have misheard. "I'm sorry, what were you saying about your...girlfriend?" I ventured.

"We went camping three years ago around the time we first started going out..."

O-kaaay. So it wasn't a mistake. *Thanks a lot Erin.*

At least Rhonda's romance seemed to be galloping off to a good start. She batted her eyes at the Michael Jordan look alike she stood next to, and there was definitely a spark of interest reflected back. It didn't come as any surprise. I knew Rhonda would likely have a boyfriend by the end of the evening.

And while I was happy for her, it just sucked that I wasn't going to snag a date myself – at a *wedding*, of all places. I discreetly checked out the other groomsmen lining the wall and resigned myself to the fact that it wasn't about to happen. None of them compared.

I smoothed out my dress and flicked my eyes back to Rhonda as she laughed at something her guy whispered. His arm rested against the wall above her head and his other hand smoothed a piece of hair behind her ear. As they shamelessly flirted, I found my gaze drifting down to Rhonda's shoes. *They really are stunning.* You'd notice them straightaway. I was beginning to notice that there wasn't anything noticeable about Rhonda's groomsman, though. No expensive cufflinks or watch. I couldn't help but wonder whether or not he was wealthy…and if he could be attracted to Rhonda because of *her* wealth. Something hot stirred inside of me, and I shot him a look of dislike as he continued to push the hair behind Rhonda's ear. Loyally, I flexed my foot. He wasn't going to take advantage of *my* friend! I'd kick him with my designer shoe if I had to, right in the shin. They'd be good for *something.*

I relaxed after further study. He didn't look down at her feet once. In fact, I'm not even sure he noticed her footwear at all – so he probably didn't realize she had money. That was great, but it also made him fashionably clueless. Then again, maybe most men are.

"So let me get this straight," Neil reiterated over the phone that evening. "You and Rhonda wasted bucket loads of money on shoes that went unnoticed. Why, exactly?"

You see? Clueless.

"Neil," I said as if explaining to a three-year-old, "the dresses were ugly. We had to have *something* that looked good. And the shoes weren't unnoticed, Rhonda's were a big hit – "

"So it was just yours then," he laughed.

"Ha, very funny."

"Ok. So what were the highlights? Other than the *shoes*?" Neil asked.

"Well," I paused thoughtfully. "Erin paired me with a nice groomsman at the wedding...I thought he might ask me out until I realized he had a girlfriend."

"You...wanted to go out with him?"

"It might have been nice. At least one date, anyway. I've always wondered what it's like to do the casual dating thing – what's your take on it?"

"It's overrated," said Neil quickly.

"But it could be good, don't you think? It would give me experience. I bet I'd know how to identify the right guy if I've dated a few of them. And it could be fun, definitely better than just staying single. I might try it some time."

There was a beat of silence before Neil snapped, "then I'll follow your career with interest."

I stared at the phone, stunned and slightly irritated. *What's that supposed to mean?*

"Is there – "

"I have to go," said Neil abruptly, "I have things to do."

"Oh…ok."

"Don't forget to send some pictures," he added warmly, as if nothing weird transpired. "I can't believe the dresses were as bad as you say…but even so, I'm sure you were still the belle of the ball."

Ok. There was something wrong with Neil. I couldn't put my finger on it but something wasn't right. It wasn't just the awkward conversation. He and Jaden seemed to be forming a friendship over the following weeks, which was *really* weird. They had nothing in common. *Nothing.* I never did understand why Jaden invited Neil to the cottage and then, after the wedding, I caught Jaden talking to Neil online a few times. I had a sneaking suspicion a prank might be brewing, and I was the target. An online conversation or two isn't incriminating evidence exactly – I just found it odd since Neil was *my* friend – and because Jaden didn't want me to see whom he was chatting with.

I padded down the hall past Jaden's bedroom one evening, and I popped my head through the open door to say hello. Jaden immediately minimized his onscreen conversation and spun around in the chair, blocking it.

"Who's online?" I asked, even though I saw.

He avoided my eye like a shoplifter sneaking past security. "No one," he said shiftily, "just chatting with Lindsay."

I moved along without pursuing it, but I'm no dummy. Cloak and dagger discussions with Neil were bad news, and I wouldn't let their cunning plans take me by surprise. Not this time.

Although…it's entirely possible I overanalyzed things. I've misjudged situations in the past – like the time I thought the cute Dairy Queen guy might have been interested, but wasn't. Well what was I supposed to think? He stared at me as I hung out with my group of friends and kept smiling at me. I thought he might come ask me out until it dawned on me that he couldn't leave his till. Duh! Feeling somewhat bold, I walked up to him myself. Well…I almost did. It turned out the hem of my skirt had been tucked up and a friend noticed and warned me before I reached the counter. He was smirking, rather than smiling, and I could have died with mortification. We left that Dairy Queen pretty quickly and I've never gone back.

But I wasn't wrong about this; Neil lived to prank and wanted to drag Jaden into it too. He'd do anything to get me from within my house. I just knew it.

I didn't end up giving it too much thought, however, because nothing more happened. I guess everyone got busy focusing on school and getting good grades – I know I was. I really wanted to get accepted into a private college known for its fashion arts program. My career goals weren't set in stone, but I knew the direction I wanted to go. I filled out the application, and a few others as backup with trembling hands, and sent them away with crossed fingers.

Then I worked on my resume. I wanted a part time job to gain valuable experience in my field of interest. This idea had actually been stewing for a while and I knew it was brilliant for the following reasons:

1. I would save money.
2. I would love it.
3. I would help people.

How many women pick a wedding gown that is completely wrong for them and end up looking horrible on their wedding day? Zillions. And it's sad because disaster can be so easily avoided – all it takes is for someone to tactfully steer a bride in the right direction…someone like me. I was going after a bridal consultant position at a local wedding boutique. I knew I'd be a shoe in for the job since I excelled in tactfulness and honesty. In fact, those qualities appeared right at the top of my resume, and I stepped through the revolving doors of the shop one quiet Tuesday evening with absolute confidence.

"Hello." I approached the woman at the front of the boutique with a smile. "Is the manager available?"

"That would be me," said the woman pleasantly. "What can I do for you?"

I launched into my prepared speech about wanting to work there and why, and gave her my resume. She skimmed it over right then, and a hopeful flutter started in my stomach. *Maybe she'll offer the job on the spot!*

She glanced up with a frown. "Do you have retail experience?"

"Well…no," I admitted.

The hand holding my resume drooped.

"But I'd do really well here! I'm familiar with all the designers and lines you carry." Impressively, I fired off names of designers and facts about their gowns.

Her hand paused and she gave me a strange look. "Well…you certainly know your stuff."

Feeling bolstered, I strengthened my case. "I also have a really good eye and love offering helpful advice, which would be very useful to brides. Take your hair for example," I eyed the frizz and bright red color, "if you changed the shade just slightly and used a product called – "

"Tactfulness!" She guffawed, startling me out of my advice. I finally noticed the expression on her face. It said I was a total moron.

"We don't have any openings at the moment." She crumpled my resume and hustled me through the door.

Honestly, what was her problem? You'd think she would have *appreciated* what I had to say. I guess I could have worded it a little differently, but something tells me she wouldn't have been impressed no matter what I said. I was only trying to help – clients don't want to buy a gown from someone looking like bozo-gone-berserk do they?

Anyway, I think she blacklisted me after I left. I couldn't find a job anywhere else, except at the movie theatre, which I turned to as a last resort. It certainly wasn't my dream job, but I couldn't afford to be picky when I needed the money.

To tell the truth, I didn't like the theatre at all. Working there was the ultimate fashion nightmare. The uniform was plain black and came with hideous non-slip shoes (I tried replacing them with a dressier pair on the first day only to be caught immediately by my chauvinistic supervisor who made me switch them), and an oversized baseball cap engraved with the theatre slogan in lurid blue, which completed the unflattering look.

I loathed that ugly, cheaply made cap – I couldn't bear the feel of it against my forehead. The stupid thing gave me a rash, so I pushed it back to avoid contact with my skin. Unfortunately, it looked worse this way but at least I was comfortable…well… as comfortable as one can be looking like a derelict. I did my best to forget this fact.

"*What* do you think you're doing?" It was my third shift at the theatre and the supervisor appeared beside me as I refilled the napkins and straws at the condiment station. He gaped at my head in open horror. "You're breaking code 176 of the employee hand guide."

"Code what?" I echoed, perplexed.

"It states that all employees must wear their uniforms in accordance with safety regulations and public appeal."

Wow. I didn't see how any part of the uniform would appeal to any public, ever.

"So you'll need to fix your cap," he said grimly and folded his arms.

"Ok. Here's the thing…I…can't. I'm having an allergic reaction to the material. It's giving me a rash."

"Where?" He peered at my forehead dubiously.

"Right here," I pointed.

He squinted. "I don't see anything."

"Well of course you can't!" I cried in exasperation. "I've worn it this way for a while now so it's probably gone!"

He bristled like a ferocious dog. *Oops.*

"But I really did have a rash!"

"Then you can bring a doctor's note to your next shift," he said implacably, "for now, you'll have to wear it properly."

I gave a world-weary sigh and adjusted the cap to his satisfaction.

I put it back the moment he left.

You know, it's true what they say – there's always a light even in the darkest circumstances. Because even though I was forced to look like a dork, even though I was in *misery* – something amazing happened. Guys were still hitting on me! And it wasn't my imagination or me misreading the situation. They really were. I'll admit the men coming to the theatre without dates weren't exactly the cream of the crop, but it gave me hope that an available prince charming might be somewhere among the crowd…and that he'd overlook my outfit.

It was another dull evening of standing in one spot, ripping tickets for hours, and catching the occasional minor sneaking into an R-rated movie, when a gorgeous blond guy in dark green khaki's bounded up to me. I didn't see a girlfriend with him, but I assumed she was in the bathroom.

"Hello darlin'." I heard a Southern drawl. "What's *your* name?"

I wondered whom he was speaking to.

"You're lookin' awfully pretty this evenin'." He winked at me then read my nametag, "Reanne."

I perked up and whipped the cap from my head. Obviously no girlfriend! His pickup lines were a little cheesy but I didn't care. He leaned against the podium where I kept the movie schedule and ticket stubs, and hung out for a while discussing movies. We were in a theatre, what else were we going to talk about?

"This looks like a good one." His lips twisted into a smile as he pointed at the schedule. "Have you seen it?"

"No, but I've heard it's really good and tickets for it are always sold out."

"Would you like to see it?" He waggled his eyebrows suggestively and I laughed.

"I would."

"Me too. So I was wondering…" He stopped and rubbed his face nervously. "If you wanted to…"

"Yes?" I gently prompted.

"If you'd be willing to…." He took a breath…"Let me into the movie without a ticket?"

"Absolut – " I froze in shock. *No. Did he just? Did he really…?* "Absolutely not!" I sputtered.

"Please?" He cajoled with large sappy eyes. "I'd be very grateful. Maybe after we – "

"Not a chance! Go pay like everyone else!"

I'm sure Mr. Dimples was accustomed to getting his way but it wasn't about to happen on my watch. Besides, if he had half a brain – he'd have asked me out before requesting a freebee. Not that this would have worked, either. I wouldn't go on a date with a guy too cheap to pay for a ten-dollar ticket. Just saying.

Then my new co-worker Terry came along and asked me out constantly. I could tell he considered himself a ladies' man but I had no idea why. I know I'm stereotyping – but he really looked like he belonged in front of a computer with a calculator rather than girl chasing. Come to think of it, maybe that's why he was so determined. I bet he spent all his spare time strategizing.

The persistent pestering began the moment Terry was hired. He asked for my number repeatedly throughout our shifts. After refusing to give it for what seemed the seven hundredth time – he took the liberty of writing out *his* number on a napkin and handed it to me in triumph.

I took it…and promptly tossed it into the garbage in front of him. It was harsh, but the guy wasn't taking 'no' for an answer. You have to be extremely clear with these types, although this time it backfired. Instead of realizing I didn't want to date *him*, he thought my actions meant I didn't want to date at all.

"You know," he placed a clammy hand on my shoulder as I swept popcorn from the sticky floor, "the company of a man can be a pleasurable experience. I have references." He gave me a cheesy grin. *Ick.*

I took in his grease mopped hair and thin head, which looked like it got squashed between automatic doors and never fully recovered…and I was truly puzzled. If women went out with him, it wasn't for his looks. But then – his personality sucked too, so how did he have references? Girls probably said yes to end the agony of his constant begging. I was almost tempted to do the same but I hadn't quite reached that level of desperation. I remained silent and started my next task.

"Need a hand?" Terry quipped as I hefted a heavy garbage bag out of a can. I was assigned all the crappy floor jobs for the night, which was bad enough, never mind Terry tagging along. But if he would actually do some work…

"Thanks, that would be nice."

I lugged the bag toward him as he clapped enthusiastically. "Good job, bravo!" He cheered.

Ha ha.

"So." He stopped chortling. "Have you realized you can't live without me yet?"

Good grief. I have to lose him.

I felt a jolt of delight as I found my escape. A crowd was at my left, and the ladies room was just behind them.

Terry followed my gaze.

"Oh you think you can lose me in the *bathroom,* do you?"

"You bet." I hurriedly pushed through the posse of people and raced toward it.

"Well not today!" Declared Terry as he zipped around the gathering, and me, in an attempt to head me off. His eyes were glued to the bathroom entrance and he was really gunning it. I stopped and watched in amusement as he charged past everyone, getting further and further away from me, becoming a dorky dot in the distance.

Wow. I cracked a smile. He totally defeated the purpose there, but you have to admire his drive.

I backed away in haste and disappeared down the hall leading to the Imax section. "Go me!" I punched the air with joy and reveled in the stillness.

My victory was short lived. Terry found me minutes later and stuck to me closer than a wad of gum on my shoe.

The guy was a pit-bull. Blatantly telling him "go away" didn't work either, and it was getting ridiculous. I finally brought in the big guns. I told Jaden. One visit from my brother sent Terry packing. I finally had relief, which turned out to be permanent. Terry stopped working at the theatre a few days later.

Jaden congratulated himself on his intimidating powers. He said Terry quit because of him. Some co-workers thought he was fired. I didn't know which it was but I did a little jig. He was gone! That's what mattered.

I would have really danced if I met a *suitable* guy, but I decided my chances of finding a match at the theatre were as good as my chances of winning the lottery. Extremely slim.

Rhonda was back in the single boat with me as well. I really thought it would go somewhere with that hunky groomsman. She had a coffee date followed by a dinner date before it all went amuck.

Rhonda said they had nothing in common and he was a bit of a narcissist, but I think the true reason Rhonda tossed him was because he kept making subtle hints about her hair. Well, maybe they weren't so subtle.

On the first date he randomly commented on the hair of other women and said what he liked about their styles…and eventually told Rhonda how sexy hers would look grown out. Which, you know, was fine – he was entitled to his opinion (and I actually agreed with that!). But then the jerk asked her to get extensions or wear a wig in the meantime. He made this request on the second date. Needless to say, there wasn't a third.

Chapter Seven

Suspicion

Prom was fast approaching and would be here before I knew it. Everyone went on shopping sprees and began borrowing each other's accessories after the New Year. It was all girls at school could talk about. I joined in on the many fun discussions but politely declined if people asked to borrow from me. Which they did. A lot. I used to lend out items all the time; in fact, I quite enjoyed it…until I met Ashley.

I lent her my favorite black Guess heels at camp once along with an attractive leopard skirt I owned. The shoes were gorgeous – all velvet and high with beautiful stitched flowers on the heels, which also appeared on the front of the shoes. I was reluctant to part with them but Ashley had just landed a date with an artsy guy who was bound to notice her repulsive footwear. Trust me, artists notice these things. She begged to borrow them, and since her shoes looked like they came from a pawnshop or maybe a dumpster, I caved.

The skirt she planned to wear was kind of tacky too. I say kind of – what I mean is – the dull skirt was *so* ugly, I volunteered mine as a loan so the guy wouldn't feel like throwing himself under a bus at the sight of it. I know I wanted to. Seeing her all dolled up and confident made me feel really good – like her fashion fairy mother.

She thanked me profusely and I thought of my loan as one small step to better the condition of the world. I even contemplated going around camp to remove some of the other eyesores with a few discreet clothing loans.

When Ashley returned from her date, her face was bursting with joy and I was excited to hear the details until I saw my shoes, which were in worse condition than the pair she owned. They were bent out of shape and caked in dry mud. I gasped in dismay. What the heck did she do on her date? Go for a hike in the rain?

My lips quivered as I stared, stricken, at the mess.

How could she be so careless? What am I going to do?

I ran my fingers along the once smooth fabric and my sadness quickly turned into a quaking rage. *She begged to borrow these. Begged!*

Desperately, I wondered if I could somehow salvage them. Anxiety clawed at me as I barreled past Ashley and ran into my cabin. I scrubbed at the shoes frantically for what seemed like hours and managed to get them fairly clean. I then snuck off the campground and walked into town to have them repaired by a shoe shop. I couldn't believe it when I got them back! They looked good as new!

Then one heel snapped off the moment I put any weight on it and that was the end of the shoes, as well as my friendship with Ashley. I didn't terminate the friendship for this reason alone. I realize these things happen and I was willing to forgive her (although let's be honest…I needed time), but then the little thief wouldn't give my skirt back! Every time I asked for it, she had an excuse: "I'm going to wash it for you first. It needs to be ironed. Oops…I can't find it."

So eventually I found the drawer it was stuffed in and just took it…and I may have spilled something on her dumpy shoes as I left.

I only ever lend to Rhonda now because you can't trust people you hardly know with your stuff (well…your *good stuff*). It's a disaster waiting to happen. And I didn't need to borrow from anyone because I had been thinking of prom-wear possibilities for *months*.

I'm sorry. I know I didn't tell you, but I wanted it to be a surprise.

I just needed to hit the stores, then Cinderella – eat your heart out. And there was one other tiny detail to take care of. My date. I wanted one. And not just anyone, someone I'd have a good time with and could ask easily.

This is more challenging than I thought.

I gave myself a little shake and cracked my knuckles. *Stop being a chicken. Just do it already!* My fingers hovered over the keys as possible segues for the conversation ran through my mind. I mean…he wouldn't say no, would he?

Neil says,
Hellooo! Anyone home? Come on slowpoke, I've typed three paragraphs to your one-liner!

Reanne says,
Sorry, I'm a little distracted. Was just thinking about prom stuff. Hey, did you enjoy yours?

Neil says,
I didn't go.

Reanne says,
What? How come??? There's no way I'd miss mine!

Neil says,
My parents booked a cruise and I went on that instead. It was our first, so it was a no-brainer really. I enjoyed the cruise, though.

Reanne says,
No-brainer! You can go on a cruise any time! You only get one prom! Well that settles it then…

Neil says,

Settles what? Exactly...?

Reanne says,

You should come to mine. You know...if you want to, since you

missed all the fun at yours.

Neil says,

You want me to be your date? ☺

Reanne says,

Yeah.

Neil says,

I'd love to!

Well that wasn't too bad – mission accomplished! Next steps: mom and dad promised to get a limo so Neil and I could arrive in style, and they were taking me shopping for the perfect gown. Yay!

"Oh my goodness!" Exhilaration swept through me as we stepped into the massive foyer of the dress shop. Photographs of ladies in Vera Wang and Alexander McQueen gowns littered the wall to my right and there was a seating area with a coffee table piled with *Vogue* magazines at my left. My head swiveled around the room taking it all in. "We're going to find something here, I know it!"

"Now take it easy," said dad seriously. "We'll examine all options." Which was code for *I'm not buying the most expensive dress here, so chill.*

"Hi there and welcome. My name is Patty and I'll be assisting you today." Patty wore silver rimmed spectacles and her hair was up in a tidy salt and pepper bun. A flowery skirt swished around her ankles as she walked. "Follow me and we'll get you settled into a fitting room, then I'll select a few pieces for you. I assume you're looking for a prom gown?"

"Yes! How did you know?" I was surprised and impressed she spotted my needs immediately.

"Oh, I've had a few young ladies in already. I'm sure we'll pick something unique and lovely for you in a matter of minutes!"

"Excellent." Mom nodded her approval.

We sat on sofas among the mirrored dressing rooms and waited until Patty bustled in with an armful of gowns. "Here you are dear, try this one first."

Mom gasped when I came out of the fitting room and dad had a hand over his mouth. I peered at myself in the mirror uncertainly.

"Fabulous!" Patty crooned. "The dress really brings out the color of your eyes!"

Yes. It does bring out the color of my eyes. I glanced at dad; tears streamed down his face as he slapped his knee. *It also makes me look like Shrek.*

"Doesn't your daughter look lovely?" Patty smiled warmly at my parents. Dad couldn't contain himself any longer. He wheezed with laughter and swiped at his eyes.

"Actually…this isn't quite what we had in mind," mom commented politely. "Let's try the next one."

It was lacy, tight and dark pink. Like something you'd see in a brothel. *I'm not going out there!* "Next please!"

I struggled into the next dress and finally emerged.

"Oh – you are stunning!" came Patty's enthusiastic voice. "This is definitely the gown for you!" Her face was alive with conviction and excitement, and I scowled at her skeptically. So did mom and dad. She was either going blind and needed a stronger prescription, or she worked on commission. I suspected the latter. There was no way I'd attend my prom looking like Dracula. The billowing black gown with the high collar was the most hideous thing yet.

"Thank you for your time." Mom stood and slung her purse over her shoulder. "We'll…have a think on a few of these gowns and come back if we decide on one."

We would never darken that door again.

"*This* place should be better." There was a hopeful lilt to my voice as I followed mom into the next shop. "Wow!" I exclaimed as we sat on the plush feathered couch and took in the impressive décor, which was Victorian and elegant. Vivaldi's *Four Seasons* serenaded us as we waited for an attendant.

"What do you think of this place?" I whispered to mom.

She glanced around the sparse yet lovely room. "I'll reserve judgment for now." Just then a door clicked. "It seems nice though," she added.

"Hello." A woman in a pink tailored Chanel suit and matching satin pumps stepped through a side door. "I'm Sharon," she extended her pale, delicate hand to my dad.

A grin split my face. *I knew it.*

"Nice to meet you Sharon," said dad jovially.

He shook her hand while I fixated on her hair. It was cascading in blond paper curls that fell just below her shoulders.

"Can I interest you in herbal tea and mint cookies while I ask a few questions to assess your needs today?"

"Yes please!" Dad stepped forward eagerly.

"Tom." Mom held up a restraining hand. "The tea is fine but not the cookies. I'll not have you complaining about your health again." Dad couldn't tolerate junk food the way other people can but it never stopped him from eating it.

"Karen! I'm having the cookies," retorted dad in a savage undertone as he tried to barge past.

Mom ignored him and caught Sharon's eye. "Just tea thanks. For my husband also."

A few moments later we sipped our tea while dad glared at mom resentfully, and Sharon sat demurely on the opposite sofa.

"Let's discuss the event," Sharon began. "The prom and wedding season is fast approaching. Do you need a gown for one or both of these occasions? I tend to have repeat clients over the spring and summer months and the earlier we assess your needs, the better." She gave a tinkling laugh. "Although I should tell you that I *am* able to work within a shorter time frame as well. We're known here for our flexibility."

"I only need a dress for Prom," I told her. "In May."

"Is there a particular look you have in mind?" Sharon gave me a once over. "I have a few ideas for your coloring and body type, but I like to incorporate personal preference as well."

"I want something graceful and slimming. Something along these lines." Reaching into my purse, I pulled out my magazine clippings from home and laid them all before her.

Sharon's eyes bugged. "Wow! Aren't you…efficient."

"Thank you!" I beamed. My clippings covered the entire coffee table.

"Well, let's get you situated in the fitting area and I'll just take a moment to look through your photos." We picked up our tea and followed Sharon. "I'll start a selection for you." And off she went to get them!

"Here we are!" Sharon wheeled in a rack full of stunning gowns. My jaw dropped as I took in the amazing assortment.

"Try this one." Mom's eyes shone as she held out a beautiful sparkling dress with a cinched waist and chiffon layering along the side. I reached for it greedily and dashed off to change.

"This is it! I love it!" I swept out of the fitting room and did a twirl. The dress gave me a perfect hourglass figure and I felt a little like Barbie. "I can't believe it! I found my dress on the first try!"

"Excellent!" Mom clapped her hands. "It's lovely on you."

"I'll take it please," I added to Sharon, happily.

"It *does* look fantastic," Sharon agreed, "but I do have another one I'd like you to try, if you don't mind?" She reached into the middle of the rack and pulled out a long, sleek gown in dazzling shades of purple and the slightest hint of well-placed turquoise.

"Ok. *This* is the one." I lit up the moment I had it on. It was the most elegant thing I've ever worn and it gave me that sought after mermaid look.

"It *is* beautiful," mom breathed as I swept the curtain aside. "We'll take this one. Thank you Sharon." Mom gave her a warm smile.

"Wonderful! Well...if you're certain, I'll take the measurements for alteration. We'll need to bring it in a bit here and shorten this strap over your shoulder – "

"We're not certain." Dad's strangled voice materialized. His eyes were glued to the price tag I hadn't noticed. $3000.00. Oh no.

The vision of myself entering the banquet hall amid admiring, thunderous applause evaporated. Dad wasn't going to pay for the gown. In fact, he was slowly backing away from my imploring gaze and clutching his wallet in a vice-like death grip. Only a pair of pliers could separate him from it now.

"Sharon, how much is the first dress?" Mom inquired calmly.

I felt a spark of hope. *Please be less...please!*

"I'm sorry, they're the same price."

"Noooo," I wanted to wail but didn't.

Mom noted my discouraged countenance and put a comforting arm around my shoulder. "Don't worry love, I'm sure we'll find something just as nice. Tom, why don't you tell Sharon our budget and we'll take it from there."

Dad scribbled a figure on a piece of paper and handed it to Sharon, who nodded tactfully, and wheeled out the beautiful designer rack. I watched it go with a heavy heart. *I'll never find a gown.*

This is what I honestly thought. However, I did find something I liked in the new collection.

The dress was cream colored with hues of pink and very flattering. It was also reasonably priced, so dad no longer appeared to be in the early throes of a heart attack. The neckline was a little low but Sharon assured us it could be modified.

"What if we add beading here and a little lace there?" Dad suggested as he studied the gown. "And maybe a flower pinned there and a sash around the middle." Dad was pretty pleased with himself.

Mom and Sharon exchanged horrified looks.

"Darling...great idea," said mom in stilted, artificial tones. "But this dress is a classic, isn't it Sharon?"

"Absolutely!" she chimed in. "I wouldn't add anything – the change would be too drastic."

"Oh." Dad looked put out but I appreciated his effort. I mean, how many dads take their daughters shopping for a dress and then actually want to participate in the process?

Take Rhonda's dad for example. She went dress shopping with him the previous week and he vetoed everything she tried on. He would only be satisfied if Rhonda went to prom dressed like a nun. In fact, it's amazing he didn't just go out and buy her a habit.

Now, I understood where he was coming from. Dressing a certain way probably *does* attract the wrong type of guy. But you can still look decent and fashionable without wearing a tent. I mean, *come on*. Rhonda wouldn't have picked anything inappropriate. She's not like that. But I get it; he's overprotective because he loves her. It's sweet, in a bothersome way.

Rhonda and I arranged a secret mission to find what she needed. We had to ditch her dad.

She slept over at my house the following weekend. Rhonda arrived with chips and popcorn and we spent most of the night watching movies and talking about the type of dress she wanted. She had the details down to an art.

"Reanne, get up already!" Rhonda huffed for the third time in the morning as I rolled onto my stomach. She opened the shutters and sunlight poured into the room.

I waved a hand at her as though shoeing away an irritating fly. "Go away, it's too early," I mumbled into my pillow.

"It's not! It's 9:00 a.m. and the mall opens in an hour…I have coffeeeee." She wielded the ceramic mug at me enticingly and I reached out, feeling around for it. My arm connected with Rhonda's bony fingers as she hauled me out of bed.

"Hey!" I complained.

"There. *Now* you can have it." Rhonda was fully dressed and ready to go.

I sipped the hot, steaming liquid and instantly felt more energetic. Next, I plugged in my hair straightener and thought about what I would wear to the mall.

As I sat down at my desk to adjust the heat settings and comb my hair, I noticed Rhonda whistling the *Jeopardy* tune. Her nails drummed incessantly against my dresser and her whistling was getting annoyingly louder.

"Fine," I said, exasperated. "I won't straighten my hair." I downed the rest of my coffee, dressed quickly, and gathered my hair into a low-slung ponytail. A cute fedora finished the look. "Ok, let's go."

Valentino. Ferragamo. Vera Wang. Rhonda tried on gorgeous expensive gown, after gorgeous expensive gown…and she didn't like any of them. By this time, I had downed two more coffees and an Iced Cappuccino. I really hoped she would find something in Michael Kors – my feet were aching.

"What's wrong with *that* one?" I asked of the sleek burgundy number Rhonda frowned at in the mirror.

"It's not sitting right on my hips. Don't you think it's bunching here?" She faced me and pulled at the fabric.

I had no idea what she was on about. "It looks great. You should get it."

"Hmm...I'll try a different size."

I plopped myself onto a chair while Rhonda changed, yet again. I suspected Rhonda's dad wasn't the reason she couldn't find something. I guess that's what happens when you're a perfectionist. Even her *underwear drawer* is meticulously arranged into the following categories: silky, sporty, stringy, and sexy. Of course it would take her forever to find a prom dress.

"Are you in it yet?" I asked.

There was a muffled reply as I watched a mother rifling through a clothing rack with her two daughters.

"Kr-ors," the younger girl enunciated with her brow furrowed. "Mommy, try this pretty Krors top!"

"Very good sweetheart!" The mother kissed her rosy cheek and tightened one of the girl's ponytails. "Except...its *Kors.* She's learning to read," the lady added to me with a smile.

"Good job!" I told the girl as she grinned proudly.

Suddenly there was movement in my peripheral vision near the store entrance and I turned my head.

Oh my!

A guy walked in with an older lady. A tall, golden haired guy with toned muscles and chiseled facial features.

Wow.

"This size is better." Rhonda came out of the fitting room and walked past me. "But I'm still looking around, so I'll put it on hold until the end of the day."

"Ok," I mumbled distractedly.

"She'll like this one, Brad," said the woman (*his mother, maybe?)* as she held out a necklace with blue and green rhinestones on a sterling silver chain. Brad took it from her and examined it.

"It's for my sister," he said to me, "what do you think?"

I hadn't realized I shuffled so close to them and my cheeks heated beneath his steely blue gaze. "Oh, I don't work here."

"That's ok." He grinned charmingly and lifted the necklace. "Would you wear this?"

"I – "

"Done!" Rhonda appeared next to me and looped her arm through mine before I could answer. "Let's hit the next store!" And she dragged me out like a super strong cavewoman.

"Wait!" I cried as she pulled me past the flashy displays of DKNY and BCBG.

"We should try Holt Renfrew next." There was a deranged glint in her eye as she sped toward it.

"Wait!" I tried again. "Stop! Didn't you see the guy I was talking to? Well…the guy I was *about* to talk to."

She slowed down. "*What* guy?"

I slapped a hand to my forehead. "The gorgeous guy that asked for my opinion on a necklace," my voice rose dolefully, "before you hauled me out like a gown possessed psychopath!"

"Ooh sorry! Let's go back!"

It was totally useless. Brad was gone. I stood in Michael Kors sullenly watching Rhonda search for him behind racks of clothing and around corners muttering, "Where *is* he?"

You see? This is what always happens. Geeks and weirdoes have no trouble finding you out and the moment you meet a hot one, he disappears before you can even introduce yourself.

"Reanne, I am *so* sorry. I didn't notice you talking to him. Maybe we can find him in the mall!"

"That's ok," I said with tremendous effort. "I guess...these things happen for a reason. It...wasn't meant to be."

"Exactly!" Rhonda cheered up and stared meaningfully into my eyes. "There are plenty of fish in the sea!"

I rubbed my face and groaned. So why was I only reeling in bottom dwellers?

Who needs to meet a man anyway? There are more important things in life to focus on...like my eighteenth birthday, which was swiftly approaching! Eighteen is huge and everyone knows it. It's the true stepping-stone into adulthood. It's first time you can be legally married without your parent's consent...among...many other things. Like...um... renting your own apartment...and...a lot of other stuff. The point is – it's a big deal. That's why I had to have a *surprise party* to celebrate the occasion. I just needed to make sure mom knew I wanted one. Subtly of course, so she would think it was her idea.

"I just *love* this episode of F.R.I.E.N.D.S," I announced one evening as mom sailed into the kitchen with an armload of potatoes and onions. It was the one where Phoebe arrives at her surprise birthday party and realizes that Joey isn't there because he's with her twin sister instead. "It must be really fun to have someone throw you a surprise party! Don't you think? Mom?"

She didn't answer so I poked my head around the dividing wall. Mom lined the supper ingredients along the countertop and consulted her recipe.

"Did you see that episode of F.R.I.E.N.D.S?" I repeated. "The one where Phoebe has a surprise party? I wonder what it would be like to have someone plan one for me."

"Don't get your hopes up love" said mom without looking up.

Right, so I wasn't subtle at all. But my parents had to give me a surprise party. I *am* their only daughter – why wouldn't they want to celebrate the joyous day I was born in such a special way?

"Reanne, please pass the cinnamon then tell Jaden I want him to take out the trash." Mom rolled her eyes toward the overflowing bin. Jaden was supposed to take it to the curb every Tuesday as part of his chores but he usually needed to be reminded.

I sprinted up the stairs to his room. "Hey whatcha doin'?"

"Nothing," he replied with a guilty shrug and hovered in front of his computer screen. Again.

I narrowed my eyes. "Mom wants you to take out the garbage."

"Yep, I'll be down in a sec."

Back in the living room, I turned on the family computer and signed into chat.

Neil is online

Aha! I knew it!

Neil is offline.

Hmm. He didn't even say hello. And Jaden disappeared right after him. *There's something fishy going on. And Jaden better tell me what it is or I'm going to clobber it out of him. Or bribe him,* it suddenly occurred to me. It's not like I could just threaten to punch his lights out if he didn't listen to me or trap him behind an ironing board…like I did when we were toddlers.

Now, before you say anything, I honestly don't remember doing these things but the second incident is documented in our home videos (Jaden followed me around the ironing board where it was propped against the wall, then I came out the other side and leaned on it…although *I* think it looks like I wanted to rest. Come on, I wasn't *really* trying to *trap* him) and mom likes to recount the other story. Apparently Jaden once asked mom if I was his mother. When the answer was "no," he asked if he had to listen to me. Then he told her what I supposedly said.

Sometimes mom's tales of my childhood makes me sound like a mini Hitler, even though she says it with a laugh. Really, I was *four*. And if it *is* true, Jaden probably had it coming because as much as I love him, little brothers can be annoying.

Siblings
By Reanne Riley (age 10)

I have a little brother

I don't know just why

He seemed to come from nowhere – maybe out of the sky?

Anyway, this little brother of mine

Has a lot of resistance

When I tried to flush him down the toilet

He didn't disappear on instance

Why won't he leave? I just don't know

No matter how hard I try, he's reluctant to go

He cries and he drools and gets in the way

Surely this kid isn't here to stay

I know! I'll do mom a favor and finally get rid

Of this tiny, obnoxious, annoying little kid

The toilet didn't work, so again I'll try

How about the oven? Surely he'll fry!

I hear him from the other room

He's crying

Maybe he needs a whack with the broom

Why can't mom shush him?

I don't understand

Mom tells me he's crying

He wants to hold my hand

My hand? I wonder why?

I'd just hit him whenever he'd cry

But to hush him now, I'll go and see

If he really is crying for me

I walk into the room and ugh, there he is

But the wailing stops and I do see

That it's true, he really wanted me!

After all I've done, he loves me still

At times he can make me ill

But I love him too

After all, he is my brother

I wish mom would take this down from the fridge. It doesn't *prove* anything. It was a poem I wrote just for fun. JUST FOR FUN. You can't get away with anything in this family.

Chapter Eight

Crash and Burn

I stretched with a loud lazy yawn and blinked a few times at the morning light filtering through the white wooden shutters in my room. Contentedly, I snuggled into my fleecy blankets and shut my eyes. I love sleeping in on Saturday mornings. It's total bliss. This time however, I wasn't drifting back into dreamland.

Did mom ask me to do something? I wondered, suddenly opening my eyes. Little particles of dust danced past my face in a sunbeam.

What was it?

I blew at the dust and watched as it twirled and scattered…and then I remembered Erin. I agreed to hang out at her house all morning so she could show off marital bliss. Don't ask me why I said I'd go.

Tossing the covers aside, I resisted the urge to dive back into bed when my feet hit the cold floor. My arms resembled the legs of a freshly plucked chicken, compliments of the drafty window dad had been saying he would fix for a while now. In his defense, he did attempt it once…but then he hit his thumb with the hammer and that ended the DIY project immediately. I'm just not sure why dad was hammering. I'm unfamiliar with tasks like this, but couldn't he have just applied silicone to the window frame? I mean – I *have* watched the occasional episode of *Holmes on Homes*. And I'm pretty sure the draft became worse after dad's go at it. Anyway.

With my blanket cocooned around me, I padded toward my wardrobe and dressed in the new angora sweater Rhonda gave me as an early gift, and made sure to wear my fur trimmed parka and boots.

There was a lot of snow on the ground and it was really cold out. I longed to borrow the car as I shielded my face from the stinging wind, but mom and dad were doing errands that day – I already checked.

I'm also not a fan of public transit with its grumpy, pushy passengers. On a bad day like today, it can turn the sweetest people into monsters. One time I witnessed two elderly ladies shoving each other because one accidentally bumped into the other…and whatever happened to offering your seat to someone who might need it more than you? Hardly anyone does it these days. And if you do – there's risk involved. Take that kind-looking man hobbling toward the back of the bus with his cane, for instance. Who would have thought he would suddenly swing it around and shriek, "How dare you, boy! You think I'm *feeble*?"

Poor kid. He didn't even see it coming…and I think he only stood to get *off* the bus.

What's the world coming to? I tell you – it's a scary place when one of your biggest fears is the attack of the elderly. Especially since they're usually armed with a maiming device or heaven forbid – pepper spray, which I've also seen used.

I made it to Erin's house unscathed.

"Welcome to our humble abode!" Erin opened the solid wooden doors wide and gave me a European peck on each cheek. "Come in, you must be freezing."

I gasped in appreciation as I stumbled over the threshold. All around me were beautiful marbled floors, high arched ceilings, and white sculptures that flanked a massive winding staircase. "Wow Erin, your house is amazing. Did you hire an interior designer?"

"Yes," she smiled modestly. "Mother told the designer to enjoy her vacation in Rome, but she insisted on coming back to decorate the house before we moved in. She's a doll. Let me give you the grand tour."

The *designer* insisted?

After a brief explanation of every high-tech gadget in the large, immaculate kitchen, and a synopsis on the imported family room furniture, I followed Erin upstairs. Cool abstract paintings livened the walls and…yep. There they were. Vincent Van Gogh and Renoir paintings.

"They aren't real," said Erin, eyeing them with disdain. "The authentic paintings weren't available for purchase otherwise we would have them."

"Oh naturally."

"And this is where our guests stay." We walked into a spectacular African themed room with leopard and zebra print everywhere. After seeing three more rooms of varying themes, we moved onto the sunroom.

"Erin, this is definitely the best part of your house! I'd spend all my time right here." There were hardwood floors with fluffy beige rugs and wall-to-wall windows. Bright, frondy plants gave it the feel of a greenhouse and I loved the stoned wall and fireplace.

"What did you say Alan does again?" I asked idly as we sat on checkered wingback chairs by the fireplace. Alan is her husband and he's seven years older than Erin. And obviously loaded. I think their parents are business associates.

"Hi honey!"

Alan popped his head through the door then grinned at me amiably. "Hi Reanne, how are you?"

"I'm well, thank you. You have a beautiful home."

"Can I get you ladies anything?"

"We'd love some tea please," said Erin.

"Coming right up." He looked at Erin lovingly before disappearing.

I had to hand it to her – she really had the perfect life. A gorgeous house, a doting husband, a nice car in the driveway…and she was still fruitlessly working on the acting thing, though she wouldn't admit it. So it surprised me that she looked wistful as I talked about plans for prom. Ok. Not so surprising – I mean – she was missing *prom. Prom!* Suddenly I felt a little sorry for her. She had everything she wanted, but she was missing out on all the final year memories.

"Alan, bring up the pastry cakes!" Erin called during a lull in conversation. This was after he already brought sandwiches and juice, and of course the tea we had initially.

Alan carried the tray in, smiling tightly. And no wonder! Three trips up and down the stairs were a lot. He placed the tray on the glass table between our chairs and wiped his red, sweating face with a napkin. "Anything else?" he puffed with a slight cringe.

"Also the – "

Now I felt sorry for *him.*

"You know what? It's ok," I jumped in before Alan blew a fuse. "We don't need anything else."

From then on, Erin carried the conversation. I couldn't get a word in, but it was ok. I let her talk about all the money they spent on their lavish honeymoon while I enjoyed the winter wonderland view through the window.

Erin offered to drive me home and I lit up as we turned onto my street. An unusual number of cars lined both sides of the slushy road and I knew what was happening right away. I finally understood why Erin invited me over. A grin split my face as I thought about what my reaction should be.

You shouldn't have! My eyes widened in shock and I covered my mouth with one hand.

No. Too phony.

I had no idea! Both hands rested on my cheeks. *Thank you so much!*

"Everything ok?" said Erin, glancing at me.

"Yes, why?"

"You were doing something weird with your face."

"Oh. Well…I'm fine."

She looked at me oddly as she parallel parked. We walked along the salted path to my house and my heart rate accelerated. My hand was already flying toward my chest in delight as I opened the door and flicked on the lights.

I was greeted with silence.

"Hellooooo? Anyone home?"

Nothing.

"Hellloooo?" I called again.

The disappointment was immediate. I really thought I was having a surprise party. Instead – the neighbors were partying.

"Mind if I have a glass of water before I go?" Erin stepped in and shrugged off her coat and boots, and then helped herself in the kitchen. "Want one?" She handed me a cold glass of water after I plunked myself onto the couch dejectedly.

I mean, I *really* thought I was having a party. It didn't have to be a surprise exactly…I just couldn't believe mom didn't plan *anything*. She always prepared something for my birthday.

Erin rubbed her arms. "Do you find it cold in here?"

"Maybe a little," I answered absently as I stared at the glass in my hand morosely. "I can adjust the thermostat."

"No!" Erin shot up from the adjacent sofa. "I think something's wrong with your *furnace*. You should have a look at *that*."

"Why? I don't know the first thing about furnaces. Neither do *you*," I pointed out.

"Actually, I do! The temperature used to fluctuate in our home all the time and then Alan showed me how to keep it constant."

Erin? Working on a furnace? I tried not to laugh. *Yeah right!*

"Ok then. Show me."

Of course I wasn't *really* going to let Erin touch the furnace. I'm not a moron. She could just explain things to me. I also saw the value in living another day. If I let Erin screw things up, Jaden would have become an only child.

I turned on the basement lights and staggered back in shock.

"SURPRISE!" everyone yelled.

Family and friends sprung forward crying "happy birthday!" while laughing and hugging me.

"Did you know?" Erin poked me in the ribs. "Or did we really get you?"

Tears stung my eyes and I blinked them back as I took in all the friendly faces. My parents, my grandparents, school friends…acquaintances…mom and dad's *accountant?*

"You really got me. I mean…I did suspect when we first pulled up, but this here," I spread my arms, "is truly overwhelming. Thank you all so much!"

"Happy birthday MG!" Rhonda swooped in for a hug, swiftly followed by…

"Neil!" I shrieked in astonishment. "What are you doing here!"

"Don't you know?" He smiled. "Surprising you is becoming my specialty. And you know me – I wouldn't miss a good party."

I playfully punched his arm. "Thanks for coming. All my favorite people under one roof! This is really special."

"And it will only get better!" Neil quipped.

Before long, mom had everyone playing games, and stories were being told in my honor. Neil kept catching my eye and grinning at me throughout the evening, and at one point Rhonda presented me with a big collage of all my favorite activities and propped it against the wall.

There was a photo of me in headphones, singing and…*har-har*. She put a broken music note next to it. And a photo of me sketching and…*No! She didn't*. She did. There were pictures of wedding gowns and bridal magazine cut outs all over the place. I groaned. Everyone snickered.

"Come on." Rhonda put an arm around my shoulder. "You know you're addicted. This wouldn't have been a real reflection of you if I didn't include it."

After everyone left, I hopped into Neil's car. He wasn't kidding about being full of surprises! He tapped the steering wheel and hummed as we drove along. I kept shooting glances at him, wondering where we were going until at last, we pulled into the parking lot of my favorite restaurant – *The Keg.*

"I love this place!" I exclaimed.

Neil came around and opened my door. "I know," he said with shining eyes.

Inside, Neil pulled out my chair as I sat down at a cozy table. The restaurant was dim, and two little candles flickered by the silverware, casting shadows on the white linen as music played softly over the sound system.

This is romantic it suddenly struck me as I glanced nervously at Neil over the tip of my menu.

"Have anything you want," he offered jovially, "the filet mignon looks good."

It *did* look good. I ordered it. Then Neil and I talked easily and bantered like we always did, and I relaxed. We were just friends out for a nice birthday dinner, reminiscing about the good old times. That's all. It was really nice.

"Remember when we planned that prank on Alex and you *bailed* on me?" Neil frowned in mock reproof as our salads arrived. "I couldn't believe you did that!"

"*Me?* What about *you?* You sailed right along with the prank anyway and then Alex blasted me. Thanks a lot!"

Neil grinned. "I was thinking it's about time to plan another one."

"Hmm, don't you think we've outgrown that now?" I said kindly.

"No, you're quite right." His laughter died away and he hailed our server. "It's probably time to begin a new chapter in our lives."

"What do you mean?" I stared stupidly at our waiter advancing with an enormous vase of red roses in his arms.

"Reanne, there's something I've wanted to discuss with you for a while now…" Neil began.

My eyes swiveled toward him in horror.

Oh no. No, no, no.

"…We're great together. We have fun, and we have so much in common." His hand edged toward mine on the table. "The last few times we've been together were wonderful and I want to explore the possibility of – "

I whipped my hand away and licked my suddenly dry lips. A tidal wave of panic rose inside me.

No, this can't be happening.

Oh God, it was.

It was like watching a train speeding toward a gaping hole in the bridge ahead. I had to divert him. Fast.

"You're right!" I exclaimed in a sudden rush. "We *should* pull another prank on Alex. It would be such fun! In fact, we should pull pranks on a bunch of people…we'll target everybody…we'll make new calling cards…we'll…"

I couldn't seem to stop myself as the waiter slipped away, discreetly taking the roses with him. I spewed out a constant stream of nonsensical babble until I finally ran out of steam and we were plunged into deafening silence.

Neil crunched on his salad and I stared anxiously at a cherry tomato as it rolled on my plate. The tension between us was thick enough to cut through with a knife. We couldn't just sit there like that. I needed to say something.

"So…how was the drive here?" I ventured.

"It was fine," came his clipped response.

"Great!" I replied with forced cheeriness.

Neil speared a cucumber with his fork and then jabbed at another one. His movements were stilted and jerky and I could see the hurt in his face.

I'm such an idiot.

Remorse poured over me.

"Neil…I'm sorry I interrupted you. I really am. Can we talk about it? Please?"

"There's no point," he said flatly, with a wounded smile. "This clearly isn't mutual."

The drive home was horrible and gloomy. Neil refused to look at me the entire time and had the radio turned up so loudly there was zero chance of talking. I slumped miserably in my seat and stared out the window at the rapidly falling snow.

What's wrong with me, anyway? Why can't I fall for a guy like Neil?

We *did* have a lot in common. We enjoyed each other's company. We could talk for hours...

I angled a look at him. His hair was slicked back, his brow was furrowed, and his hands clenched the steering wheel. There was an agitated twitching in his jaw.

It isn't my fault. I felt a sudden stab of resentment. *I can't control how I feel. It's not like I gave him any reason to think we were more than friends, now did I?*

Did I?

No. I don't think so. I told him about other guys I liked. He gave me advice. We cracked jokes.

My eyes were hot as I looked away, and in the next moment there was a tear rolling down my cheek. I knew deep down our friendship wouldn't recover. It was over. Really over...just like that.

Neil waited at the curb until I was safely inside my house before his tires went blazing down the road and out of my life.

Subject: I'm sorry

Dear Neil,

I'm at a loss for words. I want you to know how deeply sorry I am for my reaction at dinner. The situation took me by surprise and I handled it badly. I hope you know that I still value our friendship and I don't want to lose it...but I'll understand if you feel differently,

Reanne.

Subject: Not your fault

Dear Reanne,

No apology required. Not on your part anyway. I should have talked to you before arranging a big, romantic gesture like this. I can't count the times I wanted to tell you how I felt before now, or even ask you out (surely hearing that doesn't surprise you?), but each time I pushed the impulse down. I did so partly because I wasn't ready to trust again, partly because of the distance between us, and partly because I didn't trust myself not to mess things up like I did the last time. I guess I left it too late and I've messed things up anyway. I'm sorry for the way it turned out. Maybe I'll see you from time to time and we'll still be friends. Only time will tell, but regardless, you'll be in my thoughts and prayers,

Neil.

When Harry Met Sally is *so* right. I watched the movie while clutching a box of Kleenex. Neil and I couldn't be friends because attraction got in the way. On his part, anyway. I was at the scene where Harry tells Sally that men can't be friends with women they're attracted to, even if it isn't mutual. Once that vibe is out there, that's it.

That sucks. According to this movie, my friendship with Neil was doomed from the start. But it was, wasn't it? Just look at what happened.

Thankfully not all friendships end in catastrophe. In the time that followed, Jaden seemed to be getting a lot closer to his friend Lindsay. They weren't an official couple or anything, but the point is, you could tell they *liked* each other beyond friendship. The attraction was mutual. She started coming to visit at the house more often and giggled at anything Jaden said – even when it wasn't funny – and Jaden was always trying to tickle her.

And there I was – single *and* friendless. It felt like a piece of the puzzle was missing from my life without having Neil around to talk to. Who would give me an honest male perspective now? Although, if he had feelings for me…his opinions might not have been so honest. Why didn't I see it earlier? Why didn't Jaden *tell* me? That's what those secret online conversations were about. Apparently Jaden advised Neil to come for my birthday in friendship only, and he didn't listen. Familiar hurt and guilt welled up whenever I thought about Neil and how it went wrong, but each time I pushed it down. I had to move on.

Chapter Nine

The Last Days

It took a lot of shopping with Rhonda and a trip to a bridal store at Rhonda's insistence to help me get over the melancholy. I tried on some lovely gowns, which normally would have lifted my spirits immediately, but my heart wasn't in it. It wasn't until Rhonda tried on what must have been the most repulsive gown in the entire place that I started to feel a bit better. She came out of the dressing room looking so ghastly and uncomfortable in a dress with big puffy sleeves and botchy stitch work that I cracked a smile. And when she called herself "Frankenbride" and struck a pose, I totally lost it.

My mood brightened further when we returned to my house that afternoon. A stack of mail sat on the kitchen counter with a big fat envelope on the top addressed to me. From the college.

I held the envelope with slightly shaking hands and darted an ominous look at Rhonda. "This is the one I've been waiting for."

"Open it!"

Congratulations, we are pleased to offer you admission to…

"YEEEEEEEEEEEESSSSSSSSSSSSSSS!" I screamed, not taking in the rest of the letter. "Yeeeessss!" I bounced around.

Rhonda jumped and screamed too. "Congratulatiooonnnnnns! Whoooooo!"

"What happened?" Jaden burst into the kitchen in alarm. "What's wrong?"

"I-got-in-I-got-in-I-got-in!" I shoved the letter at him as Rhonda and I linked arms and danced.

"*Ahhh*. You-got-in-you-got-in-you-got-in," Jaden mocked in a high-pitched voice, accompanied by an effeminate jig.

I stopped and stared at him. "Sit down you girly man."

"Shut up you manly girl," he retorted without missing a beat. He sounded *exactly* like Arnold Schwarzenegger.

We howled with laughter.

"I'm proud of you sis," said Jaden as he gave me a gentle shove. "So…I guess this means you'll be staying in residence?" There was a definite twinkle in his eye.

Wait a minute…

I frowned. He was after my room – the little scum!

"Just so you know – you're not getting my room. I'm going to college, not moving out!" And I would still be home for the holidays.

"Same thing!" Jaden ran off to proposition mom and dad while I smirked. How ludicrous. They wouldn't give him my room. Would they?

I ran after him.

"It's finally here! I can't believe Prom is *finally here!*" Rhonda grinned at my reflection as I styled her hair. Thankfully, it was long enough for an up-do. Well…mostly.

"What do you think?" I positioned the hand mirror so she could see.

"Uh…" She crinkled her nose.

"I know, I know. I'll fix it." Little pieces of hair stuck out everywhere and she looked like a porcupine. A cute porcupine…but still a porcupine. It's not exactly the look you want for prom. I made adjustments until it was a lot better.

An hour later we descended the stairs in our radiant gowns, giddy with excitement. We posed for the paparazzi (a.k.a, my parents) then sailed out to the curb where the stretch limo awaited. Rhonda and I giggled each time we passed another vehicle. People stared at the tinted glass windows, probably wondering who was lucky enough to be inside. The noise in the limo became louder and louder with each friend we collected. There were eight of us in total, none of us with dates. I think I preferred it that way after all. We were having such fun – it couldn't have possibly been any better.

In fact, I was sure of it. All I had to do was look at Julia, sitting with her date in awkward silence at a separate table, and I knew I dodged a bullet. That would have been Neil and me.

No, it wouldn't. They don't really know each other. Neil and I would be in stitches by now...

"The rose petals jazz up the table, don't you think?" said Rhonda, pulling me from my reverie. My eyes swept over the petals to the carved candle centerpiece...and I hoped there would be a game later to win it. It was gorgeous!

"I love the costumes!" said a girl named Samantha as she strode up to our table.

There wasn't an official theme for prom, yet some showed up in costume anyway. Romeo and Juliet lingered near the buffet. Marilyn and JFK were coming through the high, arched entrance, and...

"Look!" cried Rhonda, pointing.

Oh Gross.

Aladdin and Jasmine were making out against the back wall. Way to ruin Disney. They apparently ruined it for someone else, too. "Get a room!" reverberated across the dance floor from a guy in a tuxedo that didn't fit quite right.

"Do you know what I'm really going to miss about this place?" asked Rhonda as we looked away from the make out session.

Feeling moved I nodded. Obviously she was going to say it was all the classes we had together – all the jokes and laughter. We made best friend history, and now we were going off in separate directions. I would miss it too.

"Mrs. Stoddard."

"*What?*" I gasped. "*Why?*" Not that there was anything wrong with Mrs. Stoddard. She was brilliant, actually. She was the first math teacher I had who really took the time to properly explain the equations, and then made *extra* time for students when they still didn't get it. I suck at math.

"Because of the *sneezing.*"

"What sneezing?" It was Samantha again.

"She always pauses right in the middle of a lesson and plugs her nose to stop it, but it never works. The sneezes come out in quick succession and they're really squeaky. Like this." Rhonda sneezed a Beethoven piece.

"Oh puh-lease," I said. "It's more like *this.*"

"Ouch! What was that for?" That Samantha girl elbowed me.

"Mr. Davy is coming!"

Now *he* was the *worst* teacher ever. He sped through every lesson, as quickly as possible (if he bothered to teach at all), and then had a nap at his desk while we supposedly read through the textbook. He always had a book propped up in front of him because we weren't supposed to know – but it was hard to mistake the snoring.

"Hello girls! It's wonderful to see you. Enjoying prom?" He pushed his glasses closer to his bushy brows and smiled.

"It's great!" chirped Rhonda. "You're looking well, Mr. Davy. Very *rested*."

I clapped a hand to my mouth to muffle the snort that escaped.

Samantha made a quick recovery. "Oh look, there's Ms. Kruda!"

Mr. Davy took off in a flash. We all knew he had a thing for her. And I take it back – *she* was the worst teacher ever. Did you know I averaged sixty-six percent in her technology class? *Sixty-six percent!* That's appalling. And it wouldn't have bothered me so much if I actually *deserved* the grade, but I honestly didn't. Which is why I appealed it to the principal and had it bumped up by twenty percent. And why she constantly gave me nasty looks in the school halls afterward.

I had no choice. Ms. Kruda wouldn't reconsider the grade – I asked – and she was never in the classroom! She spent all her time flirting with male staff in the corridors, or worse, in our classroom when they visited. She left us to follow complicated tutorials the entire time…and on the only occasion I ever requested her help – she sighed dramatically as if it was a huge inconvenience (which, I suppose it was. If I was still single at forty I'd probably want to spend my time flirting too) – and then clicked the mouse a few times before saying "oops! I don't know what happened there."

I'll tell you what happened – she practically wiped out my entire project! The genius techie kid in the class had to come and help me fix it.

Suddenly, the lights dimmed and a ripple of excitement went throughout the banquet hall. The speakers cracked to life. I quit brooding over the lovebird teachers as Rhonda bolted toward the dance floor. She swayed happily to the music and a small crowd gathered. They clapped, and her face was bathed in joy. She must have thought she was doing really well. The applause, however, was directed at the break-dancers as they busted out moves just behind her. Let's be honest – Rhonda's musical but it doesn't mean she can dance.

The soft lighting switched to flashing strobes and I *oohhed* and *ahhed* with everyone else. A guy actually spun on his head!

That's one thing you can always count on in high school. The guys may be immature and annoying most of the time…but occasionally they do something really cool.

"I bet I could do that," Rhonda quipped as she did some weird, wiggly move.

"Rhonda." I tried to put it as kindly as possible and placed a comforting hand on her shoulder. "You suck."

Ok. Don't panic. I can do this. It's simply a matter of deciding what I need to bring…and sticking with it. Easy. Of course, having an indecisive best friend there certainly didn't help matters.

I surveyed the mounds of clothes all over my bedroom as Rhonda once again grabbed something from the 'reject' pile and tossed it into my suitcase.

"Would you *please* stop taking items from the reject pile? I can't take everything!" I snatched a plain grey t-shirt from her hands before she could add it to the identical t-shirt she included just moments earlier.

"Fine," Rhonda huffed. "But you know you're going to need it. You need to pack *wisely* for college. This will turn out to be the one item you absolutely have to have and it won't be there. You know I'm right. Take this," she examined a narrow mauve belt. "What if you lose weight? This would be useful *and* stylish."

"I don't want to lose weight," I said dryly, "but thanks."

"You know what I mean. There will be some unexpected situation or other and then you'll wish you listened to me."

And so, my suitcase kept filling up…until I had three of them and a duffle bag. And none would close properly.

"I guess I got a little carried away," Rhonda puffed as she pressed down on one of the suitcase lids with all her might. "Quick, zip!"

"No…it isn't going to work. We won't get that shut, and I probably can't lift it, either. I only want two suitcases anyway…let's rethink this."

Rhonda ignored me and ploughed on. "Almost got it!"

I was impressed. Rhonda was red in the face and panting but the zipper was halfway there! Suddenly it snapped. Rhonda went wheeling backwards, and a pair of denim shorts went flying after her.

"Ok," she grunted, removing the shorts from her head. "Ok. You win."

Swiftly, we unpacked and started over. It took a while, but miraculously, we finally got it right. Two suitcases were stacked neatly by the door. Everything else went back in the closet. As I studied my room, the strangest feeling overcame me. The room was so…empty. I was really going away. It was thrilling and sad all at once.

"Make sure you call and email lots, ok?" said Rhonda gruffly.

There was a slight wobble to my voice. "Same to you," I told her as we hugged.

"Dad, come on!" The van was packed and mom and I waited impatiently by the front door. Well, *I* was impatient. It was a ten-hour drive to the college and I wanted to leave, pronto! *"Dad!"*

"You know your father." Mom glanced at her watch. "We aimed for 7:00 a.m. so we could leave by 8:00 a.m."

"Yeah, I know but it's still annoying." Water ran in the upper floor bathroom and I heard dad's footsteps as he padded about. When the noise stopped, dad descended the stairs…in the gaping, holy track pants – which seemed to be gaping more than the last time he wore them.

"Tom!"

"Dad!"

I dropped my head into my hands in disbelief. "Mom, I thought you hid them," I whispered.

"I did!" Mom glared at dad. "Tom…you can't wear those pants," she said in cutting tones.

"Sure I can," he replied easily. "I want to be comfortable on the road."

I glanced at his socked feet in sandals and gasped. Had he no pride? "Daaaaad!"

His grin faded as he registered our stony expressions. "What, can't a guy be comfy?"

"No!" Mom and I yelled in unison. Seriously, was he *trying* to embarrass me on the first day? For an awful moment, I thought he would wear them anyway.

Dad looked from face to face. "I guess I'm outnumbered," he said as he moseyed back up the stairs. Great. We'd *never* leave.

"Coffee?" Mom suggested, heading to the kitchen.

"Yeah." I joined her. "I guess."

An hour later…

We were on the road! Yes! I was in the back of the van with my sketching materials; mom sat comfortably in the front passenger seat reading a novel…and dad was behind the wheel, finally looking like a normal person. All was well in the world.

Except for the momentary delay at the gas station. I dashed out to the ladies' room when we stopped to fill up and when I came back the van was gone. I stayed in one spot until I saw it creeping out from the side of the gas station. Dad thought he was so funny. He pulled up beside me and I opened the door. The van inched forward before I could get in.

"Ok Tom. Let her in."

He eventually stopped and I hopped up and closed the door. You know how I said dad looked like a normal person? Well – that's it. He *looked* like a normal person, but he wasn't.

Nothing but country road stretched ahead as we drove along – and dad didn't pull any more stunts. The ride was smooth and peaceful and I was happy because I just wanted to *get there*.

Chapter Ten
College!

We drove for hours and the scenery began to change. We still passed patches of trees and the odd cluster of cows, horses and bales of hay, but you could tell we were entering a small town. The houses were quaint and spread widely apart with a few little shops scattered about. A little convenience store sat at the side of the road. It had a sign in the window reading *we rent movies,* and I couldn't believe any place still did that – everything is online these days. I was glad I didn't live in a small town. I mean – I'm sure it was nice and all…I just knew it wasn't for me. We came to a fork in the road and veered right.

The van slowed as we passed a gas station, another convenience store, and a coffee shop. Next we drove across a narrow bridge.

"There it is." Dad pointed to a little brick building just beside the riverbed.

"What are you pointing at?" I looked past the building into the copse of trees.

Dad grinned at me. "Your college residence."

He was clearly joking.

"At least you don't have to walk far for snacks!" Dad chuckled as he parked.

He wasn't kidding. Students wandered in and out of the side entrance of the building and I felt a chord of recognition as I took it all in. It was dusk now, but even with the fading light, everything looked exactly as it did on the college website. Except – for some reason, I thought the residence would be a lot bigger...

Maybe it looks small on the outside, but is actually really huge within! One could always hope.

I whipped off my seatbelt, flung the door open and nearly tripped in my haste to get out.

"Careful!" cried mom as I lunged for the back of her seat and steadied myself.

Oh the shame. Two guys were hanging out by the door directly in front of me. One got up and offered to help dad as he struggled with my luggage, and I avoided eye contact with the other guy, pretending that didn't just happen.

"Excuse me?" I tapped a blond girl with long swishy hair as she walked past. "Do you know where the office is? Or a posted list where I can find out which room I'm in?"

She grinned. "First year student? I can show you to your room if you like. What's your name?"

The girl introduced herself as Amelia Black (second year) as we followed her downstairs into the cafeteria. I guessed she was giving me a tour first. It was nice of her to show me around, though I felt a little bad for the men toting my heavy suit suitcases along.

Amelia explained the meal schedule as we passed ugly brown tables and matching doors, until we came to an ugly brown door at the far end of the cafeteria, which must have been the broom closet. She opened it with a flourish.

"Here you are!" She smiled. "I was in this room last year!"

"This is a *room*?" I echoed in shock. "Connected to the *cafeteria*?" I tried to hide my dismay, and Mom and dad exchanged skeptical glances.

"Hey, it's our roomie!" A lanky girl in a colorful outfit strode over and ushered me in. "I'm Bridget, that's Anna," she said of the robust girl silhouetted by the window.

I was speechless.

"Megan should be back in a bit. We already set up our stuff – you can settle in over here." Bridget tucked a honey colored strand of hair behind her ear and shimmied me to my section of the room: the back right corner behind the inward swinging door. Apparently I was sharing half the room with Megan, whoever she was, and we were divided by our wardrobes on wheels, which was great for privacy, but crap for space. Not to mention the lighting. Between the propped open door and the wardrobes, my corner was pretty dark. And there wasn't much improvement even with the door closed.

"What do you think?" asked Dad.

"It's…um…great."

There had to be a mistake. You can't cram four people into a room that isn't large enough to accommodate them all. Could I even fit my luggage inside? We somehow managed.

"You can come home if you want," mom whispered with tears in her eyes after folding a few shirts into a dresser for me, which wasn't even in my corner of the room.

I hesitated then put on a brave face.

"No. I'll…weather this out." Maybe I'd get used to the situation and it would improve. And if it didn't, it couldn't possibly get any worse. Right?

My parents were gone and all my wonderful clothes were squashed into the unrealistically small wardrobe that was pushed up against the end of my creaky cot. I didn't want to spend much time in the cellar like room, so I explored the rest of the building with Anna and Bridget, who were also in their first year.

The administration office was at the top of the stairs to the left – we went down the hall to the right. There was a door in the middle of the hall and Bridget peered through the glass window. "This looks like the library slash computer room," she observed.

I looked too…and the library was very tiny. And there were only two computers; a shiny black *Dell,* which I thought might work properly and the other one was old and scuffed.

Next we saw the lounge. Large windows stretched along both walls flooding the room with the last rays of the setting sun, while two girls played a match of table tennis in the center of the room.

"That looks fun!" I said to my roomies. "We should try it!" I'm actually quite good at table tennis.

There was also a foosball table against one wall and an area on the opposite side of the lounge with two sofas, a coffee table, and vending machines. I didn't see anyone else, though.

"Where *is* everyone?" I asked meaningfully.

Anna shrugged. "We have a few days before classes begin. Plenty of time for more to arrive."

Bridget caught on. "I think the men's dorm is over there."

I walked over to the window and stared at the white building across the parking lot, which I hadn't noticed when I arrived.

Well. I could see there wouldn't be many men about; their residence hall was smaller than ours.

I shifted my gaze to the river and imagined myself sitting at the bank with my sketchpad and pencils during my spare time. I wasn't sure what else I could do. I wouldn't be dating, obviously.

Movement in my peripheral vision caused me to glance back at the white building as a chipmunk scurried across the gravel.

The door down the hall creaked. It was a guy! I knew it! Bridget and I scuttled away from the window and I sucked in a breath as Alex came in.

Alex. Wearing an unbuttoned navy blazer and a short, wide tie.

You know, I should have seen this coming. I told him early on I wanted to attend this college…but I mean, isn't this a little extreme, even for him?

"Reanne, what a…pleasant surprise."

I raised a brow. "Hi Alex. What brings you here?"

"Graphic design," he said coolly, "second year."

Second year?

"And how's that going?" I asked politely.

"Great," he looked me dead in the eye. "You should know I have an amazing girlfriend. I never believed in love at first sight but now I do." He puffed himself up like a peacock and went on about this fabulous girlfriend and their 'serious relationship' for five minutes, also mentioning that he was 'off the market' several times while I half listened. At one point it dawned on me that he was no longer speaking and I found him staring at me with folded arms and pity filled eyes. Beside me, Bridget giggled.

Oh for Pete's sake.

He didn't think I followed *him*, did he*?* I really thought we were past this. And if I wasn't interested earlier, I certainly wasn't now. Alex stood before me, as pompous as ever, except now he resembled a two-legged blimp (*gosh, what do they* feed *people here?*). I could no longer avoid him because he filled half the room and blocked the exit. It didn't look like he was about to budge, either.

"Reanne, a word of advice? I'm off the market now, but if another opportunity for love presents itself, this time you should seize it and live without regret. Carpe diem I say!"

Bridget snorted and Alex glared at her.

Even she could tell he wasn't my type – why couldn't he?

Alex swung around indignantly and somehow squeezed himself into the library so we could pass. Oh boy.

"Hey guys! I have some news." A girl with caramel hair came out of the office as we approached.

"This is Megan," said Bridget.

I liked her immediately. Her manicure was perfect and I wanted to know where she bought her cute, trendy outfit! We looked about the same size...maybe she would want to swap clothes occasionally...

"I'm not staying," said Megan cheerily, instantly crushing my hopes to smithereens.

Bridget's face fell. "Aww, too bad Megs – why are you leaving?"

"This isn't the right environment for me."

"Can you say *spoiled?*" Anna murmured.

I felt a stab of panic. I didn't want Megan to go. "Why not give it a few days?" I suggested. "Some things take a little time to get used to and then they're not so bad!"

Megan smiled apologetically. "Sorry...I already withdrew."

We helped her clear her stuff from the room and I wondered if this would be my fate in a few days. I looked at the empty space as Anna and Bridget said goodbye to Megan upstairs, and felt my nose twitch. The empty space…on *my* side of the room.

If she's gone then it means…

This means…

My quarter of the room turned into half the room, and I now had two closets for my stuff! *Two!* I arranged the wardrobes side by side against the far wall and pulled the little dresser containing my stuff to where it belonged – with me. And I could *see* well. I still didn't have much light from the window since it was barricaded by Anna's stuff, but at least I had better access to the fluorescent lighting overhead. Things were looking up – a lot sooner than I thought!

The old but well maintained building where our classes were held was a ten-minute walk from the dormitories, half of which was spent trudging up a steep hill. It was a challenging trek with all my books, and I was out of breath and panting by the time I arrived each morning.

Darren began talking with me and offering rides in his little red car after the first week. He was tall with wavy dark hair, which would have looked a little better if he spent more time combing it rather than raking his fingers through it, but I didn't mind. His ruffled hair gave him a cute boyish look.

I quickly realized, however, that Darren was an outrageous flirt. His pickup lines were sweet and amusing when he used them with me, but he tried them out on other girls as well. I knew not to take his flirtations seriously, although I'll admit they flattered me. The passenger seat in his car was always reserved for me no matter who else traveled with us and he held my hand while strolling along the trail next to the dormitories. He also dropped my hand like a hot rock the minute someone we knew came along, which annoyed me, but wasn't a big deal because holding his hand was like holding a cold, dead fish, anyway.

Inevitably this bored me and I drew back from my interactions with Darren. There was no point getting involved with a guy like that. It was kind of fun, but wouldn't go anywhere. I assumed Darren would move on as well but surprisingly the opposite happened. He became persistent.

That's how I found myself at a pizza place one evening with Darren and a few of his friends. He asked me if I wanted to go and I said no.

"Why?" he asked.

I shrugged. "Don't feel like it."

He kept asking until I changed my mind, which left me wondering – *where's a muzzle when you need one?* And this only occurred to me because Darren consistently shouted 'muzzle' during class whenever a particular girl would speak, which bothered me. The girl just liked to talk…she shouldn't have had to worry that some moron was going to yell 'muzzle' whenever she opened her mouth.

So there I was with said moron, sitting in the restaurant and enjoying myself as I normally did when he wanted to be charming. His friend was in the middle of a joke when the server approached and doled out menus. I glanced at the menu and put it down.

"You're not eating?" said Darren.

"No, it's ok. It's a little expensive."

He picked up the menu and put it in front of me. "Order something, my treat."

I didn't say anything to hint. Honestly. It just seemed a little much for a meal and I hadn't planned to be there in the first place. "No thanks, I'm ok with water."

"I really want you to order something," he insisted and tapped the menu. "I *want* to get it for you." He carried on until I reluctantly perused the appetizers and salads. Darren grabbed the menu and flipped the page. "What? You think I'm cheap? Get pizza or pasta."

"Darren, I *like* salad." Was this guy going to argue all evening?

Yes. He was.

It was easier to just order a steaming dish of shrimp pasta. The food melted in my mouth and it had an intense spicy flavor.

"Thanks," I said, meaning it. "This is really good." But that was it. We weren't going out again.

Darren was sprawled on the couch in the lounge a few days later, holding up concert tickets for a group I never heard of. "It's this Saturday, what do you think?"

I peeked at him above the novel I was reading. "Who else is going?"

"Just us. I'd like to take you on a proper date."

I stuck my nose back into my book and uttered a noncommittal "hmm."

Darren sat up and moved closer. His fingers appeared at the top of my book. He brought it away from my face and his eyes locked with mine. "It'll be fun, come on."

No! My inner voice yelled, but my mouth stayed firmly shut.

"I'd like to get to know you better." His brows shot up before he wiggled them playfully. "Please?"

I laughed and wavered. "Ok."

"Great!" He beamed. "You'll love this!"

All right…I know I shouldn't have agreed to go out with the player *again*, but I couldn't help myself. Sitting around the lounge was *so* dull and Darren was nice looking in his own little way. I mean – he was no Chris Hemsworth, I'm not going to lie – but he was certainly passable. Besides, he already bought the tickets and maybe this time we'd click. I wouldn't know without giving him a proper chance. Anyway, it was just one little date. It couldn't hurt.

Darren greeted me with a wolf whistle and a "looking good!" as I walked out to his sporty car Saturday evening.

I wished I could have returned the compliment but he looked kind of deranged. His hair hadn't been combed (not even with his fingers) and there were rips in his faded jeans. I glanced down at my mauve heels, the Miu Miu skirt I borrowed from Rhonda (with the mauve belt – she was right, I did need it) and her taupe Chloe bag, and felt overdressed. My outfit was fantastic, but clearly overdone if Darren's style sense (or lack thereof) set the standard.

The engine revved and we were off.

"So is this your favorite band?" I asked conversationally.

"Yeah, I have all their CDs and I've been to all their concerts." He talked about them the rest of the way while I nodded. He didn't ask one question about my interests or likes and it didn't look like he was about to.

Great way to get to know me, I thought dourly. The thumb Darren circled on the back of my hand as he droned on did nothing to spice things up.

Darren released my hand as he pulled into the parking lot and slid into a space near the entrance. There were plenty of women tottering about in stilettos and miniskirts and I glanced at Darren.

"You're the most beautiful woman here," he said.

"Hmm," I said suspiciously.

We went inside the dark auditorium.

"You'll *love* this," Darren shifted in his seat while lights flashed and the ground shook with the pounding of drums and electric guitar. I craned my neck to catch a glimpse of the musicians through the fog generated on stage. I couldn't see anything. The moment I could – I wanted to go home.

The lead singer was in tattered leather clothing with a horrifically painted face and long gangly hair. As were the others with him. It was a rock group. I should have guessed when I spotted the crazy fan a few seats down with the same painted face and wild hair.

The screeching began and my hands flew to my ears. "How long is the concert?" I yelled over the noise.

Darren bobbed his head to the music.

"Darren!" I tapped his shoulder. "How LONG is this?"

"It's called – "

"NO." I shook my head. "Not *song*. How LONG?"

He couldn't hear me. I sat back and prepared for a torturous evening. And you know what? It wasn't as bad as I expected (though to clarify, it was *still* bad). The band only screamed the first song and I kind of made out the lyrics in all the rest.

I had a hard time hearing afterward as we sat in *Subway,* and there was a slight ringing in my ears. Darren seemed fine sitting across from me in the booth. In fact, he looked quite happy. I guess he was accustomed to being partially deaf.

"I should come over there and kiss you," I thought I heard him say as I bit into my sandwich. I'm glad he didn't…not after taking me to see the worst band *ever.*

But it was still a date; one he planned and paid for and I wanted to show my appreciation for his effort. I stood in the convenience store the following day, contemplating what to buy. I gave it a lot of consideration and finally decided to get carbonated water. Ok. Don't judge. I know the gift sounds pathetic but I *knew* he would like it. He always traipsed through the lounge chugging down bottles of Perrier. It was his thing.

I personally thought it disgusting and would never drink the stuff myself…but to each his own. And it saved me a trip to the mall where I probably would have bought something he didn't want, like a stylish tie he would stuff into a bottom drawer or a Ralph Lauren shirt he might wear while cleaning his car (dad did this once, to my utter horror). Darren didn't seem hung up on fashion anyway.

I headed to the small, refrigerated section at the back of the store and browsed the assortment of beverages. There was a selection of sodas, fruit drinks, and flavored water. I finally spotted the green glass bottles. I grabbed one, then two, and headed to the counter to pay for them.

The clerk opened the till. "Would you like a bag, miss?"

"No thanks." I planned to find him immediately and surprise him.

Feeling pleased with myself, I adjusted my Versace sunglasses and stepped out into the blinding sunlight. The river sparkled like crystal, and my step was bouncy. It always feels nice to do something for someone else; I hoped he would like the gesture.

"Hey guys!" I happily greeted two girls from my design class as they approached. They smiled back – then stopped as their eyes landed on the Perrier bottles in each hand. I didn't like the looks shooting between them.

"Are those for Darren?" Melanie asked in a strange voice. It seemed like a silly question since he was the only one constantly toting them around.

"Yes, why?"

The other girl opened her mouth then hesitated. "Um…did you know Darren is going around telling everyone you're a cheapskate?"

"No," I said, stunned. "I *didn't*."

"He said you wouldn't pay for your own meal and that you deliberately ordered the most expensive item on the menu when he took you to *Pizza Twice*. Some pasta, or something."

"That's *not* what happened!"

Why was he going around telling everyone that twisted version of events? *Why?* I pursed my lips, feeling betrayed and humiliated as I stood there, holding those stupid, cold bottles. I couldn't believe I was about to give something, however small, to a double-crossing idiot. A lying double-crossing idiot.

I marched back into the convenience store and hastily returned the carbonated crap. He wouldn't get anything from me, not even friendship.

And as with other morons of times past, I avoided Darren religiously. I sat as far away from him as possible in class and refused to look at him. I saw him in the corner of my eye, slowly inching his chair closer to mine like an evil snake in the grass. So I pierced him with a venomous look and jerked my chair away.

Darren's face snapped in shock.

You know what you did.

My glare conveyed the message. But he didn't get it because he sidled up to me after class and tried to put an arm around my shoulder, which I brushed off. "Can I speak with you privately?" I said stiffly.

"Sure." We went to the end of a quiet hall and Darren reached for my hand the moment we were alone. I felt a dart of fury and backed away.

"Darren. You and I are *only* friends – *if* even *that*."

Darren shrugged. "Ok."

"Just so we're clear."

"Yep. Whatever."

He didn't bother to ask why and was obnoxiously leaning against some other girl a few seconds later. The girl he had apparently invited to the concert before me, except *she* declined.

"Darren's a dope," said Rhonda on her end of the line as I crouched next to the payphone in the stairwell. "No. Worse than a dope, he's an ugly dope."

I giggled. Rhonda always made me feel better. "You don't know what he looks like," I pointed out.

"I don't need to know. He *sounds* ugly. He's ugly on the inside where it counts."

"Yeah. He is," I agreed.

"On a bright note," I heard the laughter in her voice, "at least you snagged a few rides in the car."

"And a yummy shrimp pasta."

"That too."

We laughed and talked for an hour, coming up with loads of nicknames for Darren, which I probably shouldn't mention. Nicknames we would use for the remainder of the school year.

"So what's the news on the home front?" I asked Rhonda. She still visited my family even though I wasn't there.

"I think Jaden and Lindsay will be officially dating soon. I can tell they're getting close."

"Ha! I knew it!"

"They're sappy with each other, it's really cute."

"And what's new with you?"

She told me all about her new music compositions and I made her promise to let me hear them at Christmas.

Rhonda made *me* promise to bring home pictures of everyone here so she could put names with faces. I was excited about the permanent black markers she suggested we use on Darren's photo.

Chapter Eleven
Amelia and Alex

The leaves floated from the trees and landed on the ground in heaps of orange, red, and yellow. I breathed in the crisp autumn air as I perched on the ledge of the wall near the front entrance of the dorm building. Fall is the best season – it's by far the prettiest and just the right temperature for sitting outside. Especially when you have to bury your nose in a textbook about contemporary art to prepare for an upcoming trip to a museum in a neighboring city. I was preparing myself for the review I would have to write afterward.

Amelia and Tara stepped outside in their identical tan windbreakers, not looking at me as they walked past.

"He's transferring here tomorrow," Amelia said with a Cheshire cat smile. She twisted a tendril of blond hair around her finger as Tara zipped up her jacket and gasped.

"He *followed* you here?" Her eyes widened. "Amazing!"

"I expected this," Amelia stated, approaching the stairs. "It was just a matter of time."

I dropped my textbook and craned to catch more of their conversation.

"So, what are you going to do?"

"Nothing. He's…"

They reached the last step and continued along the path. The wind kicked up and ruined any chance I had at hearing the rest of their conversation. Which was a shame because I was intrigued. Who was this mysterious 'he' and when would he arrive? Another guy coming to the school had to be a good thing.

The alarm sounded early the next morning and I shut it off and groaned. I wished I hadn't stayed up so late, *still* reading that blasted textbook.

I couldn't turn the clock back but I could catch a few extra minutes' sleep. I fumbled for the buttons, hitting snooze. My eyes drifted and my body relaxed.

Mmm, nice.

Colors and images swirled before me as the music announced my entrance. Every head turned in awe and the whispering began. In the distance I saw him, tall and proud – his eyes sparkled when I entered the chapel beneath a shower of shimmering rose petals. A sheen of tears glistened in my eyes as…

BUZZ BUZZ BUZZ.

The alarm interrupted once more, disturbing the most beautiful dream. I had this dream often, but sometimes the details changed – like the gown I wore or the groom's eye color…or even the wedding favors I chose for the guests. One time I turned into a wedding planner after saying my vows, and suddenly became the coordinator at Rhonda's wedding. Except she had short, spiky hair – so it was actually a nightmare.

I hated waking up right in the middle, not knowing how it would end.

I switched off the alarm and stumbled to my towel where it hung on a wardrobe hook, before continuing out the door.

So. Tired. Need. Shower.

The bedroom door slammed behind me with a thud, punctuating the shock and terror that hit me when I realized – belatedly – that I was standing beneath the blinding lights of the cafeteria. In my scummy shorts and "I don't do mornings" t-shirt (a gift from Jaden...and quite comfy, in spite of the way they looked).

I dashed across to the bathroom. There were only a few girls milling about – some dressed, some still in their pj's. No men yet, thankfully!

Whose bright idea was it to put a cafeteria and bedrooms side by side, anyway?

I discarded my pj's, turned on the shower and stepped into the inviting cascade of droplets, then screamed at the icy contact.

I was beginning to feel a little murderous.

"I'm...n-never...hitting snooze...ag-gain!" I vowed through chattering teeth. If I arrived a few minutes earlier, there might have been hot water.

"There are supposed to be *benefits* to attending a private college," I muttered darkly as I twisted the tap and grabbed my towel.

Not only did I endure cold showers, sometimes the food ran out if I didn't get there fast enough. And everyone was a busybody. News traveled faster than the speed of light. Sometimes it was beneficial, like in the situation with Darren. I'm *glad* I found out about the rumors he spread as quickly as I did. On the other hand – it really annoyed me to overhear a conversation that focused on Darren dumping *me.* What a creep.

With my pj's on and warmth returning to my body, I felt better. My damp hair formed soft curls as I checked out my reflection. A definite improvement from when I first stumbled out of bed, though I don't often look too bad in the mornings. Unlike *some* people who wake up with their hair sticking out in every direction and have ghastly bags beneath their eyes. I won't mention names, but Anna always awoke looking like that. It's good she slept on the opposite side of the room otherwise I'd have been in for a real scare every morning.

You're probably sensing some animosity here, and there's good reason for it.

Anna drove me mental. I tried to get along with her, since we were roommates and all, but there's only so much you can do when you're the only one trying.

From day one she put a negative spin on *everything* and at first I balanced that out by finding positive things to say. If she thought the potatoes at supper sucked, I'd mention I liked the meat or dessert. If she hated all her clothes, I told her she looked nice in her navy turtleneck. I thought this might lighten her up a little but it only made her grumpier. And she refused to compromise. Anna regularly left the window open because it was on her side of the room and she was always hot. I found it too cold and asked her to close it. Did she? Nope. She even opened it before going out.

I suggested getting a portable fan to keep cool but the idea didn't appeal to her. Eventually I detached and hid the window handle when she wasn't around. I mean, enough was enough.

A typed sign appeared on our door the next day, which read: *thou shall not steal.*

First of all, I didn't *steal* the handle because it belonged to all of us, and secondly Bridget didn't want the window open either. It wasn't our fault Anna overheated easily.

And there was the snoring. Every breath Anna took sounded like a grinding garbage disposal that occasionally jammed before starting up again. I wore earplugs, but I still heard it if she fell asleep before me. One night when I couldn't stand it any longer, I went over and plugged her nose for a second. That didn't go down so well…

Anyway. With my towel draped over my arm, I poked my head through the door to check for guys. There still weren't any around and I ran across to my room with plans to dress quickly and check my email before class.

"Yes! The computer's mine!" The library was vacant and I sat in front of the Dell. The other computer was unplugged with an *out of order* sign taped to the screen.

I connected the dial up Internet (yeah – *dial up*) and logged into my email to read mom's new message. I laughed out loud a few times, especially when she described her latest unsuccessful attempt to destroy dad's pants. Oh, how I missed being home.

I couldn't help but wonder if dad set up surveillance somewhere, since he managed to save the pants every time. I wanted to help.

My fingers flew over the keys as I tapped out my lengthy response and I smiled at my own genius suggestion, which was really quite simple. Mom needed to buy a shredder she could 'accidentally' drop the pants into. She would have to make sure they went all the way in or else dad would still wear them.

Someone came into the library and stopped behind me. I turned to see Alex peering at the screen over my shoulder through his black-rimmed glasses.

I minimized my email and waited for him to step back and sit on the edge of the table. I resumed typing. Quickly, because there were only a few minutes' left before I'd be late.

"I need the computer," said Alex a moment later by my ear.

"Almost done," I glanced at him apologetically as he sat down again. "I just need another minute."

I typed faster.

Alex huffed.

"Some of us," boomed Alex after ten seconds, "have vital things to work on. The assignment due for my first class is more important than your little email."

Funny he'd leave something so important until the last minute.

I bit my lip. There was no point arguing with him because I knew how that would end. One last comment to write before I could wrap up. A few seconds passed.

"Get off!" Alex exploded as he heaved himself from the mahogany table, which frankly, I'm surprised hadn't collapsed beneath him. I couldn't contain myself any longer.

"You're so rude!" I snapped as I hit 'send.' "If you're not bright enough to finish your work before the last minute then it's your own fault!" My chair slammed against the desk as I stormed out.

His vehement "shut up!" echoed through the hall behind me as I stomped out of the building. The day was off to a really bad start.

It was raining and I returned for my umbrella.

Droplets pounded it, like the sound of a thousand beads pouring into a glass jar. I enjoy rainy days, especially during a thunderstorm. Except…I prefer to watch the rain hammering the window from the comfort of my bedroom rather than walking in it, and it's more spectacular when I'm in a better mood. At least there wasn't lightning.

A flash cracked the air and split a nearby tree. Great. The scent of burning bark filled my nose. Freaked, I ran up the hill and nearly slipped. My book bag weighed me down like a ton of bricks and I shifted it to my other shoulder. I continued more slowly. I didn't want to get struck by lightning but I also didn't want to wipe out, hit my head and go to the hospital, assuming someone happened to find me lying there in the middle of nowhere.

Ow. My shoulder. I stopped and switched the bag again.

These were the times I missed that idiot Darren the most. Or rather, his car – let's be honest.

At the top of the hill, I paused, caught my breath and repositioned the book bag.

Someone suddenly took it from me and I turned around, startled.

Oh my.

Fireworks exploded like the fourth of July as I gazed at a rugged guy with laughing blue eyes. He shouldered the bag and smiled in surprised recognition.

My heart stopped. Lightning must have zapped me after all. I was dead. I had to be…and this was heaven. Or else I was hallucinating. "Th-thanks." I stammered.

The vision chuckled. "It's good to see you again…?"

I blinked away the water clinging to my lashes and straightened my leaning umbrella. "Reanne," I supplied.

"Reanne." His smile revealed beautiful white teeth. "Nice to meet you properly. I'm Brad Marshal. Here, let me get that for you," he reached for my umbrella (which was leaning again due to my distracted state of delirious joy) and raised it above the both of us as we walked and talked.

He was the transfer student. The disappearing hunk from the mall was *the transfer student!* My morning finally turned around.

I touched his strong, sturdy arm as we approached the building and thanked him for his assistance with the books.

"You're welcome," he held the door, "it was breaking my heart to see you struggle with them."

Wow!

It turned out we were in many of the same classes throughout the day and we really clicked. And best of all, he liked me back! I could tell. It was definitely fate; I couldn't wait to tell Rhonda!

"Are you humming *here comes the bride?*" asked Bridget incredulously as I tidied my side of the room.

"Er...no." At least, I didn't realize I was. But it was possible since Brad was on my mind.

Now, I wasn't being obsessive or anything. Just behaving the way any girl would when she finds someone she really connects with. Like Ariel after she rescues prince Eric and sings to him on the shore. You can't help but feel giddy!

The past few days were so exciting. I hoped to catch glimpses of Brad in every room I entered and I think he looked for me too. The only strange thing is that we didn't actually talk much after the first day. Most of our interactions took place in the library as we sat side by side at the computers chatting online. Brad used the prehistoric computer, which was finally running, and I used the Dell.

We had a great time on the computers but the lack of verbal communication was a little embarrassing. One time I giggled at something Brad wrote when Tara came into the library, took one look at us and said, "are you guys *typing* to each other? Like, why don't you just *talk*? You know?"

She had a point.

We left the library and conversed in the lounge. After that, actually talking to one another became a habit. I was noticing, however, that Amelia always seemed to be around Brad too.

Now, I'm normally not a jealous person. It was ok for him to be friends with other women. Only, Amelia was grating on my nerves with the way she batted her eyes at him and laughed at anything he said with her monstrous mouth wide open. And the constant *flicking* of her long hair made me want to gag and wish the floor would open up and suck her in. Amelia was clearly flirting with him even though she already had an off campus boyfriend who regularly came to visit her. Ugh.

"So…" I stopped tidying to ask Bridget, "what's the scoop on Brad and Amelia?"

Bridget was a bubbly, outgoing person and people tended to tell her things.

"As a disinterested third party," I added at the look she gave me.

"They used to date but Amelia broke it off. They're friends now, but he's supposedly still in love with her."

I picked up a comb and idly twirled it in my hands. "Did you hear this from him?" I paused. "Or her?"

"Tara."

Suddenly I was back on the wall ledge with my textbook as Amelia and Tara passed. Snippets of their conversation came back to me.

He followed you here? Amazing!

I expected this. It was just a matter of time.

"Do *you* think he likes her that way?"

"Don't know," Bridget shrugged. "Maybe."

I thought of the way Brad smiled at me...and the way Amelia came onto him with her batting eyes and heinous giggle. Her predatory gaze. No. He didn't like her, but Amelia still had the hots for him. Or she at least wanted his attention even though she was in a relationship. Well, she could just back off and remove her talons. I wasn't sure how I could make that happen, but for a guy like Brad I was willing to try.

"Oh my goodness! Reanne, are you *really* into Brad?" Tara bounded up to me during a break between classes and Darren, hovering nearby, swiveled around with interest.

"*What?*" I gaped at her in surprise. "Where did you hear that?"

But I already knew the answer. Bridget and I only had our little discussion the previous evening. She obviously blabbed. And so did Tara because I didn't like the cutthroat glower I got from Amelia as she stood near the drinking fountain. She took a sip then glared. Another sip. Glare. I was almost afraid to turn my head in case she actually flung a dagger at me.

"Excuse me Tara. I have to...head to the ladies' room."

Bridget and I needed to have a chat, pronto. She broke the roommate code of conduct. I didn't want everyone to know and it wasn't her place to say!

"Hey there." Brad intercepted me and smiled warmly. "How are you?"

"I'm great, just looking for someone. Have you seen Bridget, by chance?"

His smile deepened. "Just a minute ago, near the front door."

I couldn't believe it. She told him too. *I'm going to kill her!*

Except...Brad seemed pleased with the news and was more chatty than usual. In the days that followed, he sought me out more often and I came to see that Bridget did me a favor.

Brad was witty and charming and we had *so* much in common. Like, he loved to sing and had this deep sexy voice. So did I! Not the deep sexy voice of course – that would be weird. But I've always been an excellent singer in the shower, despite what that obnoxious girl said recently while I was in there. I bet it was Amelia, who definitely couldn't sing but thought she was so great.

He also had a strong family connection, which has always been very important to me. Everyone knows that when you marry a person, you marry the family too. I laughed until my stomach hurt as Brad relayed countless stories from his childhood. Especially when he described the mischief he got into with his little sister and the time he dressed her up in hockey gear and shot pucks at her.

We're so alike! I silently cheered.

Haven't I done similar with *my* younger brother? I've never had much of an interest in hockey, but if I did – I'm sure I would have done the same!

And best of all, Brad was an artist. He could draw *anything*. I particularly loved the sketch he did of me. I taped it to the wall right above my bed.

The breeze ruffled our hair and made the leaves waltz around as Brad and I sat at a picnic table by the river. He had his pencils with him and a notebook, and I guess I was illuminated by the sunlight or something because Brad wanted to sketch me.

"Don't move," he had said as his hand set to work. I was flattered he wanted to commit my image to paper and create something he could keep forever. How romantic!

I stayed perfectly still and smiled while he concentrated. I was delighted and amazed as my image appeared on the page. It looked exactly like me. He even drew the perfect flat leaf I held, on the right-hand corner of the sheet.

"There!" he exclaimed and raised it up for me to see. I waited for him to say he would cherish it forever, and reverently place it into a folder. Instead, he handed it over and said, "here you go."

"Oh," I tilted my head. "Thanks."

I guess it was something *I* could cherish forever (and I honestly will because it's really great and represents a beautiful moment).

I was on a cloud as I headed to my room with the sketch.

"I'm sorry!" Anna gushed the second I walked in. "I didn't mean to."

"Didn't meant to what?"

Anna and I had a lot of little tiffs but I was surprised to find her apologizing for any of them. That's just the way it was in our room.

"I…told Amelia you're a snob and she's telling Brad."

"Anna!"

She flinched. "I didn't mean to! I had a bad day and Amelia asked what you were like so she could warn him…and…it…slipped out. I don't think you're a snob," she added, "just a tad annoying."

"Yeah, well. Same to you."

"I thought you should know. And I *am* sorry. Look," she pointed at her end table and grinned at me timidly, "I bought a fan."

I suddenly realized the window was closed and this was her peace offering.

"Can we start over?" she asked. "I'd really like that. And I'll tell Amelia I didn't mean what I said."

I sighed. "Fine."

Her slip up really didn't matter. Amelia probably would have said something to Brad regardless, and I wanted to believe he was the kind of guy who wouldn't listen to ridiculous gossip.

I hugged my sweater tightly to me to fend off the chilly air coming through the vents. There was a swirly Claude Monet painting just in front of me, and Amelia was beside me in an extremely snug top and equally revealing pants.

I had the misfortune of being paired with her at the museum. It was worse than a death sentence. Every time we encountered a painting of a beautiful woman, Amelia found some way to relate to it.

"Oh look!" She crooned. "Her hair is *exactly* like mine. We look so alike she could be my ancestor!"

And when she wasn't doing that, she talked incessantly about how much her boyfriend, James, loved her and how much Brad cared for her as well. The heartless cow didn't love either of them back or she wouldn't have been stringing them both along. Not that she had Brad on a string. She just thought so.

"Look!" Amelia touched a marble statue. "This is almost as smooth as my skin. Reanne – do you moisturize daily? I do. Your skin could really use it."

I glanced around, wondering if there was anything I could bonk her over the head with. I wouldn't really – I'm not sadistic. The thought just cheered me.

This antique plate might do.

As we moved along, a figure trailed behind us. One that had been following us for quite some time come to think of it. Amelia stopped and commented on another piece, "I have a vintage dress similar to this!"

Kill me now.

I walked away. It was that or shove her face into the painting. And I didn't want to pay for the damage.

"Excuse me," the mysterious figure, which I could now identify as a pockmarked male in his twenties, darted forward. "I couldn't help but compare your exquisite beauty to this marble sculpture. You're flawless."

I rolled my eyes. *Great. A male Amelia.*

"I'm not interested," I said politely and stepped around him.

"Did it hurt?"

"Did what hurt?"

"When you fell from heaven." He smoothed his hair and straightened his black coat. Did the guy think he was in *The Matrix*? "Can I get your email, baby?"

"No. I don't *know* you."

"You can get to know me."

Touché. But I didn't want to. "No."

"Fine, your loss." He strutted over to Amelia and I wondered when the dark shades would come out. They were the only things missing. I watched, fascinated, as he moonwalked in front of Amelia and said, "what's up hot stuff?"

Oh man. I was going to laugh.

I thought Amelia would too but she soaked it up like a sponge and scribbled something on a piece of paper and handed it to him.

Time to walk away again.

"I gave him my email," Amelia gloated as she caught up to me near the Egyptian artifacts. "I think he likes me."

"You think everyone likes you," I muttered while trying to get away from her. She trotted beside me and flicked her pale hair over one scrawny shoulder. Then the other. Flick.

"What do *you* think?"

I think you shouldn't give your email to random strangers, and stay faithful to your boyfriend.

I shrugged.

"I'll have to tell James and Brad about this – they're very protective of me."

Flick, flick.

I hoped she *would* tell them about it so they could see what she was really like.

Chapter Twelve

Rumor Has It

So – Brad was gay. He had to be. It was the only logical explanation as to why he hadn't asked me out yet. Weeks had gone by (it was nearly Christmas) and still, nothing. Sometimes it seemed like we were getting closer…but he never made an actual move. And other times it felt as though he pulled back.

All right, I didn't think he was gay. It was Rhonda's suggestion, and that was her way of being optimistic. I guess it was better than entertaining my secret fear that he did in fact have feelings for that nitwit Amelia. And if Brad didn't have feelings for her, where exactly did that leave me? In the friend zone? It wasn't somewhere I wanted to be.

Friday night in the lounge, I worked on a sketch while Bridget and Anna played table tennis. A foosball match was also underway when Brad walked in. My heart fluttered. He looked smoking hot in dark denim jeans and a blue polo sweater, but I pretended not to see him.

"Hey you," he joined me on the sofa and peered at the drawing on my lap. "Nice work."

"Hey," I replied indifferently and continued drawing.

Rhonda read in a magazine that guys like the chase and the best way to attract one is to show less interest in him. I didn't think I was acting overly interested to begin with but it wouldn't hurt to tone it down a bit and see if I got different results.

"Christmas banquet is around the corner," Brad began as the foosball game came to an end, "and I have a few ideas for the skit."

The college held a Christmas banquet annually and it was tradition for a group of students to put on a mini performance (usually a parody of the professors). Brad was heading up the first year students.

"I'd like your input. If you don't mind?"

Would I mind? Spending countless hours planning and preparing alone with Brad? Would I MIND?

"Of course I will!" I cried joyously. "I mean…sure. Why not?"

"Great!"

Bridget and Anna dropped their paddles and bickered about who won as they left the lounge. Brad got up and grabbed one. "Feel like playing?"

"Feel like losing?" I countered with a cheeky grin. "I bet I'll win."

Brad just smiled and rolled up his sleeves. The golden hair that lined his strong, rugged forearms was an instant distraction as I prepared to serve. He was *totally* cheating.

Well…it didn't matter. I would still win. I'm *that* good.

I angled my wrist ever so slightly and launched the ball into the air and slapped it hard. I was proud of this killer serve. It worked every time. The ball hurtled through the air, spinning dizzily before hitting the left corner of the table and then veering sharply to the right. Brad hit it effortlessly and it came sailing back.

Hmm.

I lunged and barely hit the ball. Two seconds later it bounced back on my side.

I was getting hot. He returned everything, easily. I suspected he also held back in an attempt to keep it evenly matched. On the off chance I'd win, I gave it my all and really threw myself into the game. Literally.

The next shot came at me so fast that I flew toward it, twisted my ankle, and the paddle crashed into the table as I tripped.

"Are you all right?" Brad's concerned voice was beside me.

"I'm fine," I mumbled, mortified. I tried to stand. "Oww." Maybe I wouldn't get up just yet.

Brad touched my ankle with tenderness and I forgot that it throbbed. He wrapped his arm around my waist, helping me to the couch and a lock of his hair fell out of place. I reached up automatically to smooth it back.

We froze.

His arm tightened around my waist and something in his look caused a tingling sensation in my toes. He leaned in.

It worked! I couldn't believe it. Acting disinterested *worked!*

I closed my eyes, savoring the moment.

THUMP.

Abruptly, I found myself dumped on the cold couch alone, and I frowned at Brad's retreating form.

"You might want to have that checked," Brad nodded at my ankle. And with that he took off down the hall like a criminal running from the cops.

"What's got your goat?" said Bridget as I slammed our bedroom door and hobbled to my bed.

"Oh nothing," I muttered glumly. "Only Brad giving mixed signals all the time. The usual."

Bridget put down the book she was reading and leaned forward. "What did he do?"

"It's what he *didn't* do," I sighed and twisted my hands. "I'm not sure what's going on. I thought he liked me but if that's true, shouldn't he have acted on it by now? And if he isn't interested then why flirt and carry my books? Sometimes he backs off all together. I don't get it."

"Ah." Bridget's brows shot up. "I think he likes you but can't do anything about it because of the *dating strike*."

"The *what?*"

"The dating strike."

I stared at her as though she sprouted horns and began speaking Italian.

"What, I didn't tell you?" said Bridget densely.

"Noooo. You didn't. Why isn't he dating?"

"Who knows," she mused. "I only heard he doesn't want to get involved with anyone for a while."

I threw my hands up in exasperation. "Well…he could have mentioned that!"

"It's not something you would go around telling everyone," she said kindly. "It's personal."

"True, but I'm not *everyone*. So if he's on a dating strike then what's the deal with Amelia? Why does he hang out with her?"

"They're friends. He probably doesn't mind being around her because she's safe and there's no danger of them dating again, whereas *you* he actually likes, so he pulls away when he finds himself getting too close to you."

I glanced at Bridget fondly. It was a good explanation…but how did she know?

"What makes you think that?"

"By the way he looks at you. Brad's definitely interested but didn't tell you about the dating break because he doesn't want to scare you away. I bet he's afraid you won't wait for him and will date someone else!"

"Maybe," I laughed. "But there's no one around here to date!" I already tested the water with Darren and that went badly. I knew Alex considered himself an option (made up girlfriend aside – I hadn't seen her yet) but the only way he would ever be an option is if I had to choose between dating him and taking Cyanide. And I'd choose the poison. "So how long is this dating break?"

"Why not ask him?" she said simply.

"I think I will." I left the room, my shoulders set with determination.

I pushed down the mild irritation I felt when I found another girl on the phone. It was always occupied. If Brad was going to be on this dating break for *years*, I needed to know that *now*.

I tapped the girl lightly on the shoulder – "I need the phone after you," I whispered then backed away, "I'll be right over here."

I sat at the table closest to the stairwell, not bothering to care that she might not appreciate my proximity. I already learned my lesson the hard way. The last time I gave someone space on the phone, another person immediately swooped in and stole it before I could get there. It was Alex, actually. You would think I'd have been quicker than him, but he saw me heading toward it and went barreling past me.

I waited a good twenty minutes while this girl chatted about nail polish and fishnet stockings with whoever was on the other end of the phone. I was beginning to wonder if she forgot I was there when I heard the satisfying clang of the receiver returning to the base. "All yours!" She chirped and disappeared up the stairs.

Finally! I sat by the phone.

Riiinnnnggg.

Nooo!

I picked up the receiver quickly so that no one would come running to answer it.

"Hello?" came a disembodied voice. "Hello, is Amelia around?"

Click.

I hung up. It might have been her boyfriend. Or maybe that sinister museum creep. But who really cares? I waited long enough – he could call back later.

I dialed the men's dorm and inadvertently tugged at the cord. I asked for Brad and my stomach lurched nervously when he came on the line.

"Hey Brad – it's Reanne."

"Hi!" He sounded surprised. "How's the ankle?"

"Better." I was silent as I pondered how to segue the conversation into the dating strike. My palms were clammy. I should have practiced.

"I'm glad you phoned," Brad cut into my thoughts. "I was just going over who I thought would be suited for different roles in the skit...how would you feel about imitating Krista? I'm covering Calvin."

Yeeeess! I nearly squealed.

Calvin and Krista taught courses at our college and they were married. Brad asked me to play the role of his wife. It had to mean something!

"Sounds good," I replied with feigned nonchalance. "Krista always gives anecdotes about their relationship during her lectures so we have a lot of material to work with."

"So does he. The skit could start with Calvin and Krista at a restaurant, we'll reenact their first date and how it went wrong. It will be entertaining…"

Date.

I honed in on the word. My mind buzzed and my heart beat faster. This was it. The segue. It was such a perfect lead in it almost felt as if he invited me to ask him. I stood. I paced.

Come on…just do it…

" – Speaking of dates," I interjected, "what's this I hear about a dating break?" My tone was light and uninterested, but I anxiously twisted the edge of my shirt into a knot.

There was silence, apart from his breathing.

"You heard." he said finally.

I clutched the phone and waited.

"I took a break from dating to pour myself into school this year and gain some perspective on what's most important in life. It's just something I need to do right now."

"That's good…" I managed and trailed off awkwardly.

It was discomfiting with neither of us speaking and I didn't know how to ask him what I really wanted to know. *When will you date? When???*

"I might end it this summer," he eventually supplied.

I sank onto the chair in relief, my legs like rubber. Bridget was right! Brad was interested. He wanted to go out with me the summer, or he wouldn't have said anything! And I respected his reasons for not dating right now. I mean, how many guys would put their education first like that? We should all prioritize and make it a motto! How admirable!

I should have known playing Krista in the Christmas banquet wasn't going to be as simple as Brad appointing it to someone (although I couldn't see why everyone didn't just agree with him – I was obviously best suited for it).

I lined up with the others on the third floor of the girl's dormitory waiting to audition. This was a part of the building I rarely visited. The third floor contained a small music room, a vacant office where the auditions were held, and a door leading to a hall with more residence rooms.

All around me, everyone practiced his or her lines for the varying roles, including Amelia in a tight print dress for the part of Krista. She repeatedly glanced at the card in her hand and my eyes raked over her. I had the lines memorized. She was going down.

She would be Brad's – I mean Calvin's wife over my dead body. But I didn't have anything to worry about because she was really awful as she rehearsed. I'm not saying this just because she was after Brad and got on my nerves– she wasn't very convincing as Krista. How difficult *is it* to dramatize two lines? It's not like we were auditioning for *Joseph and the Amazing Technicolor Dreamcoat* (although I was about to perform as if we were).

Amelia disappeared into the room and came out a few minutes later looking pleased. "I nailed it!" She high-fived Tara.

I went into the room next and smiled at Brad who nodded back in encouragement. He suggested this role; so I knew I didn't have to win him over…I just had to convince the others. A girl named Danika and…no! Alex! What bad luck. He adjusted his glasses and rubbed his hands together like a Praying Mantis. I could already see it on his face; he wasn't going to pick me.

"You may begin," came his geeky voice.

He will *pick me. I'll show him!*

I sat on the cold metal chair in the middle of the room and then immediately shot up from it with a gasp.

"How could you?" I wailed with actual tears in my eyes. "This date is over!" I rushed toward the door with a sob and cast a tormented glance at the judges. Three astounded faces stared back at me.

"Could you do that again?" asked Danika, clearly impressed.

"Sure." I repeated it, and the second time was better than the first!

There was a smattering of applause and a wink from Brad. They offered the part on the spot.

Snow dusted the ground and flakes floated in the sky like bubbles as I headed to the first rehearsal. The earth became a blanket of shimmering white, crunching beneath my feet. The practices took place on Saturdays in the same building where our classes were held. I was almost there.

I crested the hill and caught sight of a tall, lean figure a few yards ahead.

"Brad!" I called, but he didn't turn. "Hey Brad!"

I guess he couldn't hear through the curtain of snow. Sound travels slower in winter (this is one of the few things I actually remembered from high school science).

I went a little faster, then a bit more until I broke into a run. He wasn't that far ahead. I could catch up.

I rapidly sucked in breaths of frigid air as I accelerated, but Brad's long strides kept him firmly in the distance. My legs hurt and so did my lungs and I stopped. Running through thickening snow was rather pointless.

I'm not even a runner in better circumstances. Oh, I certainly had teachers who put forth their best efforts to instill a love for running in their pupils (i.e. Ms. Bartly – grade 10 – who made us jog around the school at the start of each gym class. I tried it twice, felt like I was dying, and hid out in the bathroom until the colder months when we were no longer doing this).

He's really not far, I thought as I trudged behind him. I found myself speeding up again. I hate running but I could do it for a good cause. A few moments alone, conversing with a sweet, intelligent guy was a good cause.

"Run like Rhonda!" I chanted as I took off. *She* wouldn't let a few inches of snow stop her.

"I can't do this," I puffed a moment later, clutching my side. I made one last attempt to get his attention. "Hey Brad!"

Miraculously, he turned. Success! See what happens with a little effort?

Brad lifted his hand in a wave just as my Nine West boot sunk into the snow and hit a patch of ice.

Down I went amid an explosion of white. Brad jogged over. My face was hot and I laughed in embarrassment. "I'm such a klutz."

He grinned. "Yes, but an attractive one. Anything hurt?"

Only my pride.

And my butt.

I shook my head and he offered his arm the rest of the way to avoid another disaster. I needed boots with better traction. The pulsing throb in my rear would be a reminder throughout the rehearsal.

The classroom had been transformed into a mock restaurant. A desk was draped with a checkered tablecloth, pictures of freshly baked buns were taped to the walls, and wicker baskets filled with fruit were strategically placed. Someone even took the time to do a chalk drawing like you might see at *East Side Mario's*.

"This is really well done!" I commented as Brad and I sat with our fake menus.

"Alex did it," said Brad.

"Well…it looks great," I admitted. Although it came as no surprise, this was the type of thing Alex used to do at camp.

The dialogue we rehearsed was cute and funny. With the candles and background music, it almost felt as if we were on a real date. It was dreamy! Hey, if I couldn't go on a proper date with him, I was going to enjoy the arbitrary one.

We continued role playing and flirting with one another while waiting for the waitress to arrive. And then she came. God only knows how Amelia managed to secure a role in the skit at all, but there she was – heading toward us with a sneer on her face and a pad and pen in hand.

"Can I take your order?" She flung her hair over her shoulder and nearly slapped me in the face with it.

Well – *she* wasn't about to receive a fake tip. I envisioned a better skit than the one we were performing. One where the server gets fired. And possibly thrown through a window.

Anyway. Her part was so minor I could almost pretend she wasn't there.

Chapter Thirteen

The Mall

I had a free day the following week and decided to go to the mall. This may come as a shock…but I hadn't been there yet. I had no idea what it was like. I was desperate to check it out, of course, but it just seemed like there was never a good time to go. And when there was, something always came up. Like projects, arguments with Anna concerning when the lights should go out at night (she thought 2:00 a.m. was acceptable, and then I'd be too tired to go), or Brad knocking on my door for a round of table tennis. How could I refuse?

"Where are you off to?" asked Bridget as I bundled up.

"The mall!" I said happily. "Getting new boots – I wiped out last week." I pulled a face at the memory and then brightened at the thought of some company. "Wanna come?"

"I'd love to…but I'm having a lazy day." Bridget was sprawled on her bed in her Winnie the Pooh pj's (don't ask) with little mountains of books all around her.

"Are you suuurre?" I wheedled. I would have enjoyed having Bridget along to talk to, but it also occurred to me that I could make a few discreet suggestions for her wardrobe. The other day she wore a stretchy purple dress with bright orange leggings. I shuddered. The leggings only came to mid-calf. In *November.* "You know you want to. I'll buy you coffee," I persuaded.

"No, you go ahead and have fun." She burrowed further into her pile of books. "Maybe some other time."

"Ok." I buttoned my coat and plodded out to the bus stop.

Gosh it was freezing. I willed the bus to arrive as I hopped in place like a frog. I caught a reflected glimpse of myself on the shelter but I didn't care what I looked like. My fingers and toes already felt a little numb. Thankfully I didn't have to wait long.

The squeal of rusty breaks approached and a hiss of pollution struck the air. The bus arrived! I was on my way to the mall!

I was only after a pair of boots but visions of shops and designer labels swam before my eyes. It's always an adventure going to a new mall – discovering new stores, exploring the different levels. It would be a few hours well spent. And just maybe I'd come back with something unexpected. A bargain…something I found on sale…you never know. I'm good like that.

I should start a list of things I need in case there are deals.

I rummaged through my purse and jotted items down on a little notepad. For a while, this distracted me from the many stops made and the blasts of icy air that hit me each time the doors opened. Eventually I glanced at my Phillip Stein watch and sighed. I was right; the bus was either really slow or it was taking a really long route.

I gazed at the watch dad insisted I wear and fiddled with the leather strap. You know, I didn't like this watch at first. I wasn't in the habit of wearing a watch and I never heard of the Phillip Stein variety (until I searched online and found out celebrities wore them), but dad insisted everyone in the family wear one for the amazing health benefits. It supposedly uses natural frequency technology to relax the body and improve concentration.

Dad, always the hypochondriac, first discovered it during his Google search on sleep apnea because he couldn't drift off one night. He swore sleep apnea was the culprit and the watch was the solution. The rest of us rolled our eyes at him.

I know this sounds a little callous and I'll admit we didn't have much sympathy, which turned out to be a shame in this situation. Because dad discovered he *did* have sleep apnea after he admitted himself into a sleep clinic to find out for certain. He was even given a CPAP machine, though someone really should have told him he didn't need to have it running throughout the *day*. He looked ridiculous sitting at the computer with the breathing apparatus strapped to his face, Googling other diseases he might have had.

Anyway. How were we to know? It's difficult to believe someone when they think they have *everything* wrong with them.

Like the time dad was sawing wood in the garage. His piercing cries of "help, I chopped off my finger!" caused everyone to freak and come running, and it turned out he only slightly nicked the tip. There was barely any blood, but dad looked like he was about to pass out.

Or the time dad tried the powdered candy Jaden and I were eating. He took my thin tube, tilted his head back and poured it into his mouth and choked a little. In a state of sheer terror – dad ran around in circles like a lunatic with his hands to his throat yelling, "Karen, I can't breathe, I can't breathe!"

First of all – dad *could* breathe otherwise he wouldn't have been screaming, and secondly – mom couldn't help him until he stopped running. So we had to wait it out and eventually it cleared. So you see what I mean.

I stopped adjusting my watch as the bus pulled up to the mall. The single level mall. My heart sank. It wasn't going to be much of a shopping trip because just like everything else about the town and my college – the mall was miniscule. I frequented convenience stores back home that were larger than this. But you never know…

It might surprise me.

I wandered down one aisle of the mall, passed the food court, and then came up the other aisle.

Five minutes.

That's all it took for me to tour the entire mall, and all the stores were…well…crap. I wanted to march outside with a sign to protest the mall's very existence so others wouldn't waste their time. Not that there were many people about.

I headed back to the bus stop in total disappointment and idly stared at a map and store directory as I waited. I mean, who ever heard of *Gumby's Clothiers? Or Renata's Comfort Shoes? Or…*

Oh my goodness! Le Chateau!

I stood straighter and rubbed my eyes in case I was hallucinating. It was still there: Le Chateau. Plain as day. It was hidden in some obscure corridor next to a department store for the geriatric, but it was there. It was really, really there!

A warm happy feeling overcame me as I entered the store.

I'm home.

The contemporary music swelled and I inhaled the scent of fresh fabric. Leather, denim, silk – Le Chateau was the melting pot of stores!

My head swiveled left and right, then my eyes flew to the display at the center of the room. Immediately, I fell in love. A huge metal rack filled with shoes loomed before me. There were rows and rows of beautiful footwear. I raced over and tried them on, starting with a pair covered in simulated diamond studs followed by sparkly, lacy, and strappy stilettos. All my Christmases came at once.

Speaking of which, I needed a pair for banquet and there were at least five I liked. *Five!* How on earth would I decide?

"Those are gorgeous; I have a pair at home." The sales lady lustily eyed the glittering red heels on my feet with diamante flowers at the sides. "We also had them in black but we're out of stock. Gina bought them all – didn't you Gina?" She joked with the girl at the cash.

I made a snap decision. "I'll take them!"

I wasn't about to let those babies get away, even in a ghost mall.

Then I tried gown after gown. What good are shoes if you don't have a dress to go with them? I liked everything; they all had unique qualities. The emerald gown complimented my eyes and made them pop, the chocolate gown was elegant and rich, and the black one was like an Audrey Hepburn classic. I wanted them all. But the shoes would only go with the black dress.

The sales clerk smiled dazzlingly. This was clearly her first commission in weeks, possibly months. She finished scanning. "Your total is $425.00. Cash, credit, or debit?"

My jaw went slack. I didn't have $425.00. I didn't *have* it. Dread piled in the pit of my stomach as I stared at her. *What am I going to do?* I couldn't walk away without them. In slight panic, I asked her if she could hold the items.

"Only until the end of the day," she said in tones of suspicion.

"Thanks!"

I rushed out to the entrance of the mall and dashed to the payphones. Mom had been asking what I wanted for Christmas and I was pretty sure she hadn't bought anything yet. At least, I hoped she hadn't.

I feverishly searched through my purse for a quarter…

"Oh happy daaayyy," I sang as I skipped along the deserted hallway with my carrier bag swaying from side to side.

Don't you just *love* online banking? With a few short clicks of a mouse, mom instantly transferred the $425.00 into my account. I'm glad they finally got with the times. I also remembered to grab myself a pair of boots when I went back in, so I was all set.

It's so amazing that mom had been home. I was worried she'd be out doing errands with dad. He often drags her out to do boring stuff. The only disadvantage to the phone call was listening to dad in the background going "make sure she knows this is her only gift! I mean it! She opens nothing at Christmas!" and then roaring loudly at his own joke. Or maybe he was serious; sometimes it's hard to tell with dad.

I came out near the department store and the aroma of hot, salty fries wafted through the air.

Wow. That smells wonderful. I followed the scent to the golden arches in the food court and bought a large carton of fries. The salty steam billowed up into my nose and I bit into a piping hot fry. *Mmm. Heaven.* Such a rewarding day.

The fries were gone in about five seconds flat and my mouth was incredibly dry. I licked the remaining salt from my lips and swallowed. *I need a drink.* I sought out a water fountain, which was next to *The Body Shop* where soap and bath salts are sold.

Laughter, grating and familiar sounded as I wiped the dripping water from my chin. It came from *The Body Shop*, so I peeked around the doorway and caught sight of blond swishy hair.

I knew it. Amelia.

Breathing deeply, I darted past the store entrance, looking in as I flew by.

I stopped short.

What's he *doing here?*

Suspicion crept over me like a spider.

Why is Brad with her?

I crouched behind a poster displayed in the window and watched their secret rendezvous from the side. I wanted to give Brad the benefit of the doubt but it wasn't possible. An encounter at this location was too strange to be coincidence. And I was right because Amelia's hand rested on Brad's bicep as she belted out another round of obnoxious laughter. Tentacles of jealousy wrapped around me. And not just jealousy, hurt. He lied to me. He wasn't on a dating break.

They looked like a couple, all cozy in the store. They probably planned this trip and came to the mall together. It was painfully obvious. I shuffled over and leaned against the wall, my chest tight.

I thought Brad was better than this. I thought he was a genuinely good guy but he was really no better than Darren. I've been so *blind*. At least Darren hit on other women openly. Brad played me.

My eyes stung and I rubbed them. I thought Brad liked me. I thought…a lot of things…and now I just felt like an idiot.

The sight of my new dress hanging from the closet door did nothing to cheer me when I returned to the dorm.

"Stop moping already!" snapped Anna as she pushed the window open and fanned herself with her hand. "It's depressing."

I never did return the lever, but Anna figured out how to open the window without it. And the portable fan she was *supposed* to use was caked in dust. I wasn't in the mood for this.

"Anna – you'd better close that," I said, my voice scarily calm.

"Or what?" she challenged with a glint in her eye.

I glared at her with clenched fists. If I had to take her down – I would. She looked ready for a fight.

We stared at one another, neither of us blinking. I felt increasingly hostile with every chill that hit me, and took a menacing step forward. My eyes narrowed into furious slits.

Uncertainty flashed across Anna's face, and she suddenly scrambled back to pull the window shut.

"Fine," she mumbled before fleeing the room.

I collapsed onto my bed, relieved to be alone with my thoughts. All the dreams I had for banquet were crushed. I knew Brad wouldn't ask me to be his date…but I still imagined us having a good time together in an unofficial way, with him admiring my dress, and me pretending not to notice. Lots of jokes and flirting. It was going to be *fun*. This vision of us swirled down the drain as an image of Amelia flinging her hair and flirting with him appeared in my place, while he gazed at her affectionately.

I groaned loudly and covered my face. "Why can't she just *back off*! You have a boyfriend!" I yelled into my pillow. "YOU HAVE A BOYFRIEND!!"

I tossed the pillow aside, punched it, and bolted up. I needed to email Rhonda about this and get it off my chest. Right now.

Adrenalin pumped through my fingers as I jabbed at each key. It was cathartic. *Bam, bam.* I imagined each letter to be Amelia's conceited face as I struck it. *Bam, bam, bam.* Some of them were Brad. BAM.

A key became stuck and the one letter filled the screen. It just kept going.

I prodded and wiggled, hoping it would become unstuck, but it was firmly lodged. Fingers of fear touched me at the thought of losing this email. I wrote so much, explaining everything to Rhonda – I wouldn't remember it all if I had to write it again.

The letter K continued on my screen and another scary thought crowded in. What if I broke the keyboard?

Please, don't be broken. I wiggled it some more and it finally popped. Whew.

I continued typing, lightly this time, and glanced behind me as Brad came into the library wearing his black leather jacket. I blotted him from my mind, turning resolutely toward the screen. I wasn't speaking to him. There was nothing to say.

I *saw* them.

The only sounds in the library were the clicking of keys like that of a galloping horse as I finished writing, and the thud of Brad's leather coat landing on the table. The coat he often draped around my shoulders when I've been cold in class. Fresh hurt poured over me. Of *course* I assumed he was interested.

He's a good actor.

"Burning a hole in the keyboard?" He jibed.

I ignored him.

"That's a long email," he chuckled, "are you writing a *novel*?"

I left the library without a word. My pulse drummed in my ears as I hopped down the stairs. I would *not* speak to him even though I heard his footsteps pounding behind me.

I don't care I don't care. He can talk all he wants, I'm not listening.

I grabbed the handrail and jumped the last two steps. "Argghh," came my garbled cry as I tripped. A steel banded arm snapped around my waist and jerked me back. I collided with Brad's firm chest, and squirmed to get away. He didn't let go.

"Are you ok?" The concern in his voice rattled me and I felt sadness creeping in. I stiffened. *Not listening.*

"Reanne?" He stepped back, waiting for me to look at him. "Hey I have something for you."

Reluctantly, I followed him back to the library. I wasn't about to give an explanation as to why I was annoyed...but I hoped maybe I'd get one from him. Or at least a confession.

He pulled a small *The Body Shop* bag from his coat pocket when we went into the library and handed it to me with a self-conscious smile. I was tentative as I opened the bag, and then nearly dropped it in surprise.

"It's...vanilla lotion!"

"This is to thank you for your participation and the ideas you added to the skit."

"Oh."

"And because...you were on my mind." His look was sincere, and my face flushed. There wasn't a trace of guile in his expression...and...oh gosh. Did I get it all wrong?

He went there for me and I assumed the worst. I had to stop jumping to conclusions. Especially after Bridget mentioned that Amelia *worked* at *The Body Shop*. It wasn't a rendezvous at all.

I had to set the record straight with Rhonda. She wrote a lengthy, galvanized email about *that snake* and how she would get back at him. She was in the process of writing a song titled *Bad Brad* that she intended to take directly to a recording artist. She thought her family connection with Alanis Morisette would come in handy. I had to stop her.

When that was accomplished, I received another email from her admonishing me to get my facts straight next time, *before* she printed and revised his Facebook profile picture. Apparently it had been a lot of work.

> And by the way, she wrote, it looks like Jaden and Lindsay are officially dating!

Chapter Fourteen

Banquet

"Bridget! It's up!"

Bridget raced over to look at the seating chart for Christmas banquet, which was posted on the bulletin board in the lounge.

"We want table eight," she said, jotting down our names. "I'll have the best view of you and Brad in the skit." She winked at me. "Now see ya later babe, gotta study!"

"What's this?" Brad arrived after Bridget left. "Ah – the chart. Where are you sitting?"

I pointed to table eight and an odd look passed over his face. He added his name next to mine and smiled. "Our table can be the singles table."

Was he being funny? Was I supposed to laugh? It absolutely *wasn't* 'the singles table.' And what if I got a date, huh? Did he think no one else would ask me?

"What colors are you wearing?" He added casually.

"Black and red. You?"

"Haven't thought about it. I'll grab whatever's handy on the night."

It turned out black and red were the colors Brad had on hand for Christmas banquet, and he and I were the only two at our table who weren't officially a pair. Bridget snagged a date, and the others were established couples in senior classes.

It was so *not* a singles table, and he deliberately matched me. Unless he only did it for the skit. No. That wasn't necessary. You wouldn't try to match on a first date.

Brad was gorgeous and debonair sitting next to me. He looked so good he could have walked from the set of a photo shoot. And I was fairly pleased with my appearance. The dress and shoes were fabulous and so was the hair.

And there was Anna, two tables over, glumly picking at the potatoes on her plate. As annoying as she was, I felt a stab of sympathy for her. Her sparkly silver hat drooped off to one side and a splotch of gravy stained the front of her dress. She looked like she could use some company…maybe I'd go start a friendly chat in just a bit.

My attention drifted around the room as I took in all the little touches that made the hall so beautiful. It wasn't a very large space but each table was adorned with a lacy cloth dusted with sequins. Black material draped overhead, and entwined fairly lights gave the illusion of stars against an inky sky.

I swayed to the Christmas music coming through the speakers, which provided the background to clips of conversation and the clattering of silverware against dinner plates. The atmosphere was romantic. Especially with the photo booth in the corner where couples lined to have their picture taken under a trellis of sweet smelling flowers.

Bridget and her man were second in line; Amelia and James were posing and kissing at the front.

When Bridget returned to the table, she picked up her digital camera. "Smile," she said to Brad and I before the flash went.

I scraped my chair back and stood when the meal was over. Brad looked at me quizzically.

"Time for the skit," I said with mock severity. "Or did you forget?"

"I remember. Come on wifey." He proffered his arm and we made our way to the staging area. By staging area, I mean a corner of the room that had been sectioned off by a blanket hanging from the ceiling.

Before we knew it, we were in character.

"Here you are," said Brad, pulling out a chair.

"Why thank you Calvin. This place is lovely. It almost makes up for the journey here on your motorcycle."

Brad coughed and pulled at his collar. "Again, I'm truly sorry about that Krista."

A ripple of laughter went around the room. We sounded exactly like them! The biggest roar came when I thought out loud about the three things I always vowed to avoid in a man…and how I made the exception for Calvin. I was about to deliver another punch line when Amelia sashayed out from behind the blanket to take our order. In a black mini skirt and apron. Her low cut top revealed more than I cared to see, and she leaned over the table, facing Brad.

I felt instantly annoyed. The atmosphere was charged with tension. It snapped like static. Trust Amelia to turn a family friendly skit into something R-rated. Trust her to mess it up also, because she didn't turn to address me like she was supposed to.

"Ahem." I cleared my throat until she swung around with a sardonic smile.

"What can I get for *you*, mam?"

"I'll start with a glass of water and I'll have – "

My scream punctured the air as ice water drenched my lap. The crowd went wild…but this wasn't part of the plot.

"I'm *so* sorry," Amelia cooed, mopping up the mess. Or so it appeared. She *actually* sloshed the ice cubes around; soaking my dress further to encompass spots she missed. The conniving cow looked up with wide, startled eyes and continued apologizing.

"That's ok. Accidents happen," I replied sweetly as I stood and swept the ice from my legs in wide arcing movements.

My hand accidentally knocked the jug from the edge of the table and the remainder of ice water went flying onto Amelia.

"Look out!" I cried moments after the water splashed her bent head and blouse. I raised my hands in dismay. "Oh my goodness, I'm *so* sorry!"

I smirked and held out a dripping napkin.

Her nostrils flared and anyone else might have cowered at her pirate eye glare, but not I. Amelia slapped the napkin away and stormed out. Little puddles from her stringy, no longer curled hair trailed behind her as she went.

"I can't believe that happened," I commented to a stunned Brad/Calvin. Though what I couldn't believe was that I only drenched her head and shirt. I had aimed to get all of her.

Brad shook himself as if coming out of a trance. "You ok?" His voice was thick with shock.

"Yep. I'm fine. But *she's* not getting a tip." I jerked a thumb toward the blanket as the laughter died down.

"No. Definitely not."

We salvaged the performance and brought it to the hilarious finale we intended, but I could tell Brad was preoccupied. And you know what? If I just realized an ex of mine was a malicious psychopath, I wouldn't have been able to focus either. He must have wondered why he ever went out with her in the first place. The question certainly popped into *my* mind countless times.

The cool, icky feeling on my lap faded, as the bathroom drier zapped it away. *Take that Amelia. My dress might be stiff, but your hair will be disheveled all evening.*

"Muahahahaha!" I laughed aloud.

She had it coming. Did she honestly think she could do that and walk away unscathed?

I exited the bathroom and walked along the corridor toward the main hall. I paused with interest. Heated, muffled voices came from the balcony. The quarrel was only slightly veiled by the thin, glass doors. I knew those voices. They belonged to Brad and Amelia.

I stood still for a while as they argued and then nearly jumped out of my skin when a voice boomed next to me.

"Where's Amelia?"

James' simmering glower nearly scalded me with its intensity. I guess the skit hadn't impressed him. Or rather, Amelia's obvious flirting.

"Never mind," he muttered darkly. His eyes were fixed on the glass doors as he strode forward and concealed himself behind a pillar.

"I don't know what you see in her Brad. I don't. She has zero dress sense and an empty head."

Insulted, I gasped.

Zero dress sense? Have you looked in the mirror lately?

Amelia paced with her hands on her hips. "She's a snob! Her roommate said so. Why would you want to be with someone like that?"

"What's it to you?" Brad countered. "You're in a relationship. You shouldn't care."

"But I *do* care!" She swiveled and slapped her hand against the rail. "I care. You have no idea what it's been like for me to watch you hanging out with that…that airhead!" She spat in outrage. "She's *such* a flake – I know what I'm talking about!"

Beside me, James' face was puce.

"No Amelia. You *don't* know what you're talking about, so stop right there."

"*Please* Brad, just hear me out. I'm sorry, ok? The truth is – I made a mistake. There, I said it. We never should have broken up!"

Brad's expression was unreadable. "Amelia."

"I still have feelings for you," she continued inexorably, "I want to get back together. I know you're trying to make me jealous with Reanne. You can quit now. I get it."

"You have a boyfriend." Brad folded his arms. "How do you propose to get around that?"

"I…don't know."

"You could leave him," he said, and my heart constricted.

"I can't!" Amelia cried. "You know I can't. It would devastate him; James needs me. I need *you.* You have to get rid of Reanne – she's toxic. She's poison – "

"*You're* toxic." Brad slashed his hand down crossly. "You don't know what you want. You cheated on me, remember? And now you're doing the same to him. I told you we were through

Amelia. Stalking me and pretending we're together won't change that."

"But Reanne – "

"Enough!" Brad thundered. "I won't tolerate your trash talk or ice water assault on her." He stepped forward, his expression hard. "Just stop."

The door flung open and slammed into the wall so hard I thought the glass would shatter.

"James!" Amelia squealed as he charged onto the terrace.

"I *need* you?" His words dripped with sarcasm. "You think I can't survive without you?"

"Baby," she placed placating hands on his chest and spoke as if addressing a toddler, "you misunderstood. Let me explain…"

"Don't patronize me!" James exploded, pushing her aside.

Hastily, I backed away as Brad came in and raked a hand through his hair. He looked stressed, and then spooked to see me. "Hi," he exhaled and glanced at the bathroom door. "How's the dress?"

"It's fine."

He stared at me for a moment and then his mouth twisted into a smile. "And how are you?"

"Couldn't be better," I smiled back.

"Shall we?" Brad motioned toward the dance floor where a disco ball loomed from the ceiling. People were bopping about beneath it.

"I'd love to!" I yelled over the music. We boogied out to the dance floor next to Bridget and her guy, Fizzle. What a horrible name. His last name was Butt. He should have had it changed – I would have.

I was somewhat concerned for Bridge and Fizz as I observed them dancing. Bridget's fuchsia skirt twirled about her ankles and her arm dangled at what appeared to be a broken angle. The expression on her face was also weird and it looked like she was having a seizure. I guess she was attempting something robotic.

Brad wasn't doing too bad, but his flapping arms and bopping head did make him look like a chicken. A very tall, awkward chicken. Not that I'm the greatest dancer in the world but I was certainly doing better than they were. I had *some* rhythm, at least.

"Hey Reanne, what do you call *that* move?" Bridget chortled.

"Ha *ha*. Like you don't know." I rolled my eyes. I was *clearly* doing a moonwalk. Just because Bridget's dancing was tragic, it didn't mean she had to imply mine was as well.

I turned and moonwalked in the opposite direction and nearly doubled over at the sight before me. Bridget, Fizzle and Brad were in a straight line, rotating and freezing in sporadic, jerky movements. They *all* looked epileptic.

I giggled and transitioned into my next dance move, which to the casual observer resembles running on the spot but is actually a very complicated technique.

Now they laughed at *me*, and I grinned. We were having a blast. It's fun to laugh at yourself and just be silly every now and then.

Suddenly the music slowed. Bridget and Fizzle were in each other's arms in a flash. Her head rested snugly against his shoulder and Fizzle's hands circled her waist, landed on her bum, and stayed there.

Gee. Fizzle was a bit of a pervert.

Brad and I stood self-consciously on the dance floor and I wondered what he would do next. He scratched the back of his neck and took a step toward me, then stopped as I spun away in surprise. Darren had stepped between us and began swinging me around the floor.

"What are you doing?" I muttered through gritted teeth. "Why aren't you dancing with ten other girls at once?" He had been doing exactly that just moments earlier.

He clicked his tongue. "And leave you out? Now that wouldn't be fair."

"Wouldn't have bothered *me*."

He twirled me again and I spotted Brad sitting alone at our table. The look he sent Darren was chilling. I jerked free before Darren saluted him, smiled mockingly, and sauntered off to another girl.

Chapter Fifteen

Christmas Break

I raced from the gate towards a screaming like a banshee, jumping like a lunatic Rhonda. My entire family came to the airport, but you wouldn't have noticed them for the commotion Rhonda caused.

"Missed you too," I chuckled when she released me from the chokehold.

Jaden engulfed me in a hug. "Hey sis! How was the flight?"

"Not bad. I brought some pictures to show you!" I brandished them excitedly and immediately pointed out Amelia in the background of one. "That's her."

Mom gazed at it dubiously. "Love, you think Brad likes *this* girl?"

"U-G-L-Y, she ain't got no alibi – she's ugly! Heeey, she's ugly." Rhonda was getting jiggy with it as my luggage came into view on the conveyer belt. Amelia clearly wasn't ugly…but I appreciated the loyalty.

"He doesn't like her, as it happens. He never did." I recounted the entire story from the previous evening.

"She got what she deserves," said Rhonda, linking her arm through mine. "You know," she grinned at me, "we need to go to the mall this week. It's not much fun shopping with Erin."

"Sheesh Reanne," Jaden cut in, "did you bring the entire college back with you?" Beads of sweat trickled down his brow as he struggled to lift one suitcase. "This is heavier than when you left."

"No it isn't," came my quick retort. "You didn't drop me off so you wouldn't know. *Dad* did all the work."

Speaking of dad…he was frantically pulling at my other suitcase as it rolled past and it looked like he was about to throw out his back.

"Tom, let Jaden help you with that," mom suggested.

Together, they managed to get it down.

Rhonda looked really good. Her hair finally came past her shoulders and it was tame. I tugged a curly strand as we drove home. "This looks amazing!"

"Thanks! The long hair specialist I've been seeing is a genius with a magic touch! I swear my hair has grown quicker since he started working with it."

"Is it expensive?"

"It *is*. But *so* worth it."

I had to agree. I mean, why trust your hair to a regular stylist if you can afford a specialist? I find regular hairdressers don't listen well. If you ask them to take half an inch from the length, you're guaranteed to lose *three*.

I punched Jaden playfully. "So where's Lindsay? How come she didn't come?"

"She's at work."

Lindsay was the main subject of conversation for the duration of the drive until dad butted in with his newest health concern. We listened to him talk about it all the way home. Poor dad was terrified he might have Parkinson's because his eye twitched the other day.

I couldn't believe it. Mom and dad surprised me with a web cam the minute we got home as an early gift! They got it on sale at Costco so we could see each other when we talked. I wasn't sure how compatible it would be with the school computers but I looked forward to testing it out.

I also felt a spike of excitement at the thought of checking my email and going online. It was my only connection to Brad over Christmas, and his writing always brought a smile to my face.

I thought I'd begin the interaction with a short email my second day home.

Hey!

I arrived alive, lol. It feels great to be back. Hope you enjoy your holiday,

Reanne.

It took Brad a few days to respond, and when he did his email contained sad news. Brad's forty-two-year-old uncle was just diagnosed with cancer and wasn't given long to live.

I read this and my eyes filled.

News like that is devastating any time of the year, but how especially horrible to find out at Christmas. Jaden's appendix almost ruptured once a few years back and he had to stay in hospital for a week. He made it home Christmas day, but the whole ordeal was still upsetting. I couldn't imagine how awful Brad's family felt discovering a terminal illness. Still – he tried to remain positive, believing his uncle would recover. I replied, expressing my sympathy and best wishes for the family. After I sent the email, I wanted to cheer him up, and what better way to do that than to casually mention my new web cam, and to *use it?*

I went online and Brad was there.

Reanne says,
Hey Brad! Guess what? I got a web cam!!!!! ☺ ☺ ☺

Brad instantly invited me to do a live web cam chat and we were off!

It was *amazing*. The picture was so clear! And the most thrilling aspect was seeing Brad too. There was a web cam on his family computer. His hair was a little rumpled and he looked kind of sleepy but that just added to his allure. I enjoyed catching glimpses of his home in the background. It looked really cozy with all the family photos on the wall and the wooly red blanket draped over the sofa. At one point his sister popped her head into the room and I could see her too! She was very pretty, but looked nothing like Brad.

Ok. This web cam stinks.

I examined every inch of it the following day, wondering what the problem was. I was still glad my parents got it for me of course…it's just that it was no longer working. I didn't expect it to break after one use! Talk about shoddy!

Brad hummed as I meddled with it. His image had been on my screen for a few minutes already.

I had to bite the bullet and tell him it wasn't going to happen. The web cam was broken. I placed my hands on the keyboard and then noticed the web cam wire.

Oops. It's not plugged in.

Brad and I were having a wonderful conversation when I heard a blinging sound. I ignored it, but it happened a few more times.

Bling. Bling.

Someone was messaging me. I momentarily paused the conversation with Brad and clicked on the flashing orange box at the bottom of my screen.

What does Darren want?

The D Man says,
Are you talking to Brad?

Reanne says,
Why do you want to know?

The D Man says,
You are. He didn't answer me until now. He's not interested in you, you know.

Reanne says,
Uh huh. Trying to stir things up are you? Is that all?

The D Man says,
He likes the idea of winning you; but he'll never date you. He likes the competition. He got fired up when I talked about our dates.

Reanne says,
That's because you called me a cheapskate.

No. Scrap that. Delete.

Whatever.

I blocked him. I should have done it a while ago.

"Rhonda, slow down!" I called as she tore through the mall ahead of me and disappeared. I know we hadn't shopped together in ages, but she didn't have to go crazy. We had the entire day, and it was better to go a bit slower anyway. The mall was crowded with last minute Christmas shoppers, each one laden with carrier bags and murderous expressions.

I dodged quickly to the left as one woman in an ugly polka dot vest pushed past me, nearly knocking my Coach purse from my shoulder. "Well," I glanced behind me at the retreating polka dots. "I can forgive her. I'd be hostile in that vest too." I searched through the people milling about then yelled, "Rhonda! Get back here."

She reappeared. "Wow Reanne, didn't you get any exercise while away? You're even slower than before!"

Drill sergeant Rhonda. That's what I should call her.

She took hold of my arm and rushed forward past the decorated shop windows until we reached Santa's workshop where we waited in line. I know we were a little old for that, but it was just a bit of Christmas fun. Rhonda and I did it every year – we posed with Santa for a picture then dropped our wish lists into the little metal box by his chair. This year I was gunning for a pair of Jimmy Choos. Normally I'd also slip hints to my parents about the note I gave big red, but not this time. They already bought the dress.

We waited patiently, flanked by cotton snow while little kids screamed and elbowed one another, trying to see if the shiny presents topped with glittering bows were real.

"Amy! Thomas! Get down from that sleigh *this instant!*" A mother's voice rang out.

"Aren't we a little old for this?" I grinned at Rhonda. I mean…we were the only two over the age of ten.

"Yes," she agreed. "But we're not breaking tradition. Besides, we can't browse unless you want to get trampled by the angry heard of last minute shoppers."

"Yeah you're right. And we're already dressed up." Rhonda and I were in different shades of mauve.

"Hey mom, those girls look like grapes," a snotty nosed kid behind us snickered. His mother didn't acknowledge him.

Ok. I don't have parenting experience…and not even that much with babysitting, but rude behavior should be corrected, shouldn't it? My parents never would have let me stand there, calling someone a grape. Especially while pointing and laughing.

Anyway, we *didn't* look like grapes. And the kid looked about seven so I chose to ignore him.

Rhonda poked me. "Erin's been trying to get pregnant, did she tell you?"

"No, but that doesn't surprise me. How long has she been trying? Let me guess – since the honeymoon?"

Rhonda nodded. "They're having problems, though, and she thinks it's Alan's fault she can't get pregnant. She's talking about a trial separation."

"Really?" I tapped my chin thoughtfully. "Isn't that a little extreme? It's like they just got married five minutes ago. They need to work it out and give it more time. Have they considered testing and fertility treatmen – ouch!"

The little monster threw something at me. The same one that called me a grape. I turned and glared at him. What was it, a pebble? How did the child get a *pebble?*

"Bullseye!" He shouted. "Yes!"

"Reanne, calm down, he's just a kid." The insults and stone flinging didn't bother Rhonda until another shiny pebble bounced off the side of her head.

"Ow!" She rubbed her temple. "Why you little…"

"May I have everyone's attention, please?" A curly haired woman in a spangly green elf suit addressed the line. "Due to an unforeseen circumstance, Santa will be leaving early today. Everyone after this point," she tapped my shoulder, "must come back later."

A general moan of disappointment arose as children and parents dispersed. The pebble thrower dropped all his beads on the floor, flopped down on top of them, and screamed.

"Darwin sweetie, time to go." His mother panted as she dragged him away.

The furious, red-faced kid tossed one parting pebble, which we dodged. Rhonda and I high-fived.

I flipped through the TV channels that evening and propped my feet on the couch. I was tired and ready to relax. I wouldn't move now, even if dad said a tsunami was barreling toward the house.

I dropped the remote when I found a rerun of F.R.I.E.N.D.S. Joey and Chandler were playing foosball against Monica and she was winning. Of course.

Ping.

A noise sounded from the computer.

"And that would be a shut down," gloated Monica after she scored the last point.

Ping.

"Shut *out!*" Joey and Chandler exclaimed in frustration.

Ping.

Ok. I can't enjoy a show with a constant dinging in my ears. Even during an episode I've seen a million times.

The noise came from Facebook chat. I guess I forgot to log out the last time I was on, and the person messaging me was Brad.

Brad! I felt a bubble of enthusiasm. I switched off the TV and set up the web cam with glee. I couldn't wait to tell him about that kid from the mall – I knew he'd find it funny.

I edged toward the gifts piled under the tree Christmas morning. A large, wide box sat a few feet away and *Reanne* was scrawled across a little card on the side.

My fingers twitched…I was *dying* to shake that box and poke a little hole through the wrapping paper. Jaden and I used to do this yearly until mom caught on and began hiding the presents from us. We tried to blame Snowflake for the rips in the paper (Snowflake used to eat the fake apples from the tree, which left red stains all around her mouth– so why not the presents too? She did actually rip into a present one year – it was my gift to dad, and it was chocolate) but mom wouldn't fall for it. Since then, the presents went under the tree every Christmas Eve after we'd gone to bed. And there was no point getting up early to figure out the gifts on Christmas morning because we always got caught. I'm not sure if mom developed a sixth sense or if we triggered a silent alarm, but she always appeared in her robe as soon as we crossed the threshold to the family room.

Mom came into the room with a tray of hot chocolate and noticed how closely I sat to the presents. "Lindsay should be here soon and then we'll get going."

Beside me, Jaden's legs were crossed and he eyed the big, striped parcel. "You're gonna love your gift," he said.

"You know what it is?" I leaned in excitedly and darted a look at the box. "Give me a hint."

"Not *that* one. I have no idea what's in it…I'm talking about the gift from me and Lindsay."

"I'm sure it will be great. I can't wait," I smiled at him.

The doorbell rang in a *Jingle Bells* tune and dad went to answer it. "Hi Lindsay, come on in."

We could finally begin! I dove at the large box and was surprised at the weight of it. It was really heavy-it *had* to be something good! Next to me, Jaden arranged all of his presents into piles.

The paper went everywhere as I opened my gift with zeal. The box beneath was plain brown and gave no indication of the goody within. I peeled back the tape and looked inside. There was another wrapped box. I gingerly pulled it out and started on that one. I glanced at Jaden just as he unwrapped an X-box One and whooped. He would be on that thing the rest of the day.

Layer after layer of wrapping littered the floor as I continued to rip paper and discover smaller boxes inside. My present was beginning to look quite small.

"Goodness, you guys wrapped this like Fort Knox."

Dad just grinned.

Four boxes later and possibly a roll of masking tape – I opened the last brown box. Everyone's eyes were upon me as I shuffled through the pieces of Styrofoam and newspaper. I touched something grainy and solid and pulled it out in whirl of confusion. "Thanks so much for this lovely…what is this, a brick?"

The laughter in the room was deafening. Especially from dad, he couldn't contain himself. "I…I told you the dress was your only gift," he wheezed. "I got you! I'm brilliant!"

"And here's your real gift." Mom handed me a midsized package and the room quieted as I unwrapped it. They were trying to trick me again I just knew it. I wouldn't be fooled by the word *Mac* emblazoned on the front of the box *or* the image of a little apple with a bite out of it.

"WHOOOOOOO!" I leaped up and strangled my dad in a hug after opening the box. They actually got me a laptop!

"That web cam we gave you?" said mom with a smile "is actually ours. Your Mac has one built in. And now we can talk to you any time, and you can do all your projects without waiting for a computer!"

"Aww, you guys! I love it!"

I was beyond thrilled about my new laptop, but I didn't know how to work it. Which was slightly embarrassing, since my arthritic grandma, who had come over for Christmas dinner, was merrily typing away on her Acer laptop on the opposite sofa without a care in the world. She took a computer course. She was very proud.

A Mac is a completely different operating system, though. Nothing was where I thought it should be, and familiarizing myself with it was like learning a new language. Except, I knew I could figure it out on my own. I didn't need to ask for help.

Hmm. Where are the apps on this thing?

I clicked fruitlessly on a few icons until I found myself searching through the proper folder.

See?

I knew I could do it.

Noooooo.

The colored wheel of death was spinning on my screen – the same one that pops up on the school computers before they freeze and crash.

Ok. *Don't panic. Do not panic. This is a Mac – it will fix itself.*

The screen went black.

I killed it. I killed the Mac. Mom and dad were going to kill me. Whenever this happened at school, there was no reviving the computer unless the techie guy was summoned to sort it out. And even then he couldn't always resuscitate it.

"How's it going?" Jaden strode over.

"Well…not so good," I bit my lip. "I was trying to find the apps and somehow ended up with the wheel of terror before the laptop shut down. Shouldn't it have corrected itself?"

"It's a computer." Jaden kept a straight face. "Not a miracle machine. And you have to *download* some of the programs, depending on what you want. I can do that, if you'd like, and show you the basics."

"Thanks Jay," I replied gratefully and moved over as he skillfully booted it up. This is what brothers are for.

Chapter Sixteen

Yes! Noooo

"You'll never guess! Amelia's gone!"

It was the first thing Bridget said when we encountered each other in the dorm lounge. I stopped there before my room to see if anyone could help get my luggage down the stairs. Immediately, I forgot all about that and leapt euphorically into the air. It was fine; no one was around, except Anna who sat on the couch.

"So what happened?"

"She transferred to another college. Tara said she received an art scholarship there."

"Oh really?" I stopped shaking my booty. "For which art – the art of manipulation? No wonder she got a scholarship...she's so skilled she could teach the class."

Bridget grinned. "She didn't want to stick around and see how things progressed with you and Brad."

"Or run into James," Anna interjected, rising from the couch. She came toward me. "Did you have a good break?"

"I did! It was nice to be home. Did you?" I returned.

"Yes." Her face went a little pink. "So…I know you and I didn't get off to a good start last semester, but I wanted to say I appreciate you and hope we can do better from here on out."

Aww. If only I could believe it. I'm sure Anna meant what she said but I wasn't sure it would stick. Her moods were always up and down like a yo-yo. At least it was a beginning. Well, a new beginning, anyway.

"Bridget," I said as I finally clocked her clothes. "Where did you get that outfit?"

Black socks were hiked up over cream-colored pants. Her long-sleeved sweater was lime green.

"My mom got it for me." One hand rested on her hip and the other went behind her head as she beamed at me. "It was one of my Christmas gifts!"

No, not the mother too!

"Well, it's certainly…attractive." As in, attracting the wrong attention from the opposite sex, if any at all.

"Hey Bridge…I saw an outfit in a magazine recently and instantly thought of you. It would really suit you. Want to go to the mall together to find it? I can pick out some other great pieces for you also."

"I'd like that," said Bridget, glancing at my outfit. "Your clothes are always nice."

"Can I come?" asked Anna.

I remembered her dress from banquet and I wasn't too thrilled about the gray frock she wore now.

"Yes, let's make a day of it!"

The first day back to class I wore the Chanel tweed jacket Rhonda gave me with the matching pumps from Jaden and Lindsay. Jaden was right. I loved their gift! They must have saved for a while to get those heels and I was so touched I nearly cried. And with my shiny new Mac flipped open in front of me, I felt like a million bucks.

A guy named Tony drew near just then with a cup of coffee in hand. He headed toward the empty desk next to mine.

"Hey Reanne!" he greeted me congenially and lifted the drink to his lips. My eyes widened as I fixated on the mug of steaming, aromatic liquid. It was getting closer. As he lowered his arm, I could see bits of dark coffee swishing around the rim, spilling a little with every step he took.

Suddenly, I threw my purse onto the vacant chair beside me, sprung up and hovered above the laptop, shielding it from impending disaster.

He gaped at me in a mix of astonishment and disgust. I didn't care.

There's no way that klutz was coming anywhere near my new computer. That's not to say he would have spilled his coffee everywhere, but what if he couldn't help it? What if he *tripped*? I wasn't taking a chance.

A chair scraped across the floor as Tony glared at me and found another seat.

I breathed a sigh of relief and moved my purse as professor Rowan entered the room and began writing on the board. My fingers landed on the smooth keys and I typed every word he spoke. My laptop was awesome!

The door opened again and I looked up as Brad and Darren walked through. A tingle raced down my spine as I locked eyes with Brad. Web cam just didn't compare to seeing him in person. I missed him – being near him.

To my delight, Brad advanced and I knew he would sit next to me.

At least, he would have if Darren hadn't charged past him with a demented gleam in his gaze.

Brad tore his eyes from mine, growled and made a grisly swipe for Darren's backpack. He missed and Darren parked himself beside me as Brad reluctantly took the desk in front.

I turned to Darren and shook my head in distaste. He was extremely pleased with his idiotic self as he made the *loser* sign at Brad's back with his fingers. How adult of him. The look he gave me was pointed.

I stared right back hoping telepathy would kick in.

Get lost!

Bridget and I were playing a round of table tennis Saturday at noon, when I put my paddle down and said, "Bridge – want to go to the mall and find that outfit I mentioned?"

I needed to do something else or I would combust. Besides which, the new dress from Bridget's mother was hurting my eyes. No really. They had a thing for blinding, fluorescent colors.

"Yes, lets! Coming Anna?"

A coke can dropped in the vending machine with a clang. Anna bent to retrieve it, snapped it open, and pulled a regretful face. "It's ok, go on without me. I have other plans."

Outside, Bridget paused in front of the men's dorm just before we reached the road. "Hang on a minute," her breath came out in frosty puffs.

"What are you doing?"

She tiptoed to the side of the building and tapped at a ground level window. Her grin was cheeky.

"Bridget, don't!"

She rapped a few more times before the beige blinds were pushed aside and a disheveled Brad peeked through them.

"We're going to the mall," she enunciated. "Want to come?"

His eyes darted from her to me and I had no idea what he was thinking. He probably assumed this was my idea. Great. Why couldn't Bridget leave things alone? She always had to meddle.

After the slightest hesitation, the blinds rustled and closed. I heard a faint, "maybe next time," as Brad disappeared.

Bridget joined me on the sidewalk and sighed. "Oh well. It was worth a try. He seemed torn with you standing there."

"Bet you woke him up." I gave her a friendly shove with my hip as the bus rumbled up to the stop across the street. "And he didn't have time to get ready."

"Oh, I'm so sorry!" I glanced at Bridget as the bus arrived at our destination.

"What for?" Her expression tightened in alarm.

I forgot how bad the mall was. I brought her there for nothing. "There aren't many shops here…I don't think we'll find the clothing I was thinking of for you."

"No biggie," her brow relaxed. "I've been here before. You can find good clothing but you have to *dig* for it, I find."

"So…you've bought outfits here before, then?" I confirmed, just to be sure. That would explain a lot.

"Zack's Department is the best place to go." Her face lit up. "I bet we can find things for you too!"

I grimaced when she turned her head. I'd honestly rather step into a stream of traffic, blindfolded, than wear something from a place called *Zack's Department.*

"Is there anywhere else we could go?" There was a hopeful lift to my voice.

Bridget knitted her brows in contemplation. "I think there's a consignment store around here but I'm not sure where."

Consignment stores are often full of gems. "We have to find it!" I exclaimed. We wandered around in the cold for a while, but eventually came across it.

Wind chimes tinkled above as we stepped into the musty shop. It was the wonderful smell of undiscovered vintage. I sneezed. And incense.

"Let the hunt begin!" I raced to the accessories at the back of the store, leaving Bridget in my wake, and rifled through a bin of cool looking hats. I found a funky pink one that Rhonda might appreciate and put it on my head for Bridget to see…just as she reached for an orange, Halloween type sweater.

"*Stop*!" I yelled involuntarily.

Bridget pulled her hand back and jumped. "What*?*"

"Sorry. Thought I saw a spider. Didn't want you to accidentally touch it." I presented her with something nicer. "Try this."

As Bridget pulled the white angora sweater over her head, I spotted a burgundy and tan bag on a shelf with the –

It's a Gwen Stefani L.A.M.B. purse! My eyes widened as I recognized the logo. *For one hundred and fifty dollars*!

I had to have it. I had to. Except…I wasn't supposed to be shopping for myself.

"How does it look?" Bridget spun around and I was pleased. She looked fantastic! The sweater was similar to one I owned.

"It's really nice, you should definitely get it."

Ok. The thing about the purse is that it would normally cost a lot more than that. Like, six hundred dollars. It would have been a crime to walk out of there without it.

I stared at the purse, contemplating what to do then glanced at Bridget as she tried on an oversized, horizontally striped t-shirt. The angora sweater was balled up on the floor.

Reluctantly…I moved away, collected the sweater, and ushered Bridget to the other end of the store where I could focus and give her advice for future shopping endeavors on her own. We found three clothing combinations she could mix and match when the wind chimes sounded from the front of the shop, followed by two sets of footsteps. There was a bit of clanging as items were picked up and replaced on shelves.

"Ooh – I like this!" It was a woman's voice coming from the vicinity of the purse.

Something strange overcame me. A weird, unyielding urge. Ignoring it, I concentrated on Bridget.

"Honey, it matches my shoes!"

My fingers twitched.

"Should I buy it?"

Ack, no good!

I rounded a rack of expensive fur coats in a blur. The startled boyfriend glared at me while putting a protective arm in front of his girlfriend, as I dove and banged my shin on a low shelf. But it was ok, because I got the purse – yes!

I clutched the bag to my chest and stood. As I dusted myself off, I saw that the woman was actually quite far away, with a pair of light leather gloves in her hand, and was gaping at me like I was a serial killer about to shoot.

"Um..." I backed away sheepishly. "Lovely gloves you have there...and...uh – they *do* match your shoes. Bye!"

I shouldered my new purse and returned to Bridget before she tried on a pair of overalls.

Brad was in the lounge reading a *National Geographic* when Bridget and I returned from the consignment store. He was completely absorbed in it and wasn't aware of me standing off to the side of the sofa.

Brad is a brainy type of guy – always interested in learning and discussing intellectual concepts. In fact, it's one of the things that first attracted me to him. You know, besides his drop-dead gorgeousness, his sense of humor, and chivalrous demeanor. Basically he's the perfect guy.

I came around, sat beside him and began flipping through a magazine myself.

"Is that new?" Brad said of my purse.

You see? He also *notices* things, which is nice. "Yep, just got it!"

We made small chat for a while before moving to the subject of school.

"How did you do on the quiz we had Thursday?" Brad wanted to know. We got the results the next day.

"Aced it," I shrugged modestly. "Photographic memory." Taking detailed notes on my laptop had a lot to do with it as well. "You?"

He frowned. "Not as great as I would have liked. My grades are slipping a little."

I scrunched my face. "Really?"

"They're not *bad*," his eyes were on the *National Geographic* as he thumbed the pages. "But they could be better. So I might…extend my dating strike."

Huh? That doesn't make sense. There won't be conflict with his education if he dates in the summer.

I opened my mouth to say exactly that but nothing came out.

Darren's words were swarming in my head like a horde of angry wasps, and my mouth snapped shut at their stinging jibes.

He's not interested in you, you know. He likes the idea of winning you; but he'll never date you. It's a competition.

What if he's right?

No. Darren wasn't credible.

Then why would Brad decide to extend his dating break without giving a legitimate reason?

I slapped my magazine down on the coffee table and stood. I was angry and baffled. Why can't men talk plainly? Why can't they know what they want? Or maybe this was some twisted game like Darren said. Well, I didn't want to play.

"You ok?"

Did I *look* ok? The entire college was aware of my feelings for Brad and he called all the shots while I waited around like some lovesick puppy. Well forget it. No more. I deserved better. He could take his blasted dating break and shove it where the sun doesn't shine.

"I'm great," I answered, almost savagely, and stalked off.

I needed to toughen up in the weeks that followed and accept that Brad and I were only friends, because he was still being flirtatious one moment and distant the next. I was *determined* to not read into his comments and to just accept them as they were – nothing serious. Meaningless fun. Except, my treacherous heart refused to agree and kept arguing with my head over every little thing Brad did.

Stupid heart.

I rivaled it with Gloria Gaynor and belted out "I will survive" along with the music.

Then I switched to Aretha. "You better think, yeaaaah, think about what you're trying to do to me. Yeah you better thiiinnnk."

The louder I sang, the better. With each note I felt stronger and more determined than ever. Dancing also helped. Aretha was so encouraging and made me realize that Brad wasn't brainy at all.

He had to have a few screws loose to let go of a girl like me. Even with this realization, my feelings didn't completely melt away.

Rhonda brought him up in almost every conversation we had and she alternated between calling him a dufus and saying, "well maybe he *will* ask you out once his priorities are sorted."

Bridget wasn't any better. "Don't give up on him Reanne, he cares about you," she said to me one afternoon when I was feeling blue.

"But I *want* to give up on him!" I exclaimed in frustration. "I don't want to mope around over a guy. I have a life…and I don't need to complicate it with someone who can't make up his mind." Then I broke out into "I'll survive" again.

And there was still the issue of not knowing *why* he was hot one moment and cold the next. I was sick of Darren strutting around the campus with an *I told you so* expression on his belligerent face, as though Brad confided in him. As if he knew *exactly* what was happening.

He's such a liar.

But was he?

Really?

I wanted to get off this tumultuous rollercoaster. I sent a long email to mom about it (one of many) and asked her to consult dad and Jaden on the matter. It was time to gain male insight into Brad's behavior. I was sure they'd be able to tell me what was going on, and what, if anything, I should do about it.

That's it?

Incredulously, I read the reply again.

Seriously – that's it?

Their only advice was to simply *ask* Brad how he felt and be direct.

Like I could just walk up to him and say, "So Brad – what's the deal? Do you want to date me? And what's the real reason you won't do it *now?*"

Who does that? No one. Because it's uncomfortable.

Besides, they were supposed to review the situation and provide me with an in depth analysis of Brad's thoughts and actions. Not tell me to just *ask him* about his thoughts and actions.

I sighed.

Jaden also offered to fly out here and 'take care of Brad' (in other words – he'd pound him), which was really sweet and momentarily put a smile on my face, but wouldn't solve anything either.

Chapter Seventeen

Determination

Bridget dumped a drawer full of clothes onto her bed to sort through. All my stuff was already packed and I meandered over to give her a hand. I examined a few lovely shirts and smiled to myself. Bridget's wardrobe had improved drastically after a few more shopping trips together…and a few of these items she even picked out herself! I felt very proud of my little chick, slowly learning how to fly in the world of fashion. I knew she would continue to blossom over the summer…and of course I also planned to send her the occasional email with earmarked items to look out for.

"Thanks for lending me your extra duffle bag," I said as I gently folded a cream and burnt orange sweater. "I'll bring it back empty in September, promise."

"Don't worry, you can keep it." She eyed it uncertainly. It *was* pretty full. I guess I got a little carried away with the consignment store. There were so many beautiful things in there.

As I inconspicuously removed neon green leggings from her pile (*how* did she slip those in?), there was a knock at the door and I went to answer it.

Brad arrived to help with my luggage.

I gave Bridget a quick hug and made her promise to keep in touch, and then, before I knew it, Brad and I were standing alone in the stairwell waiting for my taxi to arrive. It was drizzling outside, and a few weeds poked through the gravel.

This is it. I twisted my hands behind my back. *Summer break.*

"So," said Brad, "what are your plans once you get home?"

"Job hunting," I replied.

I was supposed to return to the movie theatre, since I applied for a leave of absence, but when I called to pick up a few shifts over Christmas I found out that I was no longer employed there. It was petty of my supervisor to get rid of me over a hat, but I didn't really mind. I vowed to never wear it again anyway unless I was dead…and even then Rhonda would respect my last wish: for her to guard my casket with a rifle in hand and shoot on sight if anyone approached with a baseball cap.

"How about you?"

I wondered if he'd bring up the dating strike. Not that I cared. By this point I had managed to squash my feelings pretty well, and I was *glad* we were only friends. I never wanted anything more, anyhow. I had a momentary lapse in judgment and wanted my perception of Brad, not the actual Brad, who was extremely flawed and not at all attractive. I mean…he probably wasn't even a natural blond and I bet he bleached his arm hair too.

So there.

Large droplets of water pelted the glass door as the rain intensified.

"Same here – looking for a job," he answered as a blue and yellow taxi pulled into the drive. Brad darted out with my luggage and I fought off a wave of disappointment.

I wore my smartest cream suit; my hair was up in a loose chignon, and a few appealing strands were pulled out at the front. I was dressed to impress, and I definitely wouldn't make any mistakes this time. I was ready to work, and I would *not* give advice to *anyone* when handing out my resume, no matter how much their look could improve with slight changes, or tremendous ones. The key was to keep my mouth shut until *after* I got the job.

So I visited bridal shop after bridal shop, meeting managers and smiling brightly, no matter what. Because it's one thing to give advice to people when you're their personal consultant but you never do it with a store manager. Even if their shirt and pants looked like they had been made out of bath towels (store # 3). It was a real effort to keep quiet…and I did, but at what cost? The poor woman could have easily been mistaken for a fitness instructor from a 1970s workout video, rather than a bridal store manager, yet I restrained myself from commenting.

Which was really unfortunate as it turned out, because I still didn't get a job anywhere. No one wanted seasonal help even though I'd have brought such passion to the position.

This is depressing.

I sat at the kitchen table in my pj's that evening, nursing a cup of tea, with the chignon loosely falling down my back.

I should have told that woman to burn her outfit after all.

"No luck today, hun?" Dad sat down across from me with a bowl of ice cream.

"No," I sighed. "No one wants to hire just for the summer and I only want to work in a bridal shop." I traced the rim of my mug with my fingers distractedly.

"Have you applied online?" Dad asked around a mouthful of Haagen Dazs. "Try that and consistently follow up with phone calls. Show 'em you mean business and that you'd be the best seasonal employee they ever had. They'll appreciate your tenacity."

"Thanks dad!" It was good advice.

"Mmm," dad moaned on his second bite.

I was transfixed by the chunky melting glob in his bowl. Streams of goo rapidly ran down the sides of his gigantic ice cream mountain. How many scoops did he *take?*

My eyes narrowed. "Does mom know you're eating that?"

I highly doubted it. Mom was out getting groceries and I'm pretty sure the ice cream container had been hidden.

"Nope," dad grinned amiably while scooping up a chocolate drop with his finger and stuffing it into his mouth. "And you'd better not tell her."

The phone trilled in my ear for the fourth time and someone finally answered.

"Beautiful Bride, Tina speaking – how may I help?"

"Hi there – may I speak with the manager, please?"

I had applied online to *Beautiful Bride* as soon as dad and I finished talking, then I Googled the phone number. I made the call two days later, hoping it wasn't too soon.

"Brenda is unavailable at the moment," came the chipper voice. "Is there anything I can assist you with? Would you like to book a consultation?"

"No thanks. Could you please let Brenda know I phoned?"

"Certainly, what's your name?" I heard her typing at her computer.

"Reanne. And here's my number…Thanks so much!"

I gave it a few days but Brenda never phoned. So I tried again, only to be told she was with a client. I left a message indicating I had submitted my resume online, and that I was really interested in working there. I called the day after that, but Brenda wasn't in the shop at all.

I took to calling *Beautiful Bride* daily for a solid week before I actually spoke with Brenda directly, and this was because she finally called *me*.

"We don't actually have any openings at the moment," Brenda explained, and my heart sank, "but I'm very impressed by your persistence. You must really want this."

"I do!" I breathed in sudden hope.

"I'll tell you what – come see me Tuesday at 6:00 p.m. Does this work for you?"

Yes! I pumped my fist into the air.

"That's perfect, I'll see you then!"

"Very good, I look forward to meeting you."

I was ready to nail my interview! My parents peppered me with questions to prepare in the days leading up to the main event, and my answers were pretty solid. There was no way I could botch this up. No *way*.

I looked fantastic as well, which would definitely help. I wore the same cream suit as before, but this time it was paired with Rhonda's five-inch Louboutin heels and a black briefcase-like tote. I was riveted by my chic and competent reflection in the mirror as I smoothed out my skirt. Brenda *had* to hire me.

I would be the epitome of professionalism and punctuality. No – I'd be *more* than punctual. I was going to arrive fifteen minutes early.

I folded myself into mom's silver Plymouth, being careful not to rip my skirt or damage Rhonda's shoes, and placed my bag on the passenger seat. In no time at all I rolled up to the large, pristine bridal store. My palms were sweaty as I teetered to the front door and went inside.

Here I go.

I froze in the entryway when I noticed a guy manning the phone at the front desk. He was very polished, and his hair was slicked back with what must have been an entire container of gel.

Who's this? I was bewildered. I had been speaking with Tina all week.

She must be sick today. I stepped forward nervously.

"Welcome to Beautiful Bride," gel-boy spread his arms wide in an inviting gesture, "are you here for the 6:00 p.m. appointment?"

I relaxed. "Yes, I am."

"Have a seat and Stephanie will be right with you."

"You mean Brenda," I corrected.

"I'm sorry?"

"I'm here for a job interview with Brenda," I explained. "The manager?"

"We don't have a manger named Brenda. Do you mean Becky?"

Foreboding chills raced up and down my spine like a NASCAR Ferrari.

No Tina, no Brenda. I know I was speaking with Brenda.

"Wait, what's the phone number to this store?" I felt dazed as he rattled off a foreign combination of numbers. "I'm in the wrong place," I murmured in shock. "I applied here, but I've been calling the *wrong* Beautiful Bride."

I blew it. I couldn't believe it.

"Hey Alison," the guy snorted at a girl putting files away. "Did you hear that? This is too funny!"

I gawked at him. *This is* not *funny!*

My mind worked fast to salvage the situation and suddenly, something clicked.

"Wait! If I tell you the phone number I *have* been calling," I said breathlessly to the guy still chuckling, "would you be able to give me the location of the shop?"

I fired it off by memory. Thank God I had phoned it daily for a week.

I dashed to the car as fast as I could go in Rhonda's stilts, which I may have slightly scuffed, and floored it to the other *Beautiful Bride*. I beat a red light to the cacophony of bleeping horns and made it to my proper appointment six minutes late.

I stumbled through the door with my bulky bag, and a middle-aged woman with dark, French braided hair, frowned at a clock on the wall, then back at me.

"Hi, Brenda? Sorry I'm late. You'll never believe what happened!"

I probably didn't stand a chance of being hired now anyway, but I had to explain or I was definitely doomed. She waited for me to continue.

"I submitted my resume online to a different *Beautiful Bride* but have been calling your location by mistake, and showed up to the other location for our interview," I tittered uneasily, "I realized the error when I arrived, and found out I was supposed to be here by reciting this phone number and getting the proper address from the receptionist."

Brenda didn't react at first. Then, to my astonishment, her face creased and she burst into laughter.

"So *that's* why I couldn't find your resume!" Her hand flew to her mouth. "I kept searching my database and wondered how it disappeared. I'm glad there isn't a glitch with the system. Well…" She pivoted and indicated that I should follow her to an office. "You still made it here, let's proceed with the interview. You can drop off your resume later this week."

I went home, printed my resume and drove straight back to *Beautiful Bride* once Brenda finished grilling me. Brenda was an affable lady, but she was thorough and didn't seem inclined to accept seasonal help either. But I was still trying.

When I walked through the door, Brenda started in surprise. "You're back." Her eyes widened. "With your resume!"

"I thought you'd like this immediately," I said with a determined smile.

She shook her head in disbelief. "You know what? I really like you. Your training begins Monday."

Yes! Yeeeesss!

I drove home in complete euphoria, which only dampened slightly when I remembered the scuff on Rhonda's shoe.

"Never mind…it's just a shoe." Rhonda skimmed over the little mark on the right side as she sat on my bed with her legs crossed. The light in the room faded with the setting sun, so I closed the shutters and flipped on the light switch. "In fact," Rhonda handed it to me, "you can have them."

"Really?" I said in tones of disbelief. I mean, they're *Louboutins*. You don't just give them away. "Are you serious?"

She shrugged. "I bought a new pair. You can use these for work and I'll come see you in them!"

"You'll have to pretend to be a client," I winked at her, "and try on wedding gowns."

"Hmm, maybe I'll pass then. So, has the dufus mentioned anything more about his dating break? Has he emailed you?"

"No. Nothing, but we *have* chatted online…about nothing important." I pulled my laptop from its sleek case and booted it up. "I'll see if he's on now, I can tell him about the job, and you can see how we talk."

Ping.

Brad says,

Howdy ☺

Reanne says,

Hi, how are things?

Brad says,

Busy. I'm a little sore – chopped wood and mowed the lawn today.
I think I got a sunburn.

Reanne says,

Aww, poor you ☹! I've been busy today myself. Went out and got
myself a job! ☺

I filled him in on how it happened.

Brad says,

Smart girl. I knew you'd get something, beautiful girl that you are.
Talented too ;)

"Is this what he always does?" Rhonda asked over my
shoulder.

"Yes!"

"But he won't ask you out."

"No."

"Don't let him get away with it," she prompted. "Call him
out."

I hesitated.

"He walked into it with his compliments. Don't you want to know what his intentions are, or if he *has* any? Or do you really not care anymore? I think you do."

Ok. Fine. I *didn't* have feelings for Brad, but it would be nice to know that I hadn't dreamed up a romance between us. That he had some feelings for me. And all right…a very small percentage of me still hoped he would ask me out. Like…one percent…so it didn't really count.

Reanne says,
Brad, I need to ask you something.

Brad says,
Sure. Fire away! Shoot me in the leg. ☺

Reanne says,
Ok. I want to know why you're more flirtatious when we chat online, but kind of distant sometimes when you see me in person.

Brad says,
Well…I have to be. It's a necessity.

Reanne says,
Why??

Brad says,

I'm not dating right now and I didn't want to give anyone the wrong impression by spending time with just one girl.

Reanne says,

Ok...I guess that makes sense. But I feel as though you might have given the wrong impression anyway with things you've said. Like saying you were considering ending the dating break this summer, and buying a bottle of vanilla lotion for me...and the flirting. Why do you flirt with me one moment and draw back the next? I don't understand.

Brad says,

I'll tell you what; we'll hang out more in September when we're back at school.

I felt a flicker of irritation. "Am I not being clear or is he deliberately missing the point?"

Rhonda shook her head. "Deliberately missing the point!"

Reanne says,

That's not what I mean.

Brad says,

I think it's easier to talk to you online because of the writing. Words are really powerful, and spoken words are stronger than written words I guess...lol, I dunno.

What is *all this crap he's spouting?*

Reanne says,

I just want to know if you and I are only friends or if you had or
have stronger feelings for me. This is what I'm unsure of.

Brad appears to be offline.

Rhonda spat in outrage. "Did he just *leave* the
conversation?"

I stared at the screen, stunned. I finally worked up the nerve
to have this frank, mature discussion with him, and he ditched it
without so much as a 'see you later.'

Why couldn't he just answer the question? A simple yes or
no would have sufficed. Something hot and furious bubbled inside
me. Disappearing like that was flat out rude. Didn't he have a
shred of common courtesy?

"Don't let him get away with this," Rhonda glared at the
laptop. "Rip into him."

I was one step ahead of her.

Subject: (none)

Brad,

I would like you to read this email all the way through since you
severed our conversation online when you disappeared.

I'm going to be blunt here. You said you didn't want to
give anyone the wrong impression, yet I feel you misled me the

entire year by repeatedly showing interest, and then randomly backing off.

Maybe you didn't intend to be ambiguous with your comments and actions, but you were, and I am giving you the opportunity now to clarify your intent with me. You should know that I am happy to be your friend if friendship is all you're offering, but please don't play games. If you have anything to say, then I look forward to your response. If not...then it was nice knowing you. Bye.

Reanne.

I decided to stay offline while awaiting his reply. Four days went past, and he didn't send one, which was a little staggering...because even though he hadn't behaved like the prince charming I originally thought him to be...I didn't think he was *this* inconsiderate. I thought he'd at least defend himself.

I went online.

Brad says,
Hey – did you get my email??

Reanne says,
No?

Brad says,
I knew it. I knew something went wrong...wait a moment while I send it again?

Reanne says,

Ok.

Brad says,

There. Did you get it?

Reanne says,

No. Why don't you just tell me what you wanted to say here?

Brad says,

Yes...ok. I want you to know that I didn't abandon our last
conversation – I lost my Internet connection and couldn't get it
back. Also, I wrote an email the next day, which you haven't
received for some reason, and you haven't been here for us to talk.
I'm sorry for any hurt this caused you. What you said in your email
is right, though...I haven't given clear signals. The thing is, I think
you're a great girl. I do like you – I'm just not in a position to
pursue anything more than friendship presently. There's a lot going
on in my life...I need to focus.

So he *did* like me. He admitted it...but still refused to date,
for whatever reason. I guess I had to accept that and move on. I
never should have allowed myself to think otherwise in the first
place. Although to be fair, I hadn't been aware of the situation
from the start. There should have been a sign floating above his

head stating 'emotionally unavailable.' Wouldn't it be great if everyone did this? It would save some of us a lot of trouble.

Reanne says,

So...we're just friends then. That's all. ☺

Brad says,

Yeah – we're friends...for now. And may I say, as your friend, you looked beautiful on that last day of school. ☺

That's it.

Casual dating was the only way forward and I resolved to say yes to the next guy who asked me out. I doubted it would be someone comparable to Brad, but I needed to lower my standards anyway. If I kept thinking 'too short, too stocky, or too stalker like,' with every man I encountered, I wouldn't end up with anyone. The guys I met in the past probably weren't even that bad – I bet I was too hard on them.

Yes. That had to be it. It was the only logical explanation. Because what was wrong with Neil? Nothing. He was a great guy, who really cared for me, and I couldn't see myself with him. And then I got hung up on a guy who didn't even want to date.

A horrific vision of myself at the age of ninety, still assessing men by an extended checklist (too wrinkled, too gray, and too hunched) flitted before my eyes and I saw myself on my deathbed, shakily advising Jaden's many children to learn from my erroneous ways.

I shuddered. I couldn't allow that to happen! Something needed to change.

Rhonda made arrangements for me to go on a blind date. She said she was setting me up with the perfect guy. Well – actually, she described him as the *sweetest* guy, but I knew what she meant, and she knew my type so I was really excited to meet Steve.

The date was set for mid-summer because Steve hadn't been available before then – he was traveling Europe. How cool is *that*? Rhonda knew a lot about him – they were in the same musical program, and she portrayed him as utterly talented, *gifted even*, and sensitive.

That's why I didn't cancel when date night arrived. I was exhausted from working with an entire bridal party all day while simultaneously dealing with one bride who freaked out and ended up running from the store, leaving a whirlwind of *Allure* in her wake. Not that my encounter with Bridezilla was anything new. She complained about every dress I presented and made dramatic departures weekly. But I must have been doing something right because she kept coming back, despite threats to the contrary.

I soaked in the tub for a long time and let the stress of the day seep out. My foot poked a hole through the bubbles as I tried to picture Steve.

Rhonda said he was athletic too. He probably had toned, tanned calves from running the London Marathon. Or maybe he climbed a mountain in Germany or camped in the wilderness of Sweden…or…endurance hiked through the South of France! Yes! Maybe he did them all!

I was gripped by the idea of greeting an intellectual, olive skinned hunk.

Thank you Rhonda!

I lifted my wrinkled hands from the tepid water and grabbed the sides of the tub to get out. We were to meet at the restaurant in an hour, and I would recognize him by his tangerine tie. I was supposed to match.

I couldn't wait!

The hostess reached for a menu and flashed a smile. "Table for one?"

I tightened my leopard scarf. Ok. So it wasn't exactly tangerine but let's face it – orange isn't the most flattering color in the world.

"Actually, I'm here to meet St – " I stopped as I spotted him sitting alone at a table in the center of the restaurant. He wore a crisp orange tie with black diamond dots, and he dipped garlic bread in some kind of oil based dressing. His eyes closed in ecstasy as he took a bite and I felt a slight twinge of irritation. Couldn't he have waited for me? "It's ok. I see who I'm looking for."

As I drew near, I decided to let his lack of manners slip. I was supposed to be less judgmental, and he was better looking than I imagined! There were ripples in his perfectly coiffed hair, his nose was straight and strong, and he had a small cleft in his chin. Yes, I could forgive him. I was also a few minutes late. Can you blame a guy for being hungry after scaling a mountain?

Look at those arms!

I sat across from him, and his bread fumbled, landing on the plate.

"Sorry I'm late," I said. "I ran into a bit of traffic."

"Um, miss – "

I held up a hand. "Please. Call me Reanne!"

I delightedly glanced at the menu while wondering what subjects we might discuss. The pinstriped shirt he wore with the cashmere vest was top quality. Even the tie was fancy. It occurred to me that we might discuss our favorite designers.

This night kept getting better!

I could barely focus on the words before me as my eyes slid toward this gorgeous man. Talk about good fortune!

Finally!

I sensed someone standing next to my chair and I turned to address the server.

"You're in my seat." It was a slender woman with auburn hair and red highlights. She stared at me coldly, raised her left hand, then pointed to the glittering diamond and accompanying wedding band on her finger. As if I could miss it. The rock was *huge.* She waved it in front of my face. "Do you *mind* if I sit with my *husband?*"

Ahhh!

My face flamed and I shot up in mortification. "Oh goodness, I'm so sorry. I thought this was Steve," I gabbled as I backed away with hands raised. "My friend set me up on a blind date, I'm *so* sorry. – I thought this was him."

"Reanne?" A baritone voice hailed me from the back of the restaurant and I swiveled around. "Over here!"

Rhonda lied by omission. While Steve may have been a nice guy, and ok to look at, she didn't tell me he was a chatterbox or that he never washed his hair. And *how* can someone talk about composers, crescendos, and fermatas for an hour and a half straight? Seriously, *how?* I even dozed off at one point, then jolted awake…to find that Steve hadn't noticed. He was still blathering on about Beethoven and Tchaikovsky.

Now, I don't mind listening to someone talk passionately about music…in fact I encourage it. Rhonda did all the time. It's just that she recognized the glazed look in my eyes and knew when to change the subject. *This* guy didn't have a clue. I tried half a dozen times to neatly segue the conversation into theatre, art, education…even the weather, to no avail.

By the end of the date, my ears were ringing and I couldn't believe it when he leaned in for a kiss across the table. My arms were folded and my expression closed – yet there he was –

suspended above the table, his lips puckered like a fish waiting for me to reciprocate, and his hideous tie dangling in the spaghetti he had ordered. It was like something out of a slow motion horror film (*this* is my definition of horrifying).

I pushed my chair back and dropped my portion of the bill onto the table.

"Thanks for this evening Steve, but I have to go."

And I left him there with his tie still submerged in marinara.

Wagner then came onto the sound system – and you know…I don't think he cared that I went.

Maybe Rhonda should have dated Steve herself.

Chapter Eighteen

Can You Say *Psycho?*

I was finally a second year student occupying a room on the third
floor of the girl's dormitory. The *third floor*! It meant I would have
privacy this year – I could just walk from my room straight to the
bathroom and not worry about being seen by guys. Awesome!
There were a handful of first year girls staying on the third floor as
well, which I thought was a little unfair, but I guess they were just
taking the places of those who didn't return for year two.

"I'm happy to be back!" Bridget's eyes shone as she
unpacked a revolting denim dress with pleats. She obviously
hadn't followed my advice over the summer. "It will be a good
year."

"Of *course* it will be good," I agreed with confidence.

Anna wasn't with us. She was down the hall with a nice
girl named Ellen and someone else I hadn't met yet. And according
to the grapevine, Alex eloped with his girlfriend and wasn't
coming back, which amazed me.

He really did have a girlfriend. Go figure.

"I met someone downstairs," said Bridget with a happy glow. "Todd Price –he's a freshman."

That captured my attention.

"What's he like?" I asked avidly.

"*Really* nice guy, we talked for a long time. He's the one in suspenders with black, curly hair. I'll point him out when go down if he's still around. Brad was there too." Her eyes darted to the framed photo on my nightstand. It was the snapshot of us taken at Christmas banquet. "How did things go over the summer?"

"We had an honest talk and decided we're just friends." I raised my chin and looked away. "It's fine. I'm good with that."

"Oh hun, I'm sorry it didn't work out." Bridget absently folded a pair of pants over a hanger and stuffed them into her closet. "You should see Declan."

"Who?"

"Met him in the lounge – he's a freshman too, except he's twenty-seven, brawny and medium height. You might like him!" She smiled broadly.

"Yeah. Maybe."

I didn't quite trust her judgment considering her own attraction to a guy in suspenders.

"Hellooo!" A girl walked into our room wearing a red, checkered skirt and a loose black sweater. "Just making the rounds to introduce myself!"

"Come in!" said Bridget in her usual friendly manner.

The girl – Patricia Clout – sat on the end of Bridget's bed and told us she was right next-door with Anna and Ellen.

"Nice to meet you," I began with a friendly smile. "Are you a first year student?"

"I am."

"Bridget and I are in our second year. You might find dormitory life a little challenging at first but it's not too bad once you get used to it."

"It won't be a problem for me," said Patricia with her head held high. "I'm a university graduate, and I stayed in residence."

"Er…that's nice." I replied.

I doubted her university experience would be the same as staying in this tiny private college…but kudos to her if she felt prepared. Who knows, it probably would help.

"So…who's this?" Patricia meandered over to my little table and picked up my photo. "Your boyfriend?"

"No," I shrugged.

She gave me a funny look. "No?" she echoed. "Hmm."

I could see why she might not believe me…since our colors matched and we sat very closely in the picture.

"You'd make a cute couple." She put the frame down and headed to the door. "It was good meeting you, toodle-loo!"

"Is it just me?" I asked Bridget when Patricia was gone, "or is she a little strange?"

I mean…you don't go digging into one's personal life and start speculating five minutes after meeting them – do you?

"Patricia's fine," said Bridget as she pushed her suitcase beneath the bed. "She strikes me as sanguine. Whereas you're more sanguine-choleric, so she's bound to rub you the wrong way. You have to adjust."

"What are you?"

Bridget grinned. "Phlegmatic."

Ok. I don't know if I like the definition of choleric.

I looked it up, and while this personality type has remarkable traits like being efficient, passionate, and task oriented...I'm *not* aggressive, dictatorial or tyrannical. Bridget doesn't know anything.

The lounge buzzed with students and there were many unfamiliar faces. I spotted Darren chatting up a cute brunette freshman over by the vending machine, and there was a female crowd gathered in the opposite corner of the room like a swarm of flies.

"It's Declan!" Bridget whispered and pointed at the assembly. "Come on." She elbowed her way through the throng of freshmen and I followed.

It has to be said, Declan was hot. He was about 5'9," so not as tall as I normally liked, but he was certainly attractive and charismatic. You could tell by the volume of female admirers.

"And this," Declan announced as he brandished a picture, "is after I shot it between the eyes."

The photo of the dead, bloodied buck went past my face and I shrank back, feeling sick, and just a little bit faint.

"Wow Declan, you're a wonderful hunter!" Everyone shifted as girls toward the back shuffled in and craned their necks to get a closer look. I suspected they were trying to see Declan – not the kill. It was *gross*.

I had to leave.

"Don't go!" Declan noticed my retreat. "You'll want to see this next one!"

"No thanks!" I threw back over my shoulder. "I'm an animal lover."

"Morbid," Bridget muttered just behind me.

I sat alone in the grass later that day, soaking up the sun with my legs stretched toward the river, when a figure overshadowed me.

"Sorry about earlier," said a deep, male voice. "I'd have been more discreet with the pictures if I realized someone might get upset."

I looked up and smiled at Declan. "Thanks for that…but I could have avoided it by asking someone what we were looking at."

"Are you a vegetarian?" Declan joined me on the grass and draped his arms over his knees.

"I eat meat." I grinned. "I just don't like to know how it got on my plate…do you hunt a lot?"

"During open season, yes, along with fishing and camping. What are your hobbies?"

I hesitated and stared at the water. This was a great opportunity to get to know one another, but not the time to spook him out by mentioning wedding gowns and floral arrangements. He'd think I was a marriage-crazed man-hunter, even though it was only a healthy interest related to my current job and future career. It probably wouldn't bother a mature man like Declan, but I remained silent and racked my brain.

Declan leaned back on his arms as he studied me with warm, golden brown eyes.

There are plenty of activities I enjoy.

It's just a shame I couldn't think of any right away.

"I read," I eventually supplied without divulging that I love the *Modern Bride* magazine. Because…of *course* I like novels also. It goes without saying.

"Which genres?"

Gravel crunched behind us and I turned to see Patricia sauntering over to the men's dormitory, just as Brad came out and walked past her to the main building. Her head whipped around and she immediately changed directions.

I frowned.

What's she doing?

Declan waved a hand in front of my face and I blinked.

"Sorry," I said. "What were we saying?"

Brad stepped through the door with Patricia hot on his heels, and Declan observed me, with his hand resting thoughtfully against his chin. He raised a perceptive brow, and I inwardly groaned.

Crap.

Bridget and Todd began dating in the first semester, and while I was pleased for her, I found the situation a tiny bit awkward. She became this dating guru, always giving me all sorts of tips and advice. She wanted to help me get a guy also, and it was very sweet – I just wished she would help a little less. There was no way in a million years that she and I would attract a boyfriend using the same methods. Todd actually liked her mismatched clothes and hiked up socks, which is kind of romantic when you think about it. They say love is blind, and in this case it was clearly true, because Bridget couldn't see any fault in Todd either.

He tried to be chummy with me because he dated my roommate, which would have been fine under normal circumstances. But his idea of being 'chummy' was to annoy me to death. Like the time he dropped a spider in my lap when I was with Bridget and Brad in the cafeteria. A *real* spider. I couldn't stop screaming, and that was after I jumped up, spilled my water everywhere, and ran to the other end of the room like a mental patient. Everyone stared at me, except Brad who scowled at Todd.

I retaliated of course, but it was a bad idea. I should have just had a quiet word with Bridget and let her deal with him.

Getting even made Todd worse, and I decided to minimize my reactions. I figured he'd get bored and eventually stop.

And even though I wanted to scald him with my coffee the time he dropped an ice cube down the back of my shirt – I didn't. I needed to remain peaceful for Bridget. I knew everything would eventually blow over. It had to.

"Isn't Todd *sweet*?" Bridget burst into the room one evening with an armful of flowers and a silver thermos cradled in her other arm. "Look at these angel wing begonias! They're beautiful!" Bridget's face was alive with excitement as she breathed in the scent. She and Todd had already been dating for several weeks now, and he always bought her little gifts like this.

I looked at the greenish-red and slightly wilted weeds that she placed on her dresser and forced a smile. It was difficult for me to think of Todd as 'sweet' since I was accustomed to his torture tactics. For all I knew, those flowers were smeared with poison ivy in the hope that I would go over and smell them too.

"They're…nice," I managed and stepped into my fuzzy purple slippers. "I'm getting a drink; want one?"

"No thanks," Bridget uncapped her thermos and sighed dreamily. "Todd made coffee." The steam wafted up as she inhaled.

"Watch out for the laxative," I muttered, then ran out the door before she could offer any. Not that Todd would necessarily poison his own girlfriend to get at me, but I wasn't about to take a chance. He was very sneaky.

As I walked through the hall toward the stairwell, I paused by our neighboring bedroom. There was a lot of giggling going on inside, which didn't interest me at all until I heard my name. I know I did. I sidled up to the door.

Patricia hadn't done anything unpleasant since the start of school, but I knew she was the one talking about me. There was something about her that made me wary. I mean, Patricia seemed friendly enough with all the rides she offered to school in her white car (which I generally declined since Brad and I were in the habit of walking together), and she smiled often…but the smiles felt false. Like there was a current of animosity running right beneath them. She also struck up conversation regularly, but somehow we always ended up discussing Brad. Well – she did. I call it prying.

The girl was creepy, plain and simple. And it wasn't just a personality clash like Bridget suggested. I could sense her beady gaze following me as I roamed the dormitory. Why was she always staring? It was *exactly* how Snow White must have felt when she found herself running through that dark forest with the frightening yellow eyes watching her. If they ever come out with another variation of that movie, I'd recommend they cast Patricia in the woods behind the bushes. She'd even scare the hunter.

I know I seem a little paranoid, but with the type of people I tend to encounter – can you really blame me?

There was too much laughter and cavorting in the room to hear anything specific, so I continued down until I reached the dimly lit dining hall where I grabbed a Styrofoam cup from a stack on the counter, and poured myself some tap water.

I was all alone in the cafeteria. Just me and the hum of a coin-operated washing machine as clothes swished about. I took a sip of cool water and leaned against the granite countertop as a girl in striped flannel pj's came out from one of the rooms to check on her laundry in the little alcove beside the bathroom.

"Hi," I said as I took another sip.

"Hi," she replied before returning to her room.

That was me last year. I smiled. Being upstairs was so much better.

I finished my water and dropped the cup into the garbage bin by the wall, then rounded the corner to the stairwell.

A scream lodged in my throat and I froze. There was a menacing hobo crouched on the bottom step. The top of his head was bald and dirty except for white bits of hair at the sides of his face, which stuck out in all directions – and his rough, gnarled hands lunged forward to grab me.

"Help!" I shrieked and backed away. "Somebody help me!"

In blind panic, I picked up a nearby chair and took a swing at the old pervert just as the girl in pj's came running out of her room, armed with a hair dryer.

I was still screaming.

"It's *ME,*" the man yelled and shielded his face. "Stop freaking out, it's me, Todd!"

"*Todd?*" With my heart still thundering in my chest, I dropped the chair and pulled at the mask to get a look, then let it slap back into place, hard.

"Ow!" He put the mask on top of his head and rubbed his nose. "What'd you do that for?"

"What's *wrong* with you?" I throbbed with rage.

"Relax, it was just a bit of fun – and I wasn't trying to scare *you*, specifically." He nodded at the other girl. "It would have been just as fun to scare her."

Fun? Why on earth would anyone think something like this was ok or fun? It's like the time my dad dressed in an old man costume, similar to the one Todd wore, and chased his own mother down the street when she walked home from church one evening. I'm sorry, but that's not how you get your kicks. Poor Nan was quite traumatized until she realized it was dad, and then took her purse and beat him over the head with it as he tried to run back to his car. This story is almost legend now in my family, but the point is, this happened *within my family,* and dad has grown up a lot since then. This wasn't acceptable behavior from Todd, a guy I hardly knew. What did I ever do to him?

"I've had enough!" I ripped the mask from his head, tossed it on the ground and kicked it. "I'm not playing anymore, ok? Just stop!"

"You're not supposed to be here," contributed the haughty girl in pj's. She waved the hair dryer menacingly at Todd. "Get out before I report you."

It was time I had a word with Bridget.

I made it to the winter months without any further incidents with Todd. I should have had the 'I love you but can't stand your boyfriend talk with Bridget much sooner. Although I didn't put it quite like that. It was more along the lines of 'he'd better stop or I'm going to kill him,' and then she took care of it. She didn't want to be widowed...or whatever it's called when your boyfriend dies. And there was more than one way to take him out – Brad had offered on a few occasions.

"Are you sure you don't want me to rough him up a bit? Make sure he gets the message?" Brad slapped his fist into his other hand as we made tracks in the snow. It was an early Monday morning and quite dark as we trekked up the hill.

"So, you'll take care of my dirty work, like in the mafia? Does that make me the Godfather?" I flashed my teeth at him as we passed a street lamp. "It's ok...I know Bridget had a good talk with him and he won't do it again. He's actually been very tolerable without the constant tricks up his sleeve."

Just then a car rolled up and braked beside us, sliding a little in the slush.

"Well hello there," Patricia purred through the open window. Anna occupied the passenger seat and Ellen was in the back. "Fancy a ride?"

Brad and I exchanged looks as if to say *why not?* and we headed toward the road.

"*Actually*," Patricia unlocked the doors, "I only have room for one of you. Anna, get in the back and let Brad have the front. If you don't mind," she added at Anna's contemptuous glare. "His legs are longer."

"I'm sure we can get Reanne in there too," said Brad mildly. He peered into the back of her car where there was plenty of space for the both of us, and reached for the door handle.

There was a sharp intake of breath.

"A seatbelt is broken," said Patricia hurriedly. "It's not safe...or legal. I can only take one of you."

"All right," Brad moved aside. "Then Reanne can go."

Patricia's face snapped in shock, and before I could get in (not that I would have without Brad), Patricia rolled up her creaky window and the little white car gunned up the hill. A puff of smoke shot out from the exhaust pipe and the taillights blinked bright red as the vehicle quickly rounded the corner and skidded out of sight. I was amazed the maniac bothered to break at all.

Later that week, Bridget asked me if Brad and I wanted to accompany her and Todd to the mall. The four of us had been hanging out more often, and we agreed to go. I really enjoyed these outings because it felt like we were on a double date. We weren't of course, but it was nice sitting next to Brad on the bus with his arm comfortably draped around the back of my seat.

"I'm getting a new sweater from Zack's Department." Bridget and Todd were in the seat in front of us and she gazed at him with adoring eyes. "Will you help me pick one Toddy-boo?"

He kissed her nose, which was cherry red from a cold she was getting over. "Of course Bridgey-bear."

Brad snorted and I elbowed him in the ribs.

Bridget glared at him. "*What*?"

"Nothing," Brad cleared his throat. "Carry on…Bridgey-bear."

The expression on her face was comical.

Oh no.

I pursed my lips, but it was too late. A chuckle escaped.

"Traitor," Bridget mumbled in my direction.

"Oh, come on Bridge, don't be so sensitive." I patted her shoulder. "The nicknames are…endearing."

Todd turned Bridget's chin back toward him and their gazes locked. "I think *you're* endearing," he whispered tenderly.

I looked on wistfully. It was getting a little too sappy for my taste – but they were really cute together. And there wasn't even the prospect of having that for myself any time soon, which was a kind of disheartening.

"We're here." Todd offered his hand to Bridget and they filed off the bus first.

"After you," said Brad.

"So I guess we're going to Zack's first, then?" I asked once outside. "Bridget?" I looked around, thinking she might have been waiting just inside the entryway. It was empty.

Brad laughed. "I think they ditched us."

"I think you're right. Who's the traitor now!"

Brad and I walked around until we found a cozy little Starbucks.

"I'll have a tall Caramel Frappuccino, please," I said to the girl with blue hair and a metal bar through her lip. I *love* those (Frappuccino's...*not* the piercing or blue hair).

"You do know that's a *cold* drink, right?" Brad smirked as I inserted my debit card into the machine.

"Yeess."

So what?

He tugged the fur-lined hood of my coat. "You might want to keep this on."

"I'll be fine." I waved him off airily. "I always get this when I come here."

I grabbed a few napkins as Brad ordered his drink, and then we sat on large plushy chairs. The window beside us was spray painted with snowflakes and there was a soft jazzy tune playing. I took my first, delicious sip of Frappuccino with whipped cream.

Oh that's nice.

There were a few others in Starbucks: a guy studying a textbook at a nearby table, two girls having a quiet conversation on the sofa, and a guy reading a newspaper in another oversized chair. The atmosphere was perfect for all sorts of situations. Schoolwork, relaxing…I angled a look at Brad…going on a date.

I placed my drink on the table and rubbed my chilly hands together, and Brad slid his untouched cup toward me.

"Try mine."

I eyed it. His drink looked yummy too. It had a big dollop of whipped cream with chocolate shavings generously sprinkled on top. He nudged it a little closer.

"Well…ok." My hands instantly warmed as I put them around the cup and I sipped slowly to avoid burning my tongue.

I couldn't believe it; there was something better than the Frappuccino! What a wonderful blend of coffee, chocolate and a hint of something else. "This is so good!" I had a little more. "What is it?"

"White Chocolate Mocha." Brad wiped some of the dripping whipped cream from the Frappuccino, which he then took for himself. "Let's trade."

"Ok! Thanks!"

Brad was so sweet it was a shame we weren't on an actual date. He knew I'd get cold and pre-empted me by ordering a drink he thought I would like. Did he even *want* the Frappuccino? Chivalry obviously wasn't as dead as some would think.

I sighed contentedly as the warm liquid settled in my stomach, and when we finished, we headed back to the mall to look for Bridget and Todd who were nowhere to be found.

Brad and I assumed they made their own way back to the dorms, but Bridget wasn't in our room by the time I returned and there was no sign that she had been there, either. I thought there would be a few *Zack's Department* bags littering her bed with the odd lumpy sweater or pantsuit tumbling out of them, but her stuff was neat.

Mine wasn't.

Someone had completely trashed it.

I surveyed the wreckage in growing disbelief. Sheets and pillows were scattered everywhere – the mattress hung halfway off the frame, looking like a wild animal had attacked it. I was completely dumbfounded by what I saw. Most of my family photos were missing from the wall; my toiletries were strewn across the dressing table, and a plastic bottle of shampoo was cracked, with the white, oozing liquid seeping out into my favorite boar bristle hairbrush.

I drew in a sharp breath.

Oh my God I've been robbed!

But then – why didn't they ransack Bridget's things? I frantically rummaged through my drawers to see if anything had been taken, but I couldn't tell. The clothes that had been so neatly folded were now a rumpled, tangled mess. Nothing *appeared* to be missing…

If not a robbery, then what?

Fear suddenly clawed at my throat and I found it difficult to breath. This wasn't a robbery; it was a message! An evil, malicious message.

"No!" I gasped as I clocked the bedside table. *Oh no, please not that...*

The only photo I had with Brad was ripped down the middle. Sharp, jagged edges separated our smiling faces and someone had painstakingly taken the time to put the pieces back into the frame, leaving a large gaping hole between us.

Oh. My. God.

I knew she was deranged! Didn't I say all along she was crazy? I need to...no. Oh no, no, no!

The doors to my wardrobe were slightly ajar. The psychopath defiled my closet! I rushed over, flung them open, and feverishly scanned the hangers.

I almost cried in relief – she left everything in there untouched, except for –

My heart stopped.

Where is my Chanel jacket and heels?

I picked my way through every hanger once more and they were definitely gone. I really was going to cry. Out of everything she could have taken, she stole my gifts from Rhonda, Jaden, and Lindsay. I plopped down onto the floor and dropped my head in my hands. Tears leaked out between my fingers. Even if I got them back, she probably vandalized them, just like she did with almost everything else in the room.

I sat dejectedly on the floor for what seemed like hours until I found myself staring, unfocused, at my hanging mattress. I finally noticed a piece of something poking out from just behind it, and with my heart thudding, I crawled over and pulled it out.

It was one of the heels!

I dipped my head to look further under the bed and my breath caught when I saw a dark mass near the wall. My fingers grazed a bit of fabric and with one swift yank, my tangled jacket and the other heel slid out, undamaged.

"What happened here?"

Patricia appeared in my room, seemingly from thin air, and spoke in a strangely calm monotone.

Oh God.

She was there to kill me.

I sprang up from my vulnerable position on the floor, my eyes wildly zipping about. She blocked the door! How would I escape? Her muscles tensed – the lioness was about to pounce.

This is it. My life is over. Goodbye cruel world…

I just waited for her to whip out a butcher's knife and for the scary music to begin. And ok – I've clearly seen too many movies – but she seriously freaked me out.

"Such a shame," Patricia clucked and bared her teeth in a supposedly sympathetic manner. *I* didn't buy it – the windows to her blackened soul revealed the truth. Her eyes were full of barely suppressed glee as she fixated on the ripped photograph, and something inside me snapped.

"You did it!" I spat in fury. "Get out of my room!"

Her lips curled. "Did you see me?"

I thought a moment.

"No," I said almost pleasantly. "But I got it all on tape with my hidden camera."

A jolt of panic flashed across her face before she called my bluff. "No you didn't." She skittered away without another word. And just the same as if I had walked in on her holding a smoking gun with a dead body at her feet, I had all the proof I needed. She did it. Of course she did.

Bridget arrived halfway through the cleanup process and helped. It took a solid two hours between the two of us to get things back to normal, and then we couldn't stop talking about Patricia.

"You were right," said Bridget, in awe. "She's crazy. You have to go to admin and tell them what she did."

"I would if I could but I don't think they'd believe me. You *know* they like her."

This was a problem. Even though Bridget finally knew the truth – that Patricia was a total nutcase – it wasn't apparent to anyone else. All the professors and those working in the office loved her, and I'd wager it was because she was a little older, acted like the dorm mother, and was willing to spy on other students. If someone broke a residence rule (such as arriving back at the building even a millisecond after Patricia locked the main doors at night), she would immediately report it. What a Nazi.

And – I haven't said anything because I've been trying to remain upbeat…but there were even incidents recently involving the phone. If anyone called for Patricia on the upper floor – she thought whoever answered the phone should search the entire building for her, even if she was all the way down in the cafeteria so she could take the call. Did anyone oblige? No! Why would they? If she wasn't in her room, she might not have been in the building either, and why would someone waste their time looking? The person could just call back later. Or she could call them back. This is how the phone operated for everyone, but it wasn't good enough for Patricia. Oh no. She had to go and arrange a meeting with the college administrators so that they could gather us all together and give a lecture on the rules of phone usage. These rules didn't seem to apply to *her*, though. When Brad called for me, she talked his ear off until he was forced to hang up, and then she never told me about it – Brad had to.

"We'll think of something," Bridget assured me as she fell into her bed and switched off the lamp. "Or she'll expose herself…you can't hide crazy for too long. Sooner or later it's going to come out."

"Yes…well. In the meantime, I'm getting a lock for my wardrobe and keeping all my stuff in it to avoid the sequel. 'Night Bridge, thanks for the help."

"Goodnight."

At breakfast, Brad was brooding. I joined him and Declan at the table with my plate of syrupy pancakes, and stifled a yawn. I felt a little tired and miserable myself, given the previous evening.

"Don't worry, Reanne," said Declan soothingly, "*we* love you."

I glanced at him in surprise as Brad speared a piece of bacon and crunched on it moodily. I guess Bridget filled them in, and it was nice to know they cared.

"Good morning, Brad!" Patricia crooned as she arrived at our table with her breakfast. "Can I offer you a ride to school this morning?"

The girl was relentless – like a steely-jawed dog refusing to give up a bone.

Brad ignored her and vacated the cafeteria. Patricia ran after him, her tray of food forgotten.

I couldn't help but wonder if she planted a tracking device on him. She always seemed to know exactly where Brad was, and she *always* showed up when I was with him. It was so annoying. I scowled at my pancakes as Declan stood.

He squeezed my shoulder as he strode past, and whispered, "Brad cares about you more than you think."

Chapter Nineteen

Gifts

What did that *mean*, exactly?

Brad cares about you more than you think.

As much as I wanted to, I couldn't get that statement from my mind. It swirled around, jumbling my thoughts all day long. Because the thing is, I knew Brad cared for me. We had become good friends and I was finally adjusting to the fact that that was all we were. So why would Declan say he cared about me more than I thought? Why now?

Had Brad said something to Declan indicating his feelings were growing stronger, perhaps? Or was it just an observation? And…so what if he did say something? As far as I was concerned, the dating break was still on, and I was moving on with my life (you hear that Declan? *Moving on!* No confusion).

But the fact is, I was confused, and Declan's statement momentarily put a wrench into my plans. Christmas was around the corner and I wanted to buy a little something for Brad, as his *friend*. But…now I wasn't sure I should.

I debated what to do for days and by the weekend I finally decided to put Declan's words from my mind. Pretend he never said them.

The gift I had planned was small, anyway. I was getting Brad a few items that would be meaningful to him, and enjoyable.

That's why I headed straight for the snack/candy aisle at *Zack's Department* while Bridget ventured off to pick out a gift for Todd.

I grabbed a bag of Reese's Peanut Butter Bites, and also dropped a can of Sour Cream and Onion Pringles into my rickety cart, then consulted my list.

His favorite snacks: check.

Next I headed toward the music/electronic section of the store. Brad mentioned previously that he liked jogging, and I was interested in buying him one of those iPod things for him to listen to while running.

I kept my head down as I moved through the shop because the racks of clothing were becoming more hideous with every section I passed. At one point I found myself surrounded by tent-like dresses. They were everywhere. Even the pants didn't look right with big stretchy bands across the tops. The atrocity overwhelmed me and I tried desperately to find my way out of the dreadful maze of oversized clothing.

I finally stopped to get my bearings and gasped. The yellow shirt in front of me had huge gaudy zippers over the bust area. *Why?* This couldn't be proper, even for a place like *Zack's.*

My head spun as I caught sight of a sign hanging above me. *Maternity Wear.*

Oh my.

It was worse than the granny underwear aisle to my left. And ok – I know it must be extremely challenging to find flattering clothing when expecting anyway, but surely pregnant women have a better selection than *this* lot.

A heavily pregnant woman waddled past me just then, and headed for a candy-striped tarp.

I hyperventilated as I shielded my eyes.

I had to get out of there, quickly, before I made the rash decision to never have kids.

Once I escaped the ugly-fest, I stumbled into another section, which thankfully, wasn't half bad. I modeled the shiny, dangling necklaces and admired myself in the mirrors. I especially loved the lilac feather boa that I draped across my neck and shoulders.

"Hello dahling. You look simply *mahvelous.*" I winked at myself in the mirror and placed a hand on my hip.

I have to have this.

It was the best thing in the entire place. Shopping is a bit like treasure hunting. Drop me off at any dump and if there is something worth finding – I'll find it. I rolled my cart to the nearest checkout and paid for my boa in excitement. I couldn't wait to show Bridget!

"Excuse me!" the clerk called. "Do you want to purchase the Pringles and Reese's?"

Oops. I left them in the cart. And there was still the matter of the iPod.

A faint blush crept into my cheeks as I retraced my steps. "Yes, I'll get them. May I leave them for a minute while I grab another item?"

"Sure."

"Great! And where exactly are the electronics?"

I didn't buy an iPod. The crazy thing was pretty expensive. Well, the nicer ones were. For a moment I considered getting one anyway then thought better of it. That would've definitely conveyed the wrong message.

Instead I ended up trawling through a bin of miscellaneous items. I searched through the assortment of knickknacks, not quite knowing what I was searching for, until I came across these really cute mirrors with poems written on them. The first one I saw had a romantic sonnet scrawled down the middle in cursive script, with little daisies etched on either side. I really liked it, but hastily put it down. It wasn't a suitable gift…unless I wanted Brad to run screaming in the opposite direction.

Not the goal.

I continued digging and found something better.

~~**iPod.**~~

Friendship poem: check.

"Show me what you bought!" Enthused Bridget when we reconnected outside of *Zack's*.

"Look at this, it's fabulous!" Excitedly, I presented the feather boa with a flourish. "Ta daaaa."

She stared at it blankly.

I waved it around, "Ta DAAA."

"Nice stringy thing," said Bridget, without much interest.

Stringy thing???

"What did you buy for *Brad?* You know…the reason we came here today?"

"*Obviously*, I was going to show you that. I just er…the boa was on top. So naturally it came out first. Here!" I shoved the boa aside before she could comment further. "I got him these, along with something else already at the dorm."

"What's the other thing?"

"I made a copy of a CD I have – Brad likes the artist – and I wrote a personalized note on the back cover. Think he'll like it?"

"Definitely!" Bridget became animated as she reached into her purse and presented me with a small manila folder. "Especially after you've added this! There's one for you too."

I couldn't speak.

I held the snapshot of Brad and I from our first Christmas banquet. The one I thought was lost forever. Emotion must have played across my face as I was struck by an overwhelming sense of gratitude and humility. I had the most amazing, loving family in the entire world…and if that wasn't enough – I had thoughtful friends, too. What did I ever do to deserve them?

"Bridge, this means a lot, thank you." I hugged her tightly and disguised a sniffle with a laugh. "How'd you get this?"

"It was still on my digital camera – I made copies just now at the photo center." Bridget smiled in satisfaction then abruptly turned serious. "I can always get you another one of course, but still – you might want to hide that from you know who."

His favorite snacks: check.
~~iPod.~~
Friendship poem: check.
CD/Note: check.
Picture: check.

Now I just had to give it to him.

I did it the evening before I flew home. Brad sat alone in the darkened lounge, with the only light provided by the glowing Christmas tree and the tinkling lights along the windows. I stood behind him for a few moments watching the colors, wondering how to approach. Wondering how he'd react. I had already given

Bridget her gift (a Dior perfume set), but that was different. Our friendship was set in stone. I wasn't sure how this would go down with Brad, given the information (or conjecture?) I received from Declan.

I set the box quietly on the ground and covered his eyes with my hands. "Guess who," I disguised my voice.

He spun around.

"Hey," I picked up the parcel, "this is for you. Merry Christmas."

A grin split Brad's face in the flickering light as he took it. "You didn't have to do that!"

I shrugged. "I know. I wanted to."

Brad gave the box a little shake and the chips and bag of chocolates rattled.

"But you can't open it until after I leave, ok? Tomorrow." I nodded firmly. If he hated the gift, I wouldn't be there to witness his initial reaction. Although, unfortunately…I'd also miss his face if he loved it.

Brad gazed at me curiously for a while, then at last agreed.

The next day…

I fished in my carry-on and tossed the bridal magazine I purchased at the airport to Rhonda. "Check out page thirty-seven. I think this bridesmaid dress would suit just about anyone!"

Believe me, an everyone gown is almost impossible to find.

Rhonda flipped through with lightning speed. "Good pick…how do you think this might sit on, say, a pregnant woman?"

My head snapped up. "Is there something you need to *tell me*?" I demanded, glancing suspiciously at her stomach, which I couldn't see beneath her long sweater.

"Hey now." Rhonda looked a little miffed. "*I'm* not pregnant…but Erin is!"

"Whoo!" I squealed. She was having a baby.

A baby!

"What happened? Last I heard they were considering a trial separation."

"Well, Erin and I got together and had a long chat about their situation, and she blamed a lot of their problems on Alan at first, but then cried and said she loved him really, and he was the best husband a woman could ask for." Rhonda lowered her voice discreetly, as though Erin would walk in at any moment. "I think it was the hormones, poor thing. She was having injections."

"*Injections?*" I stared at Rhonda incredulously. "For what?"

"In vitro. But I asked her 'what's the rush?' They're still newlyweds with plenty of time to have a baby. I gently prompted her to focus more on their relationship and enjoy her marriage. Erin calmed down, said I was right, and the next thing I know, she's pregnant! And they weren't actively trying any longer."

"Wow…maybe it was all the pressure they put on themselves that prevented it from happening before. It must have been the *stress.* I'm really glad for her!"

Oh my gosh, I was going to be an aunt! Not a *literal* aunt, obviously, but I wanted to help Erin by providing free baby-sitting all the time. I'd get to cuddle the baby all day long…and give it back when it cried nonstop at night. You see? Win win!

Erin would get to sleep during the day.

I was glad Erin and Alan patched things up. You know, love is all that matters in this crazy world, and everyone deserves a second chance! In fact, if we could all just learn to *forgive* one another, the world would be a better –

"Hello!" Rhonda waved a hand in front of my face, pulling me from my world peace and baby bliss reverie. "I *said*, what's the deal with Patricia? Have things smoothed over, or did you retaliate?"

Right.

Most people deserve a second chance.

Not her.

"Drinks are ready!" Jaden bellowed from the lower floor where everyone waited to play *Pictionary*.

"Ok!" Rhonda and I yelled in unison.

After the fun and laughter ebbed away, I booted up my Mac while the rest of the household slept. Just for fun. Out of idle curiosity. I wasn't looking for anything specific in my inbox at 1:00 a.m., I promise. I just couldn't sleep – it was probably all the hot chocolate I had.

My stomach knotted up as I spotted an email I had no interest in whatsoever...

Subject: First Holiday Contact

Reanne! You sweet angel – you really shouldn't have! I opened your gift this morning and it was, of course...amazingly perfect. Every part played a role in this overall perfection; the way you wrapped it was interesting and the shoe box totally threw me off (just kidding- it was the whole roll of tape you used to seal it up in fact), the Pringles, and the Reese's, the friendship memento, picture, the lovely note on the CD cover...and the CD itself which I've listened to already – in the room, in the car, and it's now here where I've listened to it as I sat typing earlier on the computer. I have only one misgiving about this gift...

I really don't know how I'm going to top it. Shucks you little rotter – you seem to have a knack for winning don't you? (That's right, laugh.)

...Of course that doesn't mean I won't try.

I wasn't up in the morning to thank you personally as you guessed...the reason was: Declan and I stayed up terribly late having a deep and highly involving discussion. I finally went to bed thinking about something/someone I won't mention here (it was a good thing, mind you), and woke up rather late (sheepish grin).

I have faith that your flight went well...and by now your jaw is terribly sore from talking nonstop and on fast-forward for a few hours consecutively with your wonderful family and I look forward to hearing all about it. See you online and...

MERRY CHRISTMAS!

Brad

I couldn't stop smiling. He loved the gift! Why did I ever doubt it? Of course...now I wished I *had* seen his face when he opened the package.

The break went by in a whirlwind of family activities and long shifts at the Bridal store. I thrived in my work environment and felt so blessed to have seasonal employment with a boss who loved me. Brenda and I got along brilliantly, and she often said I was a girl after her own heart. Although, she might have liked me a little less if she knew I tried on gowns after closing hours. Then again, maybe not. It was my experience *in* the gowns that made me better at selling them. I know it.

I tried on the Vivienne Westwood gown frequently, with its blossoming flowered shoulder strap, bulbous skirt, and exquisite lace bodice. It was beautiful. A work of art...a *masterpiece,* if you will. I became this enchanting waterfall maiden when I wore it and taking it off was torturous.

Bridezilla finally bought it.

She couldn't make up her mind about what she wanted, yet again, so I described my dream dress to her one day for inspiration.

"You're engaged?" She stared at my bare left hand, amused.

"No," I shrugged. "I'm just in love with the Vivien Westwood. Let me show you."

Reverently, I brought out the gown and helped Bridezilla into it. The moment she saw her reflection, she was done. The search was over, thank God.

There was a minor meltdown concerning the veil afterwards, but that issue was easily resolved and I got a big, fat commission from the sale.

I knew exactly how I would spend it!

Chapter Twenty

Abominable Snowgirl

I surveyed my closet back at the dorm, wondering why the doors wouldn't close properly. Sure I went shopping, but I didn't get *that* much. I didn't even spend all of my commission…like…only half. This was truly puzzling.

"Can I help?" Bridget's expression was comical.

I grunted with effort as I pushed the doors together. "That's…ok," I puffed. "I think I just…about…have it." With one final shove the doors clicked closed and I looped a large metal padlock through the plastic handles. I pocketed the key in triumph.

Ha, Patricia. Try to bust through that!

"What'd you do," Bridget laughed as her eyes swiveled toward my dresser, which was laden with shoeboxes, "buy out an entire mall?"

"Oh har-di-har. I only took slight advantage of Boxing Week sales. It would have been insane not to!"

"*Slight* advantage?" She echoed. "Then why are all your clothes hanging out of the drawers?"

293

Honestly, she exaggerates. It was just the odd little belt or shirtsleeve sticking out, and that's because I hadn't folded them properly. They didn't count.

"So," I said, "did you buy *anything* during the sales? Please don't tell me you wasted the fifty percent off opportunity!"

"I did get this one thing." Bridget pulled a simple silver chain from beneath her shirt and let the shimmering butterfly at the end rest against her chest.

"Very pretty – "

"It's exquisite!" Interrupted a pretentious voice.

I cringed. The terrorist was in my room. Again.

Patricia stooped in front of Bridget, and peered at her necklace. "Can I hold it?"

I made *don't do it* neck slashing motions behind her back.

"Um…I…" Bridget reached for the right excuse, "…maybe some other time. I'd rather not take it off right now."

"Very well," said Patricia. "I came by to let Reanne know that someone is waiting for her downstairs." She turned on her heel with a martyred air and disappeared through the door.

"Guard my stuff Bridge," I said, only half joking. "I'm heading down."

Brad leaned against the doorframe at the bottom of the stairs in dark denim jeans with his leather jacket, which was wet with snowflakes.

I had a feeling it was Brad. Patricia wouldn't have bothered for anyone else.

"Hi," I looked at him quizzically as he backed into the hall until he stood outside the office. "What's up?"

He grinned as he pulled a huge silver bag with red tissue paper from behind his back and handed it to me. I laughed in delight and surprise as my eyes flew up to meet Brad's. Right away, I plunged my hands through the layers of crinkled tissue paper and began pushing them aside. As I rooted around in the bag, I darted a happy glance at Brad to see him sneaking out through the front door with an ear-to-ear smile on his face.

Hmm, so he didn't want to watch me open it, either.

And no wonder!

I caught sight of the *Victoria's Secret* label on the tissue paper and nearly dropped the bag in shock. He went into *Victoria's Secret*? Oh my God. What could he have possibly bought? I crammed the paper back into the bag and raced up the stairs before anyone could see, meanwhile picturing Brad surrounded by lingerie and shopping women. Actually...Brad surrounded by lingerie and *towering* over all the shopping women. He must have stuck out like a sore thumb. He must have been really uncomfortable in there.

What's in this bag!

I was dying to find out, and also – *where* did he even find a *Victoria's Secret*?

I jammed the key into the padlock and hid behind my closet doors as I tossed paper onto the floor.

"Oh!"

I'm not sure what I expected to find, exactly, but it certainly wasn't the cute, fuzzy teddy bear that greeted me. The large sappy eyes stole my heart, and it had the cutest black button nose. A few scented beads tumbled to the floor as I lifted the bear to my face and inhaled the flowery fragrance. The bear was soft and cuddly against my cheek…and adorably pudgy. It reminded me of…

"Your name is Theodore," I told my new little friend. From Alvin and the Chipmunks. "Teddy for short."

He got a prominent position on the bed, right next to my new banquet photo. *Victoria's Secret* was stitched in red on the bottom of his foot. How perfect is that? I would never forget this.

Next I pulled a pale pink sweater from the bag. It was thick and warm, and Brad obviously spent a lot more on his gift than I had. I slipped the sweater over the shirt I wore and put my hands in the front pocket. There was a folded paper inside.

Dear Reanne,

Merry Christmas. I hope this keeps you warm throughout the following months. Maybe now you can stop stealing my jacket. Kidding!

Brad

I didn't want to take the sweater off and almost went to bed in it, it was so comfy, but I eventually got into my pj's and settled in beside Theodore with a good book. Patricia chose that moment to walk into my room uninvited, and her eyes immediately spotted my prized bear like a hawk.

"Is that from Brad?" She ogled the bear then raked her eyes over my photograph. "Is this your *shrine* to him?"

She came further into the room, sat on the edge of the bed, and suddenly her demeanor changed and she was telling me the shrine was *nice*.

Huh?

I stared at her, frozen.

The girl was deranged.

Seriously. It's the only reason I didn't get even with her for trashing my room. I mean, let's say I retaliated by shaving her eyebrows while she slept (gosh it was tempting!). Would my body have been pulled from the river shortly thereafter? In fact, who's to say she wasn't going to off me right now? I pulled the blanket higher as Patricia went off on a tangent about what Christmas was like with four older brothers.

Her voice was animated as she spoke and the anecdotes about her brothers were actually kind of funny, I noticed. I found myself slowly lowering the blanket and listening, because despite my misgivings, she was beginning to sound like a normal girl from a quirky family. In fact, she sounded a little like…me.

Wow, was I really relating to *Patricia?* It made me question whether or not I truly had her pegged, and if she really destroyed my room. It's not like I had proof.

Right then – it seemed entirely possible that I misjudged her. Maybe she was just a normal girl who became enamored with Brad (I knew all too well how easily *that* could happen), and I had been taking her comments the wrong way.

Or not.

I wasn't sure what to think.

The next morning was the same. Patricia came out of a bathroom stall behind me and said I looked great in my pink sweater, without a hint of sarcasm.

"Uh…thanks," I said a little stiltedly, because – what was I supposed to say?

"It compliments your complexion," she added.

Ok, it's possible I misjudged her, but something wasn't quite right here…did she fall and crack her head?

I brushed my teeth and pondered this as Patricia continued to stare at my reflection, unsmiling, until at last it became clear to me. It was *so* obvious; I don't know why I didn't see it before.

Patricia had a personality disorder. Any moment now she'd reenact a scene from *Fatal Attraction.*

I resisted the urge to hurry from the bathroom, although I did keep a close eye on the chopstick in her hair in case she tried to impale me with it.

Brad's head was down as I sailed into the cafeteria and joined the breakfast line. I waited for him to look up and see me in the sweater he bought. He didn't. He kept eating.

Oh well. He'll see soon enough.

The guy in front of me moved forward and I smiled at Fran, the cook, as she dropped a strip of bacon onto my plate. "May I have a bit more bacon, please?" I asked with a friendly grin.

Fran scowled at me. "There *are* other people you know."

My smile died away. Gee, talk about stingy.

Well – no biggie. Fran was usually very nice, and we're all entitled to a bad morning here and there. I moved along and went for the next item.

"Those aren't ready yet!" the grump snapped as I reached for a freshly baked bread roll, which, by the way, looked perfectly fine to me.

O-kaaay. Would I get *any* breakfast? I waited until Fran glared at a student reaching for a boiled egg, before I snatched a bun. I stacked my waffles just as quickly then hotfooted it to Brad's table.

"Hey you!" I chirped, sitting across from him.

The look on Brad's face made my day. I was so very glad I wore the sweater.

I had the best day *ever*.

No really, it was one of the best days of my life. Who would have thought one little sweater could create so much magic?

From the moment I sat at that ugly brown table with Brad in the morning, to dumping my books on the bed after class, everything went so well. Brad flirted with and smiled at me constantly throughout the day. The spark was back! Although let's be truthful – it never really left.

Now if only I can figure out how to wear the sweater more often without it being too obvious...

"Your serve!" Bridget called out.

With my head up in the clouds, I had difficulty concentrating on table tennis that evening, but it was ok, because Bridget wasn't very good at it. She had a tendency to pop her tongue out and wiggle her bum every time the ball came near...as if *that* would help her hit it. Sometimes her paddle did connect with the ball, but I'm positive it was sheer luck. There really was no competition here, however Bridget always took her lack of coordination in stride, and cracked jokes until we clutched our stomachs with tears streaming down our faces. So playing with her was always fun!

"Ok Bridge – it's coming at ya."

The ball *very slowly* sailed through the air (it was only fair) and bounced once on the other side of the net. Bridget aligned her paddle with the ball as if it would actually connect – *ha ha* – as Declan entered the hall behind her.

WHACK.

Bridget actually hit it! I scrambled to make the return, and then she hit it again. And again. She kept sending the ball back until *I* missed it.

"You've been practicing!" I said, impressed.

"Hey Reanne, can I steal you for a minute?" Declan was in the lounge now, standing beside Bridget. "There's something I want to discuss with you."

"Ok, sure. Do you mind, Bridge?"

"No, go ahead."

I tossed my paddle onto the table, strode toward Declan then stopped. Todd ducked into the library behind Declan, with a strange smile. When I looked at Declan again, he had the same weird expression.

"Actually," I retrieved my paddle, "I'll just finish this game first."

"Come now," he persisted, "it will only take a second."

The library door creaked and alarm bells sounded in my head.

"No," I backed away. "I don't trust you."

I shrieked as Declan shot forward, suddenly throwing me over his shoulder and locking my legs against his chest.

"Put me *down*!" I sputtered in outrage, pounding his back with my fists.

"*Todd*?" Bridget's voice swelled with fury as he danced out into the hall, cackling with glee. "Stop this right now!" she thundered. "Declan! Put her down!"

Both men ignored her.

I wiggled and slapped Declan as hard as I could, also digging my chin into his shoulder.

It hurt my chin.

"Take her outside..." Todd doled out instructions.

"Stop now!" Bridget shouted, pulling Todd's arm.

"...You get the door," Declan replied.

No. They are not *doing this to me.*

I grabbed the library doorframe as it rushed past my face and latched on as Todd took a picture.

I squeezed my eyes closed. *He's dead, he's dead, he's dead.*

"Go Declan!" Todd clicked his tongue, like he would at a horse.

"Can't man. She's holding onto something. I don't want to hurt her."

"I got this," Todd sniggered as he tugged my arm. He frowned when I didn't let go.

Come on Poligrip. Please...

Todd pried at my hands. One slipped off but I put it back as he worked on the other hand. Then he went around and pulled at my feet. A shoe came off. The guys began working together.

Don't...let...go...

My fingers were burning and starting to slide.

"Nooo!"

One hand fell away and Declan pinned it. The other swiftly followed and the glass window in the library door came into view. "Brad!" I called out desperately as I caught a glimpse of him at a computer. "BRAD!"

The patterned carpet swirled before my eyes. I fell against Declan's back and felt a blast of cold air as they hauled me through the door. I made another frantic grab for the second doorframe and winced as my finger snagged.

"Todd, *stop!*" Bridget yelled. "I mean it – I'll break up with you if you don't!"

Her fiery threat fell on deaf ears. They dropped me into a snowdrift.

The cold seeped through my sweater and I sprung up, looking like an abominable snow thing. In a daze, I brushed the clumps of snow from my hair and began my agitated one-footed hop toward the dorm.

Todd's camera continued to flash as Declan scooped me up in his arms and carried me to the door where the small crowd from the library was now assembled.

Brad held the door and glowered at Declan.

"Are you ok?" he asked when my feet touched the ground. Someone else gave me my shoe.

My pinky finger throbbed where it had snagged, my clothes were soaked, and Bridget's upset voice rose as she tore into Todd outside. Everyone gaped at me…waiting for my reaction. I was not ok.

But I wasn't about to burst into tears, either. Not here. Somehow I put on a brave face, took a bow, and everyone clapped at my 'positive attitude'.

Brad stalked away without a word, Todd yelped as Bridget pinched him, and I darted upstairs.

And if that wasn't a bad enough end to the day, Bridget bounded out of bed and flicked on the lights just as I was finally drifting off that night. I could tell something was wrong by her muffled grunts of frustration, so I sat up and popped out an earplug.

"What's going on?"

Oh. I see.

Music blared from next door accompanied by thumps and hollering.

"I can't stand this," groaned Bridget, covering her ears. "I'm trying to *sleep.*"

"Want earplugs?" I offered sympathetically. "I have an extra pair I haven't used."

"No! I should go over and say something because there are rules about this and they're breaking them. This is disturbing *everyone.*" Bridget paced in agitation, and flinched when we heard a crash. "That's it, I'm going. I'll speak to Ellen – "

The door slammed and in the next moment the music stopped.

Excellent.

The lights went out, and I went back to sleep.

" – Whatever happened to *RESPECT!*" Bridget boomed a second later. "Uggghhhh!"

I bolted upright. The music started again, and so did Bridget's ranting.

I looked at her with pleading eyes, "are you *sure* you don't want to try the earplugs?"

You know, I had great expectations for college. I really did. I thought I'd make lifelong friends, get a steady boyfriend, and end up with a fabulous career. And ok – I did make close friends and I love my position as a Bridal consultant, but when you're trying to sleep after a hard day and you have someone yelling every few minutes, you can't help but think of the annoying things. Since my arrival at college I've encountered the following:

1. A tiny bedroom that came complete with a snoring, grumpy roommate.
2. Alex.
3. A womanizer.
4. A really hot guy that came with an attention-seeking ex-girlfriend.
5. A roommate I adore, but she's dating a moron who's out to get me.
6. A total psychopath obsessed with the hot guy, who is also out to get me (and who is currently keeping me awake because she's keeping Bridget awake).

Did I miss anything here?

7. Hot guy won't date.
8. I still care for him more than I should.

And the most recent ordeal was the icing on the cake. Maybe I'd have felt better if Declan at least apologized for his part in it when I bumped into him during the fifteen-minute break between classes the next day, but he just grinned and said, "hey, how's it going?" as though everything was just peachy.

9. Met another hot guy in year two, but blew it instantly by showing too much interest in hot guy number one. Way to go Reanne. Absolutely brilliant.
10. Who wants to go out with the new hottie anyway? Since he enjoys teaming up with guys like Todd and throwing innocent girls into the snow and all, and oh yeah – he's also an animal killer.

"My finger hurts," I grumbled, "and I got very little sleep last night, so it's not going too well."

"What did you do to your finger?"

What did I do to my finger?

"Actually that was you…you nearly ripped it off when it got caught in the doorway yesterday and you continued to pull me."

"*What?*" Declan reached for my hand in astonishment. "Let me see."

It was really only a small graze, but it stung like a paper cut.

"Reanne I'm sorry," said Declan, releasing my hand. "Todd said this was an ongoing game between you. He told me you'd laugh it off. Otherwise I never would have…" he trailed off awkwardly and rubbed his neck. "I wouldn't have participated."

"Todd is warped. But I forgive you – you didn't know."

"So," Declan crossed his arms, "did you see how angry your man was?"

"My man?" I attempted a blank expression.

"Brad was furious! He went to his room and didn't talk to anyone all evening. And no one's seen Todd – the guys have a bet going that Brad got rid of him."

A laugh slipped out. "Well, if Todd's missing, Bridget might have done it. She was pretty angry." And if she didn't – I'd take care of him myself. But first, there was something else I needed to do…

The stereo blasted beating drums; there was shouting and laughter. This time the overwhelming noise came from Bridget and I.

Patricia, Anna, and Ellen were getting a taste of their own medicine, *ha!*

We didn't do it as late as they had; in fact, it was just after suppertime, but if any of them tried to nap, relax, or have a friendly conversation amongst themselves, they'd have trouble. We did it to show them how inconsiderate they had been *late at night.*

I banged my row of Tupperware with the wooden spoon I found in the kitchen, and Bridget leapt high into the air, shaking her box of crackers and singing off key. We really rocked the place – the floor vibrated! At one point we were throwing balled up papers at each other, which was followed with a pillow fight and we couldn't stop laughing. I even forgot why we did it all in the first place until the knock came. I had just whipped a pillow past Bridget's head after she tripped me, when we heard it.

Bridget increased the volume and slipped into her platform shoes. Her feet crashed against the floor in an almighty thud every time she jumped.

The knocking became urgent.

We grinned at each other and I lowered the music as Bridget clomped to the door with her lips silently moving. She was practicing her sarcastic remark. Anna had been rude to her when the situation was reversed. I wasn't sure if Bridget could pull this off because she was just too nice – but I admired her for trying. You can't let people walk all over you. Sometimes you just have to stand your ground.

Bridget took a deep breath and flung the door open.

"Oh sorry!" She gasped, closing it again. Bridget turned around, her face white. "Well that backfired," she muttered miserably and switched off the stereo.

It wasn't Patricia, Anna or Ellen at the door. It was some girl from the other end of the hall. She was trying to study, and she was *really* ticked. Oops.

Twenty-one

Everyone's Lost It

Bridget didn't break up with Todd. I thought she'd end it for sure after he tossed me into the snow but they were still going strong. Though I guess the silver lining came in the form of Todd apologizing and admitting that he genuinely didn't realize how upset his actions made me feel, and promised to stop. And Bridget was happy, so things were looking up.

Until they weren't, because – there's always something, isn't there?

The upstairs phone rang for the fourth time one quiet evening, and no one went to answer it, so I finally did.

"Hello?"

"I'm calling for Patricia," came the female voice amid crackling background noise. "Is she there?"

"Just a second, I'll check." I left the phone dangling and headed to Patricia's room. As I knocked on the door, a girl named Janet stepped out of her bedroom, which was directly across from the phone, and wanted to know who was calling.

I didn't know who called and just said, "don't worry, it's not for you."

I cracked the door open an inch. "Patricia? Are you in here?"

The room was empty. I went in, helped myself to a pen and paper, and jotted a note, which I left on her bed.

"Patricia's not in," I told the girl on the phone then hung up. When I turned around, Anna stood before me with blazing eyes.

"That was for Patricia, *wasn't* it?"

I didn't know what Anna's problem was and I *definitely* didn't appreciate her tone.

Wasn't it?" She repeated.

"Yeah, but I don't see why that should matter to *you*."

"You do this on purpose!" Anna took a step forward and jutted a menacing finger at me. "You think you own the phone, Reanne. Patricia never gets her calls!"

Ooh. Not this again. It was getting very, *very* old.

"Who died and made *her* Gestapo of the school?" I snapped. "Anyway, this has nothing to do with you, so please get out of my way."

She didn't.

"*Excuse me*." I advanced. "Anna, move."

"Or *what*?"

Seriously? She seriously wasn't going to move?

"Or *this*!" Without quite realizing it, my leg shot out and kicked Anna in the shin. Her face crumpled.

"Guuuys," Anna fled down the stairs, wailing. "Reanne kicked me!"

Cries of outrage arose from the lounge.

What just happened?

I stood stock still, feeling dazed. How did I go from having a peaceful evening in my room to *this?* The situation was like a jigsaw puzzle someone dumped all over the ground. Nothing made sense. I couldn't piece it together. And I felt horrible.

I didn't *mean* to kick Anna. I honestly didn't. Suddenly all the stress of the past few weeks, the past two *years*, seemed to press in on me all at once, crushing me like a ton of bricks. A lump formed in my throat and I picked up the phone to call Rhonda.

Janet stormed through the doorway right then, where Anna had disappeared. "Who do you think you *are?*" She growled.

I turned away from her scathing gaze and pressed the phone tightly to my ear. Janet's finger landed on the latch, disconnecting my call. I couldn't deal with this – it was too much. I slammed the receiver down and ran to my room before anyone else arrived to gang up on me, locked my door, and quietly cried into my pillow.

I sat across from Patricia in the dean's office, squirming in my seat. I didn't stand a chance. In this room, innocent until proven guilty didn't exist. It was all over the dean's face – Patricia could do no wrong.

"Let's review the facts." The dean finished perusing the letter Patricia had composed, and stared at me reprovingly. "Reanne, I understand you refused to pass along a phone call Patricia was expecting? Followed by an assault on Anna and Janet? Is this correct?"

"No, it isn't!" I cried. "The call *clearly* wasn't expected because no one was around to answer the phone, so I did, and *then* I went to Patricia's room to tell her about it, but she wasn't there. So I left a note on her bed."

"*Was* there a note on your bed?" He glanced at Patricia, who reluctantly nodded.

"As for Anna…*she* threatened *me*. At least, I felt threatened. I was trapped beside the phone and I asked her to step aside so I could pass and she wouldn't!"

"So you admit to kicking her!" Patricia crowed. The Dean silenced her with a raised hand and turned to the door.

"Anna, please come in. Show us where Reanne kicked you."

I felt sick and shaky. What if she had a big ugly bruise?

Anna waddled through the door, sat down, and propped her leg on a chair. She hiked up her cotton pant leg, grimacing in pain. My stomach churned with dread. I must have really socked it to her.

"Right here," said Anna with a wobble to her voice.

"Where?" I frowned.

"There."

There was nothing but a tiny dot. Why did she make such a fuss? "Anna – are you sure that's not a freckle? Or a cookie crumb, perhaps?"

"Why…you…it's a *mark*!" She screeched. "You maimed me! It might be fractured. You can't always tell at first," she added to the dean. "I could sue you for this…I could have you *charged.*"

The dean cleared his throat and waved Anna down. There was obviously no evidence, just a lot of hearsay. "There is still the matter of Janet – "

"I didn't do anything to Janet!" I interrupted. "She," I pointed to Patricia, "is trying to sabotage me with her lies!"

"You slammed the phone down on her finger!" Patricia barked.

I mentally assessed the scenario.

"No I didn't. Janet harassed me immediately after Anna, and disconnected the call I was making to a friend. All I did was hang up before going to my room to get away from her. If her finger got caught, I'm sorry, but it was an accident. She shouldn't have put her finger there."

The dean smoothed the letter flat against his desk and looked around the room at us. "Apparently there's been a misunderstanding…"

I sighed. *Thank you!*

"…Reanne should apologize to Patricia and do better to pass along her calls in the future."

What?

The dean was officially insane.

Patricia nodded. "She does this all the time. She doesn't pass along anyone's calls."

Out of all *the girls in the dormitory – I am the* sole *reason everyone misses their calls?* Cow.

"And I suppose you give Reanne all *her* messages, Patricia?"

Every head turned in surprise toward Bridget, standing like an archangel in the doorway. "I don't recall you coming to get me when Todd has phoned, and when Brad wanted to talk to Reanne, you didn't even *pretend* to look for her. You talked to him instead!"

"Why do they need to phone here," Patricia muttered, "you see them every day." She clapped a hand over her mouth the moment the words escaped, and Anna looked away.

"Young lady, you are not involved in this discussion," the dean admonished Bridget. "Wait outside."

"With all due respect sir…this isn't a fair meeting. Reanne hasn't done anything wrong. Patricia's been bothering Reanne because she's obsessed with Brad and is jealous of Reanne's friendship with him."

"I'm not!" spat Patricia, her face pink.

"Oh really?" Bridget smirked. "Then why do you always try to get him alone for private conversations, and then all you want to do is badmouth Reanne?"

"I don't!"

"You do. Brad is outside. Maybe he should testify."

Wow. If I ever get into any real trouble I want Bridget's representation. She should have gone to law school.

"Ladies, enough!" The dean sounded at the end of his tether. "This behavior is unacceptable. Clearly there are personal issues among you that need to be resolved, and I suggest you work it out like adults. On your own."

Patricia adopted a humble tone and turned beseechingly to the dean. "May I just say – I don't have anything against Reanne? Hand on heart," she looked me straight in the eye, "I love you. You know that."

"No you don't." Bridget shuffled me through the door. "So cut the act."

And *then* Brad disappeared near the end of March. And I don't mean for an hour or two – three days passed and there was no sign of him anywhere. He didn't show up for class, I didn't see him in the cafeteria or lounge, and he was never in his room. I had a guy check. He just vanished without a word and I knew something bad happened. You don't just disappear without telling someone, unless it's beyond your control. Dreadful thoughts ran through my mind over and over, and I couldn't stop them.

Maybe he got into a horrible accident or was lying helpless in an alley somewhere. He might have been mugged. These things happen all the time you know. What if he committed suicide? Maybe he was so depressed that he and I weren't dating that he threw himself off a bridge! Ok, unlikely. But whatever the reason, I needed to find out. I had to speak with Declan.

I went over to the guy's dorm and knocked on Declan's window.

"Where's Brad?" I asked when he came around to the door.

His expression was grave.

Oh no, oh no. I knew it.

The women around me were in buckets of tears while the men they were with comforted them. I sat in a side pew sniffling quietly as tears trickled down my face and dripped onto my black cotton dress.

"I can't believe he's gone," the woman next to me whimpered before openly weeping into her sopping hanky. "He was so young."

"I know Gwen. I know." A man with salt and pepper hair and a dark mustache rubbed her back in small soothing circles.

I stared at the picture beside the wooden casket covered in flowers, and felt a fresh wave of sadness. In the next moment, I was sobbing too. A gentle hand landed on my arm, with pale lacquered nails. "How did you know him, dear?" Gwen dabbed at her mascara-smudged eyes.

"I'm a friend of – "

" – Oh you poor thing! You must be devastated." Her voice cracked. "Here dear, have a tissue."

For one horrifying moment I thought she would pass me her own hanky. Instead, she reached into the pink purse that matched her nails and handed me a fresh Kleenex.

"Thank you."

"Excuse me dear, I *must* give my condolences to Elena. Elena, *darling!*"

Brad's aunt Elena stood next to her husband's casket at the front of the parlor and began shaking when Gwen hugged her. It was all so sad, and yet touching at the same time. The reverend had so many wonderful things to say about his life and those he influenced that everyone was crying again in no time. At the end, Brad somberly carried the casket out with five other men, and I didn't have a chance to speak with him until after the burial at the reception.

Bridget and I helped serve food and did dishes all evening. They didn't really need an extra set of hands, but it was the least we could do to show our support. I saw Brad standing off to the side with an older gentleman at one point, and chose that moment to break away and approach.

"I'm sorry for your loss," I said, not knowing what else to say.

"Thanks for coming." Brad turned to the man. "Dad, this is Reanne."

"This the one you told me about?" remarked his dad and shook my hand as Bridget joined us.

We talked quietly as people began clearing out. The sky had gone black and we were in for an imminent downpour. Rain started splattering the window.

"We'd better go too," said Bridget, removing her apron. "Before it gets worse."

We hugged Brad, said goodbye to his dad, and headed out with everyone else.

Brad returned to campus after missing a full week of classes. I gave him copies of the notes I took, and advised him of a test we were having the next day. He thanked me, but didn't show up to write it. Or show up to any of our other classes for that matter. I didn't see him until the next morning at breakfast when he asked to borrow a glue stick.

"Why do you need one?" I asked, puzzled.

His smile was cryptic. "You'll see."

I went upstairs and got it for him.

Then I didn't see him again all day until the evening before the doors were locked. He handed me the glue stick and a handcrafted envelope that had my name decorated on the front. He thanked me for the glue and left.

I studied the thick envelope in my hands. There was a cute, hand drawn caterpillar next to my name, and underneath were the words: *Spring has sprung; the grass has riz…so here your letter is…*

I sat on my bed, carefully pulling out the papers. There were pages, and pages of words and pictures of Brad and I pasted among the writing. Writing that…

I gasped. Did it really say what I thought it did? My vision blurred as I read it again.

Dear Reanne,

This last day of March, one before April Fools, has been for this guy one of the most amazing, inspiring, and life-altering 24 hour periods of my young life. But truly – I've been doing a lot of hard, focused thinking about some major and deep issues in my past, present, and future.

I want to begin by apologizing to you. You put so much work into helping me catch up after missing class because of my uncle's funeral, and then I return and become virtually invisible. I know that would appear as if I didn't appreciate what you did voluntarily for me – however that's not true. You've consistently been the best of friends.

I'm very glad to know you, Reanne Riley – and I could think of nothing better than to write you the letter I should have written months, maybe years ago. So yes, there are things I want you to know about me…although this comes from a purely selfish motive, because I will thereafter request to know more about you, hun.

I feel as if I've managed to lose some of the information you've given me about yourself over time, which you have undoubtedly noticed and it must annoy you. I don't try hard enough I guess – which I am ashamed of. I have to develop more skills with memory, or rather, listening closely to learn and store information.

You challenge me Reanne. You remember so much of what I've told you about myself – I am in awe and again in shame for my in-qualifying efforts.

So then, I guess the first thing you've figured out about me is that I'm definitely not in any way perfect – especially in areas of memory. I really hope you can help me with it. Over time, I'm certain I can get better. I want you to know that I recognize my weaknesses and faults and I hide from people who I want to think highly of me – whom I respect. You are definitely one of those people. I withdraw to my room and pull back in social situations and just from stupid habit. I don't want to get too close to people – because loving people means opening up and risking being hurt. I know this annoys you most about me so I want to try my best to fully explain. I really, really like you – always have – and I didn't want to get too close, so I began to avoid you, although I will have you know that I'm always looking for you. I'll let you in on this secret – lately – everywhere I go in the college area – every room, everywhere I walk – I'm subconsciously looking to see if you're there, and whom you're with.

I've been lying to myself and to you about how I really feel about you. I waited and waited because I wanted the timing to be just right. I needed to figure things out in my own life before I involved your emotions and feelings. I sense, I hope correctly, that you want to share more of my life as well. Is this true?

I'm over thinking every step I make because I want to be honest and clear with everything – totally transparent.

If you ever wondered if there was something I disliked about you that was causing me to avoid showing any emotion toward you, please know that it was never the case. It has always been about me, making sure I was ready, that I was more sure of myself after Amelia, and that I would be able to treat you like a special friend – or more closely – more than a friend. I'm not interested in dating for casual fun…I know dating is fun, but you're a person, a very intelligent woman with an amazing, loving family, with talent and ambition…and so much.

When my uncle died, I found an opportunity to love my aunt and cousins – and be there for my family. I felt so useful and purposeful and it finally dawned on me where my priorities should lie. I have a sense that you know me – or that you want to know me. You've seen a lot of my shortcomings in the past two years, and you're still my closest friend – which amazes me again and again.

Summer is approaching, which would mean a long distance relationship over the next few months and at other times, which I don't like as I haven't seen many of those work out, however the hope of sharing something phenomenally special with you in the future would make the time apart bearable for me. But what about you? This I leave up to you (laugh) I feel like I'm proposing, not asking you out!!! I'm way too serious sometimes, forgive me ☺

I just really want to treat you as if you are the most fun, loving, beautiful, reliable, intelligent, inspiring, precious, and special daughter of parents who I'd be afraid would kill any man or boy (in my case) that would play with your heart in a trivial manner.

So, I've said my piece – you know now clearly how I feel about you. Thanks for reading, and oh – by the way – thanks for lending me your glue! Couldn't have done all this without it!

Yours,

Brad.

I wiped my wet face. My heart thudded. Brad asked me out. He *actually* asked me out. Oh wow. After two years, after I accepted that it would never happen, the guy I wanted, wanted me too. I finally had a boyfriend.

I finally had a BOYFRIEND! Rhonda was going to flip.

Chapter Twenty-two
Anything I Should Know?

I emailed Rhonda and mom immediately, and the upstairs phone rang two minutes after. Rhonda's voice blasted my ear in an elated screech. "MG! What color am I wearing at your wedding? How did this *happen?*"

I threw my head back and laughed joyously, then somehow restrained myself. "Let's not get ahead of ourselves," I said, feeling very mature. "He only just asked me out."

Although I can't say the thought didn't cross my mind as I re-read the letter. I love a good wedding, everyone knows that, but it didn't mean I wanted to skip the fun of dating and jump straight into marriage. Honestly, I'm not *Erin.*

"True. You might not get married for a few years. Maybe you'll have one of those long engagements and I can help with all the planning!" Rhonda's voice rang out in a bubble of glee.

Who said anything about a *long* engagement? Oh dear lord.

"What if it *does* take him ten years to propose?" I asked in sudden panic. "Look how long it took him to ask me out in the first place!"

"Don't think about it," Rhonda soothed. "It will all work out the way it's meant to be. You're together now – that's all that matters. This is huge!"

"You're right. You're absolutely right!" I laughed again. "I'm just *so* happy to be where we are."

Patricia came by just then, pretending she wasn't eavesdropping. I stopped talking until she was gone.

"We'll need to communicate in code or strictly by email from now on," I whispered. "I don't want this getting out just yet."

In the morning, I passed the men's dormitory with a smile plastered to my face and Brads words still floating around in my mind. It was so surreal. If not for the letter safely locked away in my wardrobe, which I read at least five times already, it would have been difficult to believe it actually happened.

The door to the men's building crashed against the wall and I jumped. Brad ran out with puffy cheeks and his shirt half buttoned. He held up one finger then ran back inside.

I stood there, waiting for my boyfriend. The stupid grin on my face widened. *My boyfriend.* Nothing could ruin this day. *Nothing.* Not a tornado, a freak blizzard, or even Patricia.

And speak of the devil (literally)…she was just getting into her car off to my left.

"Want a ride?"

It took a minute or two to realize she was addressing *me*.

"That's ok, I'll walk."

"Sorry." Brad joined me on the sidewalk. "Had to finish my mouthwash."

"Do you *both* want a ride?" Patricia looked from me to Brad and I could almost see the wheels turning in her head (assuming she had any).

"No thanks," said Brad, and we strolled away.

I kept the secret for seven whole days, which means I didn't tell Bridget either. I wanted to, but it was the only way to keep Patricia from knowing, and I wanted her in the dark as long as possible.

Except, I kept singing and humming everywhere I went and Patricia was no longer the only one looking at me with suspicion. Patricia finally said something when she caught me singing 'Oh Happy Day' in the bathroom.

"You've been in a good mood lately," she noted.

"Yep. Sure am!"

She perched on the counter as though we were about to have a girly chat. "Is there anything I should know?"

"Nope," I beamed at her. "Have a great day."

I dressed and decided it was time to tell Bridget. Right then. The news spread throughout the dormitory like firecrackers exploding one after the other. There were squeals and shrieks every time someone found out. Girls congratulated and hugged me all day; it was all they could talk about. I overheard someone at lunch saying, "it's about time – the sparks have been flying for *two years.*"

It wasn't much different with the guys, except they were clapping Brad on the back going, "way to go man," while he smiled deliriously.

Epilogue

One year later…

"Karen! Where are my track pants?" Dad called from the top of the stairs in his t-shirt, boxers and socks.

Drawers banged closed and I heard the thud of a belt buckle hitting the floor as dad searched his room again.

Mom shook her head and rolled her eyes when dad rounded the corner, frenzied.

"What happened to them!" he wailed. The track pants were in his hands, completely mangled. "You ruined them!" He accused, pointing at mom. "You've always hated them!"

"Dad," I cut in gently while trying not to laugh. *"Everyone* hated them."

His face was a mask of reproach. "Reanne, don't take her side."

"Oh Tom, would you just forget about those decrepit pants?" Mom huffed. "They went in the laundry with the bleached load by mistake. They were worn out from overuse and couldn't take it. Anyway," her eyes narrowed, "why were you looking for them? You couldn't have worn them today."

"No reason," said dad shiftily. "I just wanted to know where they were."

"Yes…well now you know." Her look was pointed. "Now please put them in the trash and get into your tux so that your daughter isn't late for her wedding."

"Fine," he grumbled and trudged up the stairs.

"Mom you're a genius," we slapped hands.

"I knew I'd find a way to get rid of them. We couldn't have your father looking like a hobo in the photos."

My eyes were damp as I laughed. Quietly…so dad wouldn't hear.

"I still can't believe you're getting married," Rhonda sighed as she buttoned my Vivien Westwood gown (I know. I could hardly believe it myself. My parents saved for my wedding for years and never told me!). "You're about to be a married woman. Things will be different now."

"Nothing will change between *us!*" I vowed. "You will always be my best friend…we'll still make lots of time for each other."

"I know," Rhonda dabbed at her eye. "I know, you're right. I just can't believe you're already at this stage in life. You and I were always on the same track, moving at the same speed. Now it feels like you're going ahead without me. But I'm really happy for you. You look stunning."

"So do you." Rhonda was in a deep purple dress and looked exactly like Audrey Hepburn on the cover of 'Breakfast at Tiffany's.' Gloves included. "You look perfect for meeting – "

"– The photographer," Bridget cut in neatly as she entered the room. "She's here. And I finally separated the lovebirds," she said of Lindsay and Jaden.

Lindsay blushed as she followed Bridget. "What can I say? We love being together."

"I know," I agreed fondly, and surveyed my bridesmaids in their dresses. Each girl wore a different style to flatter their individual shapes and tastes, but they were all in the same royal violet. The photos would look amazing!

The violinists raised their bows and Rhonda's rendition of *Canon* filled the church. "Here we go," Rhonda whispered in excitement. I was excited about getting Rhonda to the altar to stand near Declan, who already waited there with Brad. I paired them up for the day.

Bridget went next, and she sailed out toward Todd. Yes, I know what you're thinking. Why have this goofball in my wedding? He really cleaned up his act in our third year and is a really nice guy, as it turned out. I finally saw in him what Bridget recognized all along, and so did Brad.

Erin rushed up and gently placed her baby daughter in Lindsay's arms. "Am I late? I got here as fast as I could – we had a diaper emergency."

"It's fine." I smiled adoringly at my beautiful little flower girl, with the fattest rosy cheeks and cute frilly bloomers beneath her dress. She made bubbles with her puckered mouth, and my heart melted.

Camera's flashed as Lindsay carried the baby down the aisle and there was a collective "awww" echoing throughout the church.

And before I knew it, I was at the altar staring at the love of my life, listening to those ancient, magical words. "Dearly beloved, we are gathered here today in the sight of God to join..."

Brad tenderly squeezed my hand as a bridesmaid behind me sniffled. Then I realized it wasn't a bridesmaid, it was dad, and I began feeling emotional myself. His only daughter was about to become a married woman. He would miss me, unless his tears were falling over the loss of his pants. It was one or the other.

"Is there any reason why these two should not be joined together in holy matrimony?" The minister paused meaningfully and my grip on Brad's hand tightened.

Please don't let the psychopath show up.

I almost enlisted security just in case, but I didn't think she'd go that far. Besides...she didn't know we were getting married. On the day of our graduation, Patricia *admitted* to trashing my room the previous year. I guess she wanted to gloat since she didn't get the guy, but in the end I didn't hold a grudge. I really just felt sorry for her.

I released my breath as the ceremony continued. "By the power invested in me, I now pronounce you husband and wife!" He grinned at Brad. "You may kiss the Bride!"

And boy did he ever.

ABOUT THE AUTHOR

Rachelle Chedore grew up in Toronto Canada before venturing to the Maritimes for post-secondary education. She enjoys creative writing, live theatre, coffee shops, and the color purple. *Undaunted: One girl, many morons, and the search for Mr. Right* is her first novel. She still resides in the GTA with her two children, and two crazy dogs.

www.ingramcontent.com/pod-product-compliance
Lightning Source LLC
Chambersburg PA
CBHW070643180626
46817CB00006B/2227